Out of Print

A Novel by Sean Rogers

Out of Print
by Sean Rogers

First Edition: August 2022

Published by Onyx Neon Press
www.onyxneon.com

Editor: Chastity West
Cover design: Phil Poole

This book was typeset on Ubuntu using Pandoc and LaTeX. Many thanks to the open source developers who make these and other projects possible.

Follow the author:
Twitter: @Sean_T_Rogers

ISBN: 978-0-9854519-9-8

For all the booksellers I've worked with, and for the ones I haven't.
Give'em hell

1.

The Future of Bookselling

QUEENS, New York, October 26, 2009. At the bookstore, God-awful early on a Monday morning.

Management had scheduled a meeting to discuss a secret matter with the staff. This had never happened before. Every year we gathered as a group in October to go over the store plan for the holiday rush. And once, a full-staff party was thrown for a retiring manager. Never a cloak and dagger affair like this, though. The whole event was curious. I don't sleep much—one of the consequences of being over seventy—so the early hour didn't piss me off as much as it did the others. But really, five o'clock? There was nothing so pressing that it couldn't wait till seven. And someone could have had the decency to brew coffee.

Don, the store manager. Gray hedgehog hair, scraggly mustache, blocky glasses, red eyes.

—Good morning, everyone.

Don was a notoriously late riser. On the few occasions he worked early shifts, he was known to set up the registers and then disappear into his office for hours while the sales floor buzzed with rumors that he was napping, hung over as hell. The inside dope said Don was a drunk, but I didn't buy it. Some people are born with big, lazy eyes and are prone to this accusation.

While the staff watched in silence, Don sat down at one of the café tables, removed his glasses, and began to violently rub his big, lazy eyes. Michael M sprang to the center of the floor like a genie released from a lamp. Michael M was an assistant manager—slender-framed, Laotian, sharply dressed and universally disliked. He was known to be involved in a training program with the hopes of ascending to the store manager position himself one day.

Michael M.

—Hello, everyone.

His actions smacked of kiss-assy desperation.

—We're going to take roll call. Please shout *here* when I call your name.

He held a pen and yellow pad. Eagerly reading down the list of names, he relished those moments of silence when he was able to mark a no-show employee. There were fifty-one of us in all—that's including the baristas and receivers. A sizable group to be squeezed into the café. Michael M sang over us all.

—Charlie Mueller!

I raised my hand half-mast, almost imperceptibly past my shoulder. Minimal effort to show my displeasure with the early hour.

—Right here.

My protest went unnoticed. Michael M continued to call out names while Michael P, the other assistant manager, who had just emerged from the back offices, passed slips of paper to the weary masses. Grumblings from the booksellers flowed in a wave as the written message reached different employees. I didn't have my slip of paper yet and the complaints were tantalizing.

Voices from the crowd.

—What, are we in the FBI now?

—No one ever listens to me anyhow, so this really doesn't matter.

—I knew it would come to this.

I finally received my note. I tilted my glasses forward on my nose. I smoothed down my white mustache as I read. I was almost a lawyer once, so I recognize a basic nondisclosure agreement when it's handed to me. What the hell was this about?

Michael M shouted over the babble.

—What Michael P is passing out is a promise.

He politician-paced, hand pumping his lined notepad with each syllable.

—It's a promise that you will keep the exciting Black Friday news that we have for you this morning *to yourself*. No newspapers, no television, no reporters…

The booksellers grew incredulous grins. Susan M and I shared a particularly sarcastic look. Who did management think they were talking to, here? A room full of movie stars? Which person sitting in the café right now had the ear of a reporter? What a crock of shit. So, there's a new Black Friday sales initiative. So what? We woke up early for this?

Don's murmur rose through the din, sewage into the basement.

—And no chat room discussions. No MySpace posts about this, no Facebook, no whatever else you people are doing…

That made more sense than the reporters, I suppose. One of the baristas, a spunky teenager who really had no business speaking.

—What are we talking about here, Don?

Radio silence from Don. He nodded his hedgehog head at Michael M and then pushed his knuckles against his brow, continuing the rubbing assault. Michael M flipped over a briefcase on an espresso-freckled four-top. He snapped two latches up and opened the case. From my angle I could see that there were three identical items inside—rectangular things with white trim. I didn't know what they were. Had no clue. Michael M savored our ignorance.

—What I am about to show you cannot become public knowledge until Black Friday, when it will debut. In order to have an experienced staff by Black Friday, we're starting a series of training sessions beginning this morning. If you've been paying attention to rumors on the internet, you might already know what I'm going to tell you.

Michael M pressed a button on each of the rectangular things. He then closed the briefcase and stood erect, opened his eyes owlishly.

—Anyone? Does anyone have a guess as to why we're here this morning?

A long pause of excruciating silence passed over the café. One of the industrial dishwashers in the back room gurgled in discomfort. Everyone wished they were dead. Or that Michael M would die. Something—anything at all—to end this unbearable moment. Then the many-braceleted arm of Susan M rose.

—Is the store closing?

Don was spurred into alertness with the suggestion. He hummed like a beehive at Susan. Michael M cut in abruptly.

—What part of what I just said would lead you to that conclusion? No, Susan. Anyone else?

Voices from the crowd.

—Are we getting a toy department?

—No.

—Is there going to be a big author signing?

—No...

—We're going to start selling cigarettes?

—Of course not.

Suspecting that the group was being less than earnest, Michael M put the kibosh on the guessing game. He produced one of the rectangular things from the briefcase. Its face was a darkened screen. Then, the screen came to life as Michael M lifted it, changing from black to white, with words inscribed in the center: *Read Forever*. Foreboding, almost. Michael M held it up like a sacrifice to the demigods of the novel that sat quietly in a field of bookcases behind us.

Michael M, a sanctimonious gleam in his eye.

—This is the Miles of Books SwiftFoot©. It is an E-Reader. And it is the future of the bookstore.

We nodded in understanding, working hard to hide our smirks. When I could be sure that none of the management team was watching, I turned to Susan M and rolled my eyes. It wasn't long after this day that I was fired.

2.
The Third Strike

THE story of my firing begins with the SwiftFoot and ends with a young man named Jake Fletcher. It was February 2010 now. The SwiftFoot had debuted like a lead balloon during the preceding holiday season, and Jake had been with us since the previous summer.

I'll be honest; Jake was an annoying hotshot when he started working at Miles of Books. He had been gracing us with his presence for only eight months and for the last five of those months held the head cashier position. To his credit, he hadn't received any complaints. The head cashier is the first line of defense against those hobgoblins of retail that are invalid returns and expired coupons, and therefore a whipping boy for the ornery rabble. Not a single complaint was lodged against Jake during all those months. The kid had done well for himself. And he strutted around like he *knew* he had done well for himself.

He was a schmoozer, ingratiating himself to anyone within the Jake Radius of Charm. Because of his bottomless desire for friendly conversation, he was a natural seller of the Miles of Books membership discount card. His sales pitch was hardly a sales pitch at all. Instead, there was a veneer of intense concern that the customer did not *already* have the card. He seemed stunned during each and every encounter when it came to light that the customer had somehow missed the boat on this stupendous opportunity of owning a Miles of Books discount card. And maybe he *was* shocked. Anyway, it worked. While the rest of us struggled to move one or two membership cards, Jake sold over ten of those suckers every day, even though he was granted merely a hundred or so transactions in which to accomplish the task. It was a neat trick, I guess. He also managed to keep the impulse line well merchandized and all the supplies—the pens, the shopping bags, the receipt paper—fully stocked.

I'll offer up that I was a little sore about Jake's promotion to head cashier. Honestly, I thought it might go to me. But I didn't want to work the forty hours a week that the head cashier job required, and I guess that took me out of the running. There was no financial reason to take a promotion. I had a little bit of military money coming for an old injury—still do, actually—and I'm lucky enough to receive social security checks. But in the back of my mind, I had the idea that Don might decide to promote me to head cashier. Just in the mornings. And then Susan M, who worked mostly nights, sharp as an auditor, could take the other shifts. I never suggested this to Don, but I did spend some time thinking it through. It seemed like a good plan to me. No matter. It was fine. Jake was doing a fine job as the head cashier.

Right up until he wasn't.

One day Jake was different, and no one knew what brought about the change. His discount card sales plummeted, the impulse merchandise went feral, and cashiers ran out of plastic bags in the middle of the afternoon, forcing them to call the manager on duty, or MOD, for replacements. Jake became distant and dreamy, a balloon loosed to the fickle winds. The worst part of it was that he started losing money.

Miles of Books enforced a strict policy about losing cash, and long was the list of booksellers booted to the curb over the monetary equivalent of a latte with an extra shot. A cashier was granted three strikes—meaning, their register could be off by five dollars three times and forgiveness was granted. But a fourth miscount and the axe fell. No questions asked; no quarter given. Jake, who was on to the penny for so many months, had now depleted his three strikes in quick fashion. The store held its breath every time Jake's till was being balanced. No one wanted to see him go, least of all the management team. And I'm no villain; I didn't want him fired either. I wouldn't wish firing on anybody, believe me. In a couple of weeks, he was scheduled away from the cash area to train in the receiving room. At that point, he would be bereft of money-handling duties and the pressure would fall off. I privately hoped that he made it out of the head cashier phase and used the experience to humble himself.

The daytime customer service person called off on a Friday, so they asked me to stay late. This happened every now and then. I normally worked from 7:00 a.m. to 11:00 a.m., but management knew that I had an open schedule and could always work later if needed. To help out, I stayed until four o'clock, covering the floor and the cash registers. It was a busy day. The hours zipped by in a happy whir of books and games and coffee and money. The phone calls and floor recovery and recommendation requests blended in a rhythmic flow. I was pleasantly tired by the end of the shift.

A bell sounded overhead. It was a request from the cash area for backup. It was past four and I was officially done for the day. I lifted the phone at the customer service counter and paged the MOD.

—Michael P.

—Hi, Michael. This is Charlie. I'm supposed to be finished for today, but I think I'm the only one who can answer that cash page. Would you like me to go up front?

—Nope.

The lion's share of humor practiced by the management staff consisted of saying *no* when the answer to a question was clearly *yes. Can I take my break? No! No breaks for anyone today!* That kind of thing. Michael P tended to overdo it.

—Yeah, actually that would be great, Charlie. Thanks.

Phil rang by himself on register seven. Jake's shift had just ended, so I assumed he was in the back offices counting down his till. A line of five customers had formed. I hopped on register two and welcomed the next guest.

I felt good, in the zone, and smiled unintentionally. I small-talked my first customer and inquired whether they had the Miles of Books membership discount card, and since they didn't have it, did they want to sign up today? And were they sure they didn't want to become a member with Miles of Books, seeing as how they would save three dollars and seventy-five cents on this purchase alone? The next customer had a young child with them. I let the child carry the bag, building him up with the suggestion—*You're a big kid, right?* The next customer wore a black hat with gold writing proclaiming his status as a World War II veteran. He bought a book concerning the Battle of the Bulge and asked if I, too, were a World War II veteran. I said *no, Korea.* I checked the clock, and it was nearly twenty minutes past four. The line was still too deep for Phil to handle alone. I kept ringing.

Between customers I called out.

—Phil, is somebody else due in?

—No, not at the cash register. Just leave, Charlie.

Phil nodded his head toward the queue. They could hear his every word.

—These people can wait.

I figured I would assist two more customers and then skedaddle. I would tell Don on my way out that Phil needed help up front. Simple as that.

Then, Jake returned to the cash area while I attended to the second of these customers. He was pale and walked briskly. He marched behind the counter to inspect the register he had worked that morning. He punched the no-sale button and timidly peered inside at the empty tray like a child checking for monsters under his bed. He moved the machine out from its place and gazed behind, over the minute trashscape of dust, paper clips, and crumpled receipts from years past. He found nothing of worth. Looking down, he scanned the green and maroon carpet, praying to spot the money that Phil and I could tell he had lost once again. This was it. Jake was out of strikes and would be fired. I took one more customer.

The line eventually dissipated. Jake slouched at Phil's register. The two of them whispered furtively as I watched out of the corner of my eye.

Phil.

—I would, Jake, but I don't have the cash on me.

Jake nodded and put his hand on Phil's shoulder. Phil looked like he might cry. Jake took a deep breath and gallows-walked back down the row of registers. He passed behind me as I finished the transaction with my customer. He made the turn back to the office to report that he could not find the money.

—How much did you lose?

He turned to me.

—Twenty dollars. Even.

I studied the security camera over my shoulder like a pitcher holding a runner at second. It wasn't out of the realm of possibility that we were being observed by management. Was I risking my job for this kid whom I didn't even like? I honestly don't know why I did it, except that there was a sad and embarrassed young man in front of me and I had the power to be his salvation. I slipped a twenty-dollar bill free without removing my wallet from its back pocket. I bunched it in my fist and covertly handed it to Jake.

Jake, whispering.

—Thanks so much, Charlie

I felt pretty good about it.

Jake marched back to the office. The line of customers was gone so I decided it was time for me to go as well. Phil raised his eyebrows to me. He knew what had transpired. I was nervous as I crossed the sales floor because I had just done something for which I could be fired. I was certain that in my long career as a bookseller I had participated in some skullduggery that could have led to a firing. But even with this certainty, I couldn't recall a worthy example, at least nothing that was as blatantly deceptive as this. I walked into the breakroom to retrieve my bag and felt dizzy with nerves.

Michael P from the cash room.

—Oh, thank God. Jesus Christ, Jake. Please be more careful. You know we can't protect you if you're off again.

—I'm sorry. I don't know what's wrong with me lately. I'll get it together.

—You better. You're in a really good position here, and I don't want to see you screw it up over something trivial.

I collected my things and exited the breakroom. Normally, I would sit down and eat something, but my presence when Jake escaped unscathed from the cash room might seem like a demand for thanks. That scene would be uncomfortable for both of us. Better to be long gone. My nerves settled like sediment as I approached the front of the store. I had done something very selfless, I realized. I saved the kid's job, and no one would ever know except for me, him, and Phil. This made me feel like a charitable person. I enjoyed that idea. I daydreamed that I might start volunteering. A soup kitchen or something. Maybe I *would* do that.

As I passed through the front door, footsteps rushed to catch up with me. It was Jake. He wore a sheepish smile. Apparently, he didn't want to let this awkward conversation pass.

—Thank you so much, Charlie. You really saved me there.

—It's all right.

—Let me take you out to lunch.

—No, don't worry about it.

—No, I really want to. And you must be starving. You worked a whole day when you were supposed to only work four hours.

He was right. I was uncommonly hungry. This definitely swayed my decision. Plus, Jake was relentless.

—We'll go to the bagel place. They serve tuna salad on a garlic bagel. It's amazing. And they have an ATM. I'll get you that twenty I owe you.

Tuna on garlic? I reluctantly agreed.

3.
The Shelving Lesson

HUNGER wasn't the only reason I agreed to Jake's late lunch at the bagel shop. Just like the acceptance of most invitations, there was a degree of guilt involved. I had needlessly said some inconsiderate things to Jake during one of his first days. The memory of my thoughtlessness had chaffed me since the previous summer. And even though it was a small indiscretion, it kept me up some nights. Social interactions gone sour tend to stick with me. My own cruelty is the worst jailor and this one had been running his night stick down the bars for months. Jake probably didn't even remember the incident.

Like I said, Jake irked me from the first day I met him, with his smothering loquaciousness, his careless efficiency, his complete exuberance to be in New York City. He was tall, tow-headed, straight from college, fresh as windowsill pie, like so many others before him. His permanent red cheeks were obviously unable to sprout a beard. He had piercing blue eyes that could only have come from Ohio—eyes that had studied the shifting, brown water of Lake Erie, I imagined, or eyes that had peered through car windows while rocketing through the flatlands of neatly tilled cornfields. It was my fourth decade as a bookseller when I met Jake, so you must understand that I had met a long line of his doppelgangers going all the way back to the late sixties. I was impervious to the Radius of Charm. His type had become a routine annoyance.

A natural salesman, sure—but he was also polite to a degree that made the other booksellers anticipate sarcasm. Not only did he speak with acute correctness but said *please* and *thank you* and often held doors when he knew a woman followed. I once overheard him say *excuse me* to a book-laden dolly cart that he almost bumped into.

He became the talk of the store among the old ladies. The young girls, the ones that were Jake's age, acted like they didn't even notice him. They were scared, I think, intimidated. But the old hens, they didn't care. They squawked every time he walked out of the breakroom. *He's so handsome*, they clucked, *and such a gentleman*. Then they would say to the youngest girl within earshot, *Honey, if I was your age, he'd have my phone number by now*. It ruined several of my lunch breaks over the course of a half year. I wiped my hand down my mustache. I adjusted my glasses obsessively. I harrumphed. The chatter was implacable. *He'll be moving back to Ohio before the year's out*, I thought. *You just wait and see.*

But he didn't go so quickly. And when he was ready to be trained on shelving, I was given the task. Jake already knew how to use the registers, had been taught to make a cappuccino, was schooled in the art of our handheld scanners, to look up a book on the computer, to place an order for a customer. Now it was time to meet the old man. Shelving is the most important task a bookseller can be assigned, and I was the most experienced shelver at Miles of Books.

He shook my hand firmly.

—Hello, Charlie! Ready to shelve some books?

Honestly, that's how he talked. Like he walked straight out of a Garrison Keillor story. Absurd.

Miles of Books was what they used to call a Big Box Bookstore. This was meant as an insult, I believe, insinuating that it was an obnoxiously large, publicly traded corporation that carried a generic, unimaginative catalogue. And I suppose this was true. But I still loved her. A chain bookstore is different than a chain clothing store or restaurant—it can maintain the integrity of its soul despite its size. Or so I thought, on all those mornings while I diligently filled its shelves.

I waited outside on the dewy, dank sidewalk every morning while the store was dark and the sun was just coming up, until the manager arrived with the key to let me in. I saw the store wake—the lights coming on were the stretching of her arms, the small messes left from the night before the crust in her eyes. In the morning, dust on bookcases showed like wrinkles on a face, unnoticeable until the sun's rays hit at a certain angle.

Shelving is the most important task because if the books aren't where they are supposed to be, all the goals of the store become unattainable. Obvious, right? You'd be surprised at the remiss with which many booksellers treat the process. Shelving is the store's breakfast. It is her foundation. I remember relaying this sentiment to Jake. He nodded seriously, as if I had just given him directives for an assassination. *Good*, I thought. I began my spiel.

Shelving is a game of details. It begins in the receiving room. The receivers lug the boxes through the back door and sort the books onto H-carts—large, brown, albatrosses with wobbly wheels and eight metal shelves. The shelver pushes the cart onto the sales floor to a particular section. The sections are like Russian dolls, one main category loaded with layers of smaller, more refined categories. The sections can be dizzying in their minuteness and exactitude.

Example? Picture a Health and Fitness section where areas labeled Heath or Fitness are nowhere to be found. Instead, it is made up of subcategories—Exercise, Nutrition, Calorie Counters, Alternative Medicine, Diseases. And it doesn't stop there—each subcategory is packed with sub-*sub*categories. Within the Diseases subcategory there is Cancer, Back Pain, Crohn's. And that's where it ends, right? Wrong! Within Cancer there are sub-sub-*sub*categories: Breast! Thyroid! Prostate! Every section is like this—universes inside the nutshell. Sometimes these subcategories are misleading. Camping is a subcategory to the Sports section. Sleight-of-Hand and Magic in the Games section. Death and Grieving is a subcategory in Self-Improvement. Is this last grouping a nihilistic commentary on our very existence? Don't question! Just shelve!

Everything fits into the sections. Let me repeat that—*everything fits into the sections*. There were booksellers who had the habit of pushing a cart back to receiving at the end of their shifts that still carried half the books they were supposed to shelve, claiming that the sections were too tight to fit them. This drove me over the fucking ledge. There is no reason for this, folks. The books always fit onto the sales floor. If they don't fit on the shelf where they belong, then the bookseller should look down the aisle. The bookseller should look at all those bays and bays of books. Is there not one space on the shelf that can be scrunched? Is there not one book faced-out that can be spined? Yes, of course there is. There *always* is. The bookseller should make the adjustments and shift to create space. The books always fit.

I remember telling Jake to shelve honestly. It was difficult and time-consuming to do everything right—to put your books in the correct subcategories, shift where you should, bring your cart back to receiving empty. *Many succumb to dishonesty*, I told him. *Like*

Terry Fernando. I shouldn't have named names, but I did. Terry was the worst. Booksellers (like Terry) might come across strays that the recovery team from the night before had missed. It is tempting to leave them where they lay. There is so much to do in such a short period of time. That stray book had been someone else's responsibility, hadn't it? There is a full schedule of booksellers who are free to get that tome back where it needs to be, isn't there? This isn't our responsibility...

No! That's Terry Talk! Booksellers should silence these thoughts. They should help this wayward traveler back to his home. There are often empty coffee cups and other debris left on the shelves. Throw them away! There are often holes left where titles were purchased the day before. The bookseller should spread out the books left behind. They should make a beautiful display of each bay, emptying their carts and filling up the belly of the bookstore. *This is your responsibility*, I told Jake, *when you are the morning shelver.*

Jake was a natural, of course. He shelved like a black belt practicing the kata—calm, graceful, wise. He bent down and shot back up in ways that I would never dare, lest my lower back or right knee betray me. He asked a lot of questions, and I had a lot of answers. We shelved for two hours and then at nine o'clock the doors opened for business. This was when the real test began. This was when the juggling act commenced.

To keep up with store standards, we were to finish the shelving by 11:00 a.m. Most of the work should have been accomplished before opening because after the day started, focus was compromised. Customers asked questions, the phone rang incessantly, the bell sounded overhead to page a helper to the cash registers. Time dwindled. After the front doors were unlocked, shelving, the main objective of the shift, became one in a list of priorities.

Jake performed admirably. He was polite when customers interrupted him and divided his attention seamlessly between task and distraction. A talker caught him at one point, a relentless regular named Bernie, and Jake had waved the chatterbox along with him while he shelved, keeping up with the meandering drivel as he emptied the Teen Fiction cart. I'm no doctor, but I feel comfortable saying that Bernie was an insane person. Every bookstore has one. Many have three or four of them. Bernie's particular breed of insanity was deceptive in that he always had a clever, inquisitive look on his face, and had the scent of one coherent enough to shower once a day. In respect to the latter, I suppose we were pretty lucky. Bernie was also savvy enough to begin his interminable diatribes with something that might interest his subjects. He always tried to reel me in using baseball as bait. *You see those Yanks last night, Charlie?* That was his first mistake. I'm a Mets fan. But, if I showed any spark of interest—really, if it appeared as if I weren't going to be outright hostile to him—he would commence with a chaotic stream of nonsensical boasting, both unbelievable and tiresome. It went something like this: *Yeah... Jeter, Jeter, Jeter. When are they gonna learn, right? If you ask me, Mr. Jeter spends too much time staying up with the ladies. Oh, you don't think that can break your concentration? It can. Let this guy right here set you straight before God and all his angels, those ladies can distract you. You ever been down fifty-seventh? Between fifty-seventh and fifty-eighth? The Mackerel House? Don't. Don't go. Not if you like your life the way things are right now. I lost my badge down there. Went in, didn't leave for three weeks. Mackerel House kicked me out when the money was gone. By then—no wife, no kids, no car, and they took my badge from me. Yeah, the badge. You didn't know I used to be CIA? Well, it's not really CIA. It's more secret than that. I'm not allowed to tell you the organization's name. But I will. C'mere, lean in. I gotta whisper. Lean in, I won't bite. It's called The Secret Armada of Super Killers. Don't tell anybody that. If you do, you won't wake up the next day, let me be the one to tell you, in front of God and all his angels. Yeah, but they took my badge after the Mackerel House. Said they couldn't have an agent with that kind of libido. I impregnated four hookers in three weeks. Then I lost my badge. I'm writing a book about it. A memoir. You guys are gonna have to make space for it on your shelves. Probably up there with the best sellers. I hired an editor for it and everything. After he read my writing, he said I was a genius. I don't know. Maybe I am. I mean, he would know, wouldn't he? He's an editor. Maybe you heard of him, his name's John Updike? You ever heard of John Updike?*

This is not an exaggeration. I promise, that's almost a verbatim account of something Bernie has told me. This was the type of dialogue Jake was dealing with while he finished both the Teen and Study Aids carts. But he somehow sent Bernie ambling back to the café, smiling and whistling, while keeping the shelving speed to standard as far as productivity is concerned. Jake had a way about him that charmed these yahoos like snakes in a basket.

—Good job today.

Jake and I wheeled our last two empty carts back to receiving.

—Do you have any questions? Anything I didn't cover?

—Questions…

Jake brought his cart to a halt. He donned a philosophical expression as if he might ask whether an interventionist God was responsible for our fates.

—What kind of coffee do you drink?

—Excuse me?

—Are you a latte man? Mocha?

I don't know why, but I spoke gruffly.

—I just drink regular coffee.

—That's great. Let me buy you one. As a thanks for training me.

Actually, I *do* know why I spoke gruffly. He was just too smooth. Jake was too oily for me.

—No.

The word came out much colder and with more force than I intended. I do that sometimes. When confronted with oiliness. Jake raised his eyebrows.

—No problem.

He sounded pale; my tone had stung him. I softened up a touch.

—I already had one this morning.

—All right.

—But thank you.

I am vinegar. We separated.

Not a big deal, right? Not something that should cause me to toss and turn in the night, I guess. But it bothered me. Jake was abrupt with me for the next few shifts. His Radius of Charm was disabled, replaced by a monk-like silence as we shelved. I've never been good with silences. The pauses in conversation, the amount of time it takes for someone to return a phone call, moments after a prayer in the dark by my bed—these times make me anxious. They loom over my imagination—redoubtable, unfriendly. A large part of a person's happiness hinges on how these silences are interpreted, but I just can't see sunshine in a Rorschach. Oily or not, Jake had tried to be kind, respectful even, and I answered him rudely.

This awkward encounter early in our relationship may explain why I agreed to let Jake take me out for lunch. Normally, I ate in the breakroom and then caught the train home. These days I rarely socialized with the other employees outside of work, and certainly not with someone so much younger. I used to run with the young crowd. Lord knows I used to.

I knew it was a bad decision and I thought about skating out of there before Jake had time to collect his things from the break-room. I didn't. I stayed. Maybe I shouldn't have, but I stayed.

4.

The Chelsea Thing

I had walked past the bagel shop many times but had only entered once. On that occasion, the bookstore had closed due to snow, and I had wanted a coffee on the way back to my apartment. The restaurant was as I remembered it—white and orange counters, a mezuzah hanging in the door frame, trays of lox, and hummus and cream cheeses of every variety. The women who worked there were young and Israeli, brief with the customers but efficient and pretty. Both Jake and I ordered the tuna bagel, and I got a coffee as well. We sat down at one of the round, orange tables, the dying sunlight of the winter afternoon in our eyes. We unfolded our bagels from the wax paper.

At the time, I did not frequently go out to lunch or order food at restaurants. The fragile ecosystem of my budget could not handle such expenses. I had long ago learned to live without the comforts of take-out and deli counters. I ate breakfast at home—two eggs, scrambled with cheese, coffee splashed with whole milk, a piece of toast. Lunch was taken in the bookstore breakroom immediately following my shift. I packed tuna fish, a good helping of cottage cheese, some almonds or cashews if they were on sale, and a piece of fruit, usually an apple. Dinner was a wild card. It depended largely upon the sales at my grocer. There was a basic rotation that consisted of baked chicken and broccoli, pasta of some sort, or a cut of red meat with salad and potatoes. I had been eating like this for years, decades maybe. The only things I bought out were slices of pizza and coffee. The coffee was often purchased from the Miles of Books café where I received a fifty percent discount.

So, a tuna fish bagel, with its tomato, lettuce, and strange hint of *za'atar*, was something of a delicacy. I drank my coffee, sipped water from a clear plastic cup, and ate my bagel while listening to Jake talk. Let's face it, I was enjoying myself.

—So, you're off at eleven every day?

—For the most part.

—And what does life look like after that? What do you do with yourself?

—Oh, this and that. I read a lot, of course. And I try to catch most of the Mets' games in the summer.

—Cool. I tried watching the Mets since I can't see any Cincinnati games on TV out here. But I can't get into it. Baseball's just not the same if you don't watch your hometown team.

We talked in this manner for some time. I'll admit, I had been nervous while walking from the store to the bagel shop. I had regretted accepting Jake's invitation. But now, with my belly full and my coffee half gone, the tightness in my chest relaxed. The words of our conversation came to me easily. I was comfortable and confident and chatty. *This must be the way Jake feels all the time,* I thought to myself.

Of course, our conversation naturally settled on books. Jake spoke quite poetically about Jeffrey Eugenides, an author whom we had both read. Things were going smoothly, and Jake had many insights that hadn't occurred to me. But then, inexplicably, he lowered his voice halfway through a sentence about hermaphrodites. Just ground to a halt like his batteries had died. My hearing has held up well over the years, but I can't abide mumbling.

—I'm sorry?

Jake's eyes looked through me. I turned around in my seat to follow his gaze. He spoke quietly to the back of my head.

—It's nothing, Charlie. Turn back around.

Jake was studying a customer waiting at the counter. She was short with curly, dark hair and an attractive curve to her body. I didn't take Jake for someone to stare lasciviously at strangers. I was about to ask if he knew the young woman when I realized who it was. I waved my hand.

—Chelsea!

Chelsea was a new employee, one I had trained to shelve just last week. She had been diligently learning the ropes as a bookseller for over a month now. I really took a shining to her. Don't take this the wrong way, but I still enjoy talking to nice, pretty girls. Yes, I'm several decades older than her. And I understand it's hard to hear this and not think that my motivations are untoward. But they're not. I just appreciate her company and it doesn't hurt that she's pretty. Call me a creep if you want.

I glanced back at Jake; my hand raised in the air to flag Chelsea down. Upon reading his expression, I let my hand fall back to the table. He didn't look good. Beads of sweat had broken out on his forehead, his eyes cast down to the orange table, crazy with worry, like he was in the throes of a malaria dream. Turning back to Chelsea, I noticed that she seemed to have caught the same fever. She dawdled for a moment with a brown bag in one hand and a large coffee in the other, interested in nothing, seemingly, except the tops of her sneakers.

—Hey, Charlie.

Then, she shuffled out of the bagel shop without looking at Jake, letting in a cold burst of wintry air through the door. Jake moaned under his breath like he had just stubbed his toe. His bagel waited on its wax paper half eaten. He dropped a napkin over it.

—I'm going to have to quit.

Hold on, hold on.

Let me take this opportunity to tell you about Chelsea, because she is at the heart of this story almost as much as Jake.

Chelsea had been hired the previous month just as the part-time holiday workers were leaving. Chelsea is a nice girl. Quiet and polite. Her hair is a warm front of inclement weather—curly, brown, and untended. The curls fall in front of her large—some might say googly—eyes. She is beautiful, but not in a way that everybody can agree upon. Like I said, the wide eyes and curly hair are an acquired taste, but her hooked witch's nose is downright polarizing. I've always liked a woman with a remarkable nose, but that's just me. Another point of contention might be the way in which she speaks. Chelsea has a mush mouth. I suppose today they would say she has a speech impediment or a lisp or whathave-you. Where I come from, it's called a mush mouth. It's as if her tongue is too big for her teeth, her bottom jaw too jutting. Something about her mouth isn't right. I found it endearing. I still do. The best singers have voices littered with imperfection.

It was the end of winter now, but spring was coming, and with it, spring employee turnover. Many booksellers worked while they attended college. Students showed up in the city, regular as cicada infestations every fall. When the semester ended, they burrowed back to their homes across the country leaving a large coverage gap through the spring and summer months. Chelsea should have been one of these—she was a college student—but she was remaining in New York straight through the year for reasons unknown to me. The store was slower in the spring and summer, but we still usually brought on one or two people as temps to fill this void.

I liked everything about Chelsea save one thing: She was going to school to become a teacher. Evaluating her character, I didn't think she would finish the program. She was just too sweet to join that thuggish profession.

The greatest secret of every bookstore is that we are prejudice against teachers. Chelsea hadn't uncovered this fact yet, but it would rear its ugly head soon enough. Our bias must be kept a secret, not only because we are in the business of customer service, but also because teachers supply the store with steady business and lucrative school-related events. We must be nice to their faces. But our intolerance for educators is well founded, let me assure you. The problem is complicated. Its roots run as deep and labyrinthine as Middle Eastern border disputes. But I'll try to explain briefly.

Because of the money involved, stores often set up discount programs for teachers. Our store, for instance, had a teacher's discount card which allowed twenty percent off books that they bought for the classroom. Please note the caveat: *for the classroom*. When this program was first introduced, the cashiers were instructed to enforce the rules and remind the teachers that their personal purchases were full price. Only those books that were intended for the *children in your class* should be discounted the twenty percent.

Well. The uproar was mighty. Teachers are prolific complainers—litigious and penny-pinching at every turn. They wrote emails to the corporate customer service in droves. The teachers who were aware of the policy told lies to the cashiers. On more than one occasion, I have had a teacher approach my register and lay her discount card down saying, *These are all for my classroom,* while stacking trashy romance novels in front of me, her educator's discount card indicating that she teaches first grade. They stare me in the eye, these educators, daring me to contest, already composing the customer service complaint email in their minds.

These discount thieves believe that they are the most undervalued people in America because it occasionally suits a politician's campaign to say so. They believe they are not paid enough and that no one respects the fact that they are molding the generation of tomorrow or whatever. In many ways, I suppose this is true. But let's call a spade a spade; they get summers off. There are a lot of things I would put up with if I got every summer off in return.

I've worked with several teachers over the years, and I will begrudgingly admit that they were by and large excellent employees. They possess strong work ethics and are skilled at conversing with customers. But that's beside the goddamned point. Everyone who ever worked in a bookstore can retell an incident when a teacher was inhumanly nasty to them. I dreaded the day when Chelsea's spirit would be crushed under the power of that job. I didn't want to see it.

I realize I'm a little off track here. Thinking about teachers gets me fired up. Back to Jake, then.

—Quit the bookstore?

Chelsea had exited the restaurant, huddled with her purchases, and rushed down the sidewalk. She didn't look back.

—Why would you quit the bookstore? What just happened?

—Chelsea and I don't get along very well.

I did my parrot impression.

—Don't get along very well. . .

He didn't elaborate.

—I wasn't even aware that the two of you knew each other.

—Yeah, no one at the bookstore knows about it.

Flabbergasted and embarrassed, I didn't know how to proceed. All the gruffness that had peeled away during our lunch grew like tree bark around me again. Jake's silence pecked at me, trying to extract empathetic questions. But I didn't *want* to know anything else. Yes, curiosity would get the best of most people in this situation. How did they first meet, you might wonder? What caused the distance between them? Was there love in the air? Nope! No thanks. To me, the whole matter was entirely distasteful. I hate knowing other people's business, particularly if romantic elements are involved. I didn't want to know that the girl Jake liked wouldn't go out with him. I didn't care. I got divorced young, so I had enough of that garbage to last a lifetime, thank you very much. I wasn't good at consoling people, and I didn't aim to get better. I know this world can be rough; I'm human. But I just didn't have the patience or the desire to be a sounding board. I pushed my chair out.

—Well, thanks for lunch.

—Chelsea's from Cincinnati too.

And here we go...

Halfway out of my chair, I slid back down. My coffee was almost gone, what was left grown cold. The door and the bitter winter winds beyond called to me like sirens from the other side of the windowpane.

—Is that so?

I actually knew Chelsea was from Cincinnati. During training she mentioned that she was raised in Ohio and had worked in a library there for some time before coming to New York for college. It didn't register with me that she and Jake were from the same town. They're all from Ohio, these kids.

—Did you two used to see each other?

—Yeah.

Jake shook his head.

—And I broke up with her before I went to college.

—Is she still mad about that?

—No. She recently found something out about me.

And did I ask what she found out? No. No, I didn't. I would be keeping all of this to myself, were I Jake. I hoped that my silence might suggest he put the brakes on the soap opera. Jake saw nothing but a green flag.

—We used to talk on the phone occasionally, even though we weren't together anymore. Chelsea was here, in New York, and I was at Pitt. Then I graduated from college and Chelsea still had two more years at St. Johns. She stopped calling me, and I don't know, I guess I missed her.

—So, you moved to Queens?

—I told her that I got an internship and would be coming to New York.

—But there was no internship?

—No.

—Where did you say you were interning?

—The *New York Times*.

—Really?

—I was making it up on the spot.

—But the *Times*? Wow.

—Anyhow, I didn't actually have the internship. I didn't have *any* internship or job or anything. I just came here to be with her. But when I got here, I found out she was dating someone else. That's why she wasn't calling me.

I raised my eyebrows and looked towards the exit.

—These things happen.

—Yeah. So, I stopped calling her. But then she got the job at the bookstore. *My* bookstore. She knew I'd been lying about the internship.

—How did she know?

—Because I told her.

—You could have said you were still interning part-time. Or that the internship was over.

—Well, I didn't. I told her the truth.

—That was a mistake. You should have continued lying.

—I told her that I came to New York for her. And she hasn't spoken to me since.

I considered this.

—Shit. Maybe you *should* quit.

—Thanks, Charlie.

Silence fell over our table again. I took this opportunity to once again push my chair back from the table.

—Thanks so much for lunch.

—Hey, don't worry about it. Thanks for saving me at work. I'll be more careful from now on. I just have to get this Chelsea thing out of my head and concentrate on what I'm doing.

I stood up.

—Good. Good luck with that.

5.

Push the button, Charlie

MARCH 15, 2010. Back office. Acrid smell of boxed reams of paper and too much aftershave. Both Michaels, me, and a little black machine. Seeing the two assistant managers in the close quarters of the tiny office was like witnessing a sketch comedy gag waiting to start. Michael P was so much taller than M, so much heavier, and carried so much more corny energy. P winked at me as I walked in and M took notes about God-knows-what, a slight frown on his face. A single metal folding chair formed a triangle with their padded black swivels. Since Michael M was busy writing on his notepad, I spoke to Michael P.

—Should I sit?

—No, Charlie, this is a standing session. You have to stand the whole time we talk.

I chuckled heartlessly. Michael P broke character.

—Of course, Charlie! Have a seat.

After I made myself comfortable, we jumped right into it. Michael P led the conversation. M didn't seem to be paying attention.

—All right, Charlie, what have you learned about the new Color SwiftFoot©?

I was silent for too long, thinking. Start talking, Charlie.

—I haven't learned as much as I'd like. It's in color, so it's better for magazines.

P waited for me to continue and M now finally raised his head from his notetaking. But I didn't have anything else to say. I looked from one to the other, smiling my best friendly-old-man smile. When it became clear that I had fired all my ammo, Michael M broke into a wry smile. He spoke to me but looked at Michael P.

—Soooo, you've learned that the *Color* SwiftFoot© is in *color*.

Michael M was always saying things like that. The impertinent son-of-a-bitch.

Let me catch you up. A black-and-white screened SwiftFoot debuted on the Black Friday before Christmas. I didn't have much to do with the proceedings. During the all-store meeting where they had introduced the new product to us, they had indicated that the staff should take its sales seriously, but I found myself outside the loop. Michael P and Michael M had stressed how imperative it was to sell a bunch of these suckers during Christmas, but half of my shifts took place while the store was closed. Who was I supposed to sell them to? The other shelvers?

At the time, the SwiftFoot seemed unnecessary to me, as if someone wanted to add a thesaurus to my coffeemaker. Books operate just fine. We don't need a software upgrade. But this new device was now in the store, so to a degree, it became part of my life. I was aware of E-Readers before Miles of Books put one on the market but had never used one. It was small and rectangular, almost the size of a thin book. The screen was gray, the back cover white. As I understood it, the SwiftFoot connected to a website to buy digital books that appeared somewhere in the machine. Then you just read and pressed a button to turn the pages. My understanding never went beyond these facts because it never needed to.

The SwiftFoot did not do well that first Christmas. The managers became intense about its sales and then abruptly eased up after the new year. The holidays are Game Seven of the World Series to a bookstore. Win this one or scrap the whole year. There are always plenty of new sales initiatives during the Yuletide—the bag of tricks is turned upside down. The previous year, they wanted us to solicit emails so that we could send the customers coupons. Another year, they wanted us to push hardcover books over paperbacks. The management staff kept wildly inaccurate tracking-sheets on the number of hardcover books each employee claimed to have sold. BOGO deals, exclusive editions of *Monopoly*, blankets with literary quotes on them—there was always something, some magic bullet that was going to help us make our sales plan during the holiday. This year it was the SwiftFoot, and next year it might be lap desks with cup holders or a cardboard popup version of *Fear and Loathing in Las Vegas*. Who knows! The best thing to do, as a bookseller, is to duck and cover. Tell the bosses what they want to hear and by January it'll be back to business as usual. The stick-to-itiveness of the management staff left much to be desired.

In their defense, the desperation during the holidays was unavoidable. Here's a startling fact: A retail store will do nearly thirty percent of its business in the weeks between Thanksgiving and Christmas. Thirty percent! It is vital to use every advantage to sculpt this small chunk of time into a success. I understand this. I understand the gravity of those forty days. But these niches became the focus of the entire store for the winter season and then melted away in the spring. It was easy to forget they were ever there.

And so went the SwiftFoot, I thought. By February of the following year, it was hardly mentioned. We still carried the thing and people occasionally asked for it, but the drive to sell was dead. Deader than dead. In fact, on one occasion, the battery ran out of juice on the display model, and nobody noticed for days. It was just an unusable slice of plastic, displayed at the front of our store under signs of Ozymandian proportions, boasting its innovative importance to society. But just like all the other holiday initiatives, the SwiftFoot had gone the way of the audio cassette book; it became extinct like brass bookends and *The Hardy Boys*. So much for the future of the bookstore.

Then, a few weeks out from Easter, we received a new E-Reader. This one was faster and smarter (whatever that means) and held more books. It came in color, and one could manipulate any part of the screen by touching it. It was as if a child had yelled *game on* after a car passed down the street. Michael P and Michael M were back on the prowl. The two assistant managers solemnly vowed to train everyone on the new Color SwiftFoot.

I dared to hope they might pass me over. It isn't that I'm bad with technology. I'm not *that* kind of old person. I keep up with things—I own a Blu-ray player and I'm aware of Beyonce. But I was at a point in life where I could see the failures coming before they arrived. Adept at identifying the markings of a short-lived fad, I didn't want to be a part of this one. I kept my head down and quietly did my shelving until they finally snatched me into the back office.

—Is there anything else you've picked up about the Color SwiftFoot©, Charlie?

Tall and wide-framed, Michael P managed to hover around three hundred pounds while not looking overweight. He kept a trim goatee and gel in his hair. He wore a small pair of glasses when he read and they looked alien on his hulking frame, like a satellite dish on a cathedral. Michael M was as petite as Michael P was large. Like I've mentioned, M was surly. But he also spoke with an amazing vocabulary. I often walked directly from our conversations to the dictionary section. Michael M wore ties to work and no one else on the management staff ever did. He and Michael P were always together in the store whispering furtively. It was rumored that the two of them were secretly dating.

I floundered along with the conversation.

—Sure, that's not all I know. It has a touch screen. Customers like that. You can subscribe to newspapers on this one, right?

Michael P agreed.

—Yes, you can. But there are a lot of other things to learn about the product if you're going to sell it. We need you to help us with this, Charlie. It looks bad if members of the staff aren't fully trained. The district manager is coming for a visit today. What would happen if you had to troubleshoot a problem with the Color SwiftFoot© in front of him? You need to get a better handle on it.

—Well, that's what we're doing here, right? I thought this was a training session.

I looked from one Michael to the other. Michael M smirked again.

—Sure, Charlie. It's just that many of the other employees took the initiative to *seek out* information on the Color SwiftFoot©.

I didn't reply, but there were many things I could have said were I quicker on my feet. Other employees worked more hours a week than me. Other employees planned on buying an E-Reader and had a vested interest in how it worked. Other employees were scheduled in the café or at the customer service desk and therefore had more downtime where they could fiddle with the SwiftFoot.

I came in every morning and had a time-specific task to accomplish. When was I supposed to study the new fad? But even if my mental acuity had allowed me to access these ideas in a timely manner, this wasn't the moment to say them. Sometimes you have to swallow it.

The Color SwiftFoot crouched on the desk between the Michaels like a repugnant beetle. I picked it up and pressed the button to bring it to life. The background was blue and green, a picture of a clear day on a bucolic field. It looked pretty and perfect and I wished I were there instead of here. A worry grew in my chest, but I shrugged my shoulders and looked Michael M in the eye.

—All right. I guess I have some catching up to do then. Where do you go to buy a book?

For the next half hour Michael M drove me through the ins and outs of the Color SwiftFoot, stopping when we arrived at functionalities he thought would be helpful to point out in a sales pitch. Michael P whistled to himself during the lesson and banged his sausage-link fingers against the keyboard of his computer. When the technical training with Michael M began, P had been constructing schedules. But by the time M and I were finished, he was reading a webpage about celebrity gossip.

My attention wavered during the session like the refraction above hot coals. I was so frustrated and so angry about the way Michael M had talked to me that my brain malfunctioned. I drifted. I tried to listen, but my mind wandered through a forest of imaginary conversations where I told Michael M exactly how I felt, pointed out with precision how he had wronged me. By the time we reached the end of the lesson Michael M had said many things and I had learned very few. But he sat back satisfied in his swivel chair and held me in his smarmy gaze. This time he looked at me but spoke to Michael P.

—I think it happened, Michael.

I smiled to give the impression that I found his coyness amusing. I didn't.

—What? What happened?

—You had your *Aha* moment.

—What's that?

—It's the point where everything suddenly clicks, and you understand. Your mind says *Aha*!

The Michaels swiveled back and forth in their chairs as if they were working out of the same hive. Michael M was ablaze with glory.

—Everyone in the store has been having them with the Color SwiftFoot©. It happened to you too, didn't it, Charlie?

~~~~~

Look, I'm old. It wasn't always this way.

I was born in Queens, New York, the only child of Helen and Harry Mueller. My mother was a quiet woman, cold and austere on the surface with strange streaks of kindness that, even at this age, I don't fully understand. She would, quite literally, not talk to me for days at a time. And then—sometimes for an hour, sometimes for a week—she wouldn't let go of me. Hugging me, kissing me, buying me toys and treats.

She worked as a secretary in Manhattan, and I was left alone for large swaths of time beginning at a young age. I grew to enjoy being alone. My father was still married to my mother but was often absent. I don't know what my father did for money, but I know he drank a lot. They never fought, as far as I can remember, but they never talked much either. It was like they were living
~~~~~

two completely separate lives weakly held together by the obligation I represented. They split some years after I moved out of the apartment, in 1954 maybe or 1955.

I remember them being pleasant with each other once on a trip to Fun Land. I've seen pictures of the three of us at different vacation spots—beaches, boardwalks, county fairs—but I only have a memory of this one trip, to Fun Land, which was just across the river in New Jersey. It was a rinky-dink amusement park by today's standards, but it was something else back then. There was a rollercoaster, for one thing. Not all the amusement parks had rollercoasters. The Rumbler, as the wooden death trap was named, put Fun Land on the map. I rode The Rumbler and many other whirlabouts and loop-de-loops with my father.

Fun Land, despite the insinuation in its name, did not have a fun house. It did not have a house of horrors either. What it had was The Land of Tomorrow—a building that housed life-sized dioramas dedicated to the world to come. You know the shtick—flying cars, talking robots, dummies of men and women in monochromatic jumpsuits. My father was something of a futurist, I guess, always looking ahead to the automated life. He wandered through The Land of Tomorrow with undisguised wonderment, pointing out massive computers to my mother, fidgeting with a mechanical arm, standing still and laughing to himself as a moving walkway ushered him down the sidewalk past all the metallic storefronts of Jules Verne Street.

He scooped me up in his arms when we entered The Recreational Room of the Future and placed me on his shoulders. My mother stood next to us, her purse held by both hands in front of her waist, her pointed brown glasses hanging from the tip of her nose. My father kept one hand on my back, steadying me on his shoulders, and one around my mother. She leaned into him, pressing the side of her body against his.

A booming narrator described the scene from The Recreational Room of the Future on a recorded loop. We listened to it twice through. Two mannequins sat on a couch as amenities were showered upon them by mechanical servants—an automatic wine pourer, a dinner of roasted duck on a conveyer belt, a television that rose from beneath the floor. And they never had to move. The man pressed a button and their desires appeared before them.

My father was over the moon. The Recreational Room of the Future was all he talked about on the drive home from Fun Land. He couldn't wait until the future was here. He kept pestering my mother, when did she think they would start building houses like that? When would they be affordable for normal people like us? Did she think that an apartment, one like ours, in Queens, would be fixed up like that? My mother laughed in her patronizing, almost mean-spirited way, *Any day now, Harry. Any day.*

As we walked from our car to the apartment building, my father lifted me once again and put me on his shoulders. It was early evening in June. I remember this moment clearly, even after all these years. The stars were just beginning to come out. The street smelled of exhaust, but layered underneath that smell were the scents of flowers and pollen. The darkness was punctuated with soft neon pulsations of lightning bugs. There were lightning bugs in New York City back then. I wished the exhaust was gone, that all the cars of the city were gone, and that I could smell the spring like the kids in the country could smell the spring. This time of year reminded me of the movies I'd seen. It reminded me of Dorothy running through poppy fields in *The Wizard of Oz*, of Errol Flynn riding a horse in the *Santa Fe Trail*, of the kids running through the farms in California at the end of *The Grapes of Wrath*. It was a fantasy of mine to be there one day, be in a place of pure nature where there were no tall buildings, no cars, no exhaust fumes. On my father's shoulders, we were a totem pole, one face looking to the past, another looking to the future and the Land of Tomorrow.

—What do you think of that, Charlie?

He paused for a moment, and I didn't answer because I wasn't sure what he meant.

—How would you like to press a button and get whatever you want?

6.
Philosophical Phil

PHIL was an interesting specimen. Phil once told me that during his senior year of high school, the other children voted him Most Likely to Wear a Top Hat in College. They made up the category specifically for him, he said. Phil took pride in this unique tribute, but I suspect that his pride was misplaced. The award had the ring of mockery.

With long, curly hair beginning to gray around his ears, he was tall and thin, eyes pensive, cattish even. He was pushing fifty but moved through the sales floor with lithe movements, like an aged Puck thirty midsummers later. He wore short-sleeved, button-up shirts that during his shift slowly became undone to reveal images of cartoon characters—usually Marvin the Martian—on the undershirts beneath.

A young kid stopped and loitered at the information desk around noon. Phil had just finished a phone call, and I was pulling an empty H-cart back to receiving. The kid was blotchy and awkward and looked a bit lost.

—I need a book for class.

Phil was a member of the British Royal Guard. The kid looked at Phil and Phil didn't move. Waited. The kid continued.

—I need to write a report.

Nothing from Phil. Hardly blinked. The thing was, if Phil wasn't asked a direct question, he assumed the customer was just making conversation. Phil was a skilled question-answerer. Not so good with conversation, though. The kid eventually found the magic words.

—. . . can you help me?

There ya go.

—Ok. What are you looking for?

—Nonfiction, I guess. Where's the nonfiction section?

Oh, and then he ruined it! This was going to get ugly. Phil exhaled, exasperated. He squinted and massaged the bridge of his nose. The boy turned to me, frightened, but I cast my eyes to the floor and began to push my cart. You're on your own, brother. I mean, come on—*nonfiction section*? Geez. You get what you deserve for that one. Phil began berating the young man as I walked away.

—See the section behind me? The one labeled *fiction*?

—Yeah. . .

—Beyond that section is Mystery, Romance, and Science Fiction. Everything else—everything else in the *whole, entire store*—is nonfiction. So, you might want to be a little more specific. Or maybe I'll send you back to class with an Audubon Society Field Guide about mushrooms. Would you like that? Would you like to write your little report about *mushrooms*?

Hey, don't look at me. I don't know how Phil didn't get fired. I mean, I hate the nonfiction question, too, but talking to people like that? I mean, *Christ*. Oh, well. Phil wasn't really that bad. He just got worked up over certain things. He was generally a sweet guy and would probably find the young man a good book for his report. Phil knew his stuff; that's for sure. He knew his books but had no clue how to talk to people. Or maybe he *did* know how to talk to people and chose not to do it correctly. You never know with Phil.

I punched in the code on the receiving door and swung it open, almost hitting Jake.

—Watch it there, Charlie. I'm in a precarious situation here.

Jake Fletcher, high wiring on the top rung of an old, traitorous ladder. Jake had straightened out his money-counting issues. He'd been doing well since our lunch at the bagel shop. Management had trained him in every section of the store at this point. They loved him. And why wouldn't they? He had a kind word for everyone he met and accomplished the work of three employees each day.

Many employees made this impression when they first started. The new guys often had bright dispositions and good work ethics. But, in most cases, this attitude fell apart once they became comfortable. Their breaks lengthened, their recovery of the store grew sloppy, and they started leaning against the counter at the information desk, speaking flippantly to customers. But not Jake. Not yet anyway. He worked like the ink was still wet on his application. I could tell by the way he navigated the receiving room that he could probably run the place.

The receiving room was an elaborate contraption. Many booksellers worked long careers without ever fully understanding its complexity. Receiving rooms were different in every Miles of Books location, and a small or oddly shaped receiving room could handicap a business. Even with our large space in receiving, November and December were marked by towers of boxes, swaying obelisks of books, threatening to topple. But this dangerous condition was not the norm for Miles of Books, simply a holiday hazard. At my Miles of Books location, the receiving room was strictly ordered—almost obsessively so. It was the kind of room that made you consider separating your M&M's by color before eating them. It takes a good receiving manager to keep things straight. Someone tough and organized, smart and no-nonsense. Becky was this type of woman.

She was morbidly overweight, but no one seemed to notice. She was one of the nastiest people I ever met, but for some reason her anger was funny. She would call an employee a son-of-a-bitch for forgetting to break down a cardboard box, and he would walk away chuckling. Her greasy, brown hair was forever strapped back in a swaying ponytail. And I swear, her black eyebrows were so expressive they could lift and drop nearly two inches on her forehead as her anger undulated. She wore sweatpants to work every day, moving her considerable bulk around that cramped room like a slalom skier through the sloping flags.

Becky spent her days opening box after box after box, looking at the covers of each book and separating them onto the different shelving carts. Every tenth book or so, she would regard the cover with skepticism and mutter to herself, *Look at these fucking idiots.* I don't know whether she realized she was saying the words out loud. The sentence held a trance-like cadence. She most often applied her catch phrase to group photos, almost always men, such as baseball teams, 1920s union protestors, war stories. Now and then she would ask the ether to look at fucking idiots of mixed company, such as the Supreme Court or a nun floating in a sea of ragged orphans. But it was mostly men. I suppose this was telling.

I carried a stack of returns in my left arm. I had to be careful to sort them correctly. Everything depended on organization, and Becky guarded the integrity of the return shelves like a rottweiler in a prison yard. When a store returns books, the books go directly back to the publisher. Since my stack of books went to myriad publishers, it needed to be sorted. The names of publishers were printed on the face of each shelf to help with this sorting, but because of the different quantities that go back to each publisher, they could not be put in alphabetical order. For example, the major book houses—Simon & Schuster, Random House, Harper-Collins, Penguin—needed to have more space than the smaller ones—Kensington Publishing, Oxford University Press, Thomas Nelson. So there needed to be higher shelf space for the larger publishers and lower shelf space for the smaller publishers. To accomplish this, the major houses all needed to be on the same row of shelves thereby destroying any chance that the publishers could be sorted alphabetically. Many booksellers had to ask Becky where certain publishers were, which annoyed her, and many booksellers made mistakes with the sorting, which annoyed her even more. Terry Fernando, that asshole, just plopped his stack down on the Random House shelf each time without even attempting to sort.

Becky insisted that there was some logic to the setup, that they were alphabetical linearly or some bullshit, and if you just looked at it the right way it all made sense. I don't know about that. I often stood in front of the return wall for minutes, hypnotized almost, searching for John Wiley & Sons.

I was in just such a trance, searching the returns area for Ingram, when Jake interrupted my thoughts.

—Which one you looking for, Charlie?

—Ingram. Don't worry, I'll find it.

Jake scanned the shelves and pointed.

—Top left. Next to Houghton Mifflin.

I nodded and reached up to place the book.

—One second, Charlie.

It was Phil's voice. I didn't even hear him come in.

—Is that supposed to go back to Ingram or Ingram *Paper*?

Oh, shit.

I already knew that Phil was right, but I zapped the book again with the handheld scanner and looked at the Vendor Return section. Ingram Paper. Phil crowed.

—That's what I thought. You boys need to develop some attention to detail.

Phil shook his head at Jake and me, unbuttoning the top of his shirt to reveal the uppermost part of Marvin the Martian's helmet. I placed the book on the Ingram Paper shelf, but it was too late. Becky migrated across the room. Her voice limped with fragile patience.

—Charlie, you know that Ingram and Ingram Paper are different, right?

Her eyebrows climbed to her greasy widow's peak in a searching arch.

—I know.

—You know they go to two different places?

—I know, Becky.

—So, if you send an Ingram Paper return back to Ingram, it's going to the wrong place. They'll ship it back and we'll have to pay for it.

—I know.

—The district manager is coming today. He might pop in back here. I need everything to be perfect.

—The district manager is coming again? He was just here last week.

—He didn't show last week. But he's coming for real today. You have to put the returns in the right place.

—And I usually do. I didn't see that it said *Paper*.

Becky stared in my face for an unusually long time, trying to root out any false ideas about the differences between Ingram and Ingram Paper. I'm sure that reverberating in her head were the words, *Look at this fucking idiot*. After a lengthy stare-down, she nodded.

—Ok.

She walked back to her computer, clearly suspecting me of chronically misplacing returns. Her suspicions were baseless.

I still had a handful of returns to place and was hypervigilant through the rest of the process. Phil lingered next to me as I separated the books. I thought he was waiting for me to make another mistake. This, of course, infuriated me. How dare he watch me like this, like I was a child handling a steak knife? I wouldn't even accept this treatment from one of the bosses, and Phil was certainly not one of the bosses. My face grew hot, and I made huffing sounds as I shelved, but Phil didn't move away. He also didn't seem to notice my frustration. He finally spoke.

—Twenty-nine.

—What?

—Twenty-nine Philosophy titles on the return shelves. Ridiculous.

—Shut up, Phil.

This was Becky, her face bathed in the electric glow of her computer. Her voice was tired, like a boxer rising from his stool who can't believe his beaten foe is going to fight another round.

—I won't shut up. Do you know how many titles are in Philosophy all together? Two hundred and eighty-one. Returning twenty-nine titles means we've just gotten rid of another ten percent of the Philosophy section. It's *decimation.*

Becky and I made eye contact and shook our heads in unison. Decimation. Oh man. Here we go again. I started shelving the returns faster so that I could get out of there. You see, Phil liked to memorize things, like the exact number of books in the Philosophy section or the first five pages of *Crime and Punishment*, and then use these tokens to impress people. He had a fact-a-day calendar in his head and would often steer conversations toward these facts so that he could impart his knowledge. Both Becky and I had heard the decimation trivia a half dozen times. Jake was fresh meat.

Phil directed his words to me even though he knew I'd been to this rodeo several times.

—And it actually *is* decimation. Decimation is Latin and was first used to describe Roman battles. If you lost ten percent of your soldiers, you had been decimated. It literally meant losing ten percent.

Jake The Rube.

—Really? That's so interesting. I've never heard that before.

Phil grimaced like a cartoon wolf tying a handkerchief around his neck and licking his lips. Becky turned her face from the computer. Her eyebrows hung low. She had something on Phil, I could tell.

—Wait a second. The last time I heard this factoid it was the other way around. Decimation meant *leaving* ten percent and *losing* ninety.

Phil was quiet, pulling the hairs on the end of his chin.

—I don't think so. I'm not sure.

—Well, I *am* sure. I'm sure you're full of shit.

—I'll have to look into it.

This was one of the most grandiose concessions Phil had ever made. He stood next to me, statuesque, thinking. It was uncomfortable. Then he continued as if he hadn't paused.

—Either way, home office is stealing all our Philosophy books. They took eighteen titles from the section the month before and twenty-one the month before that.

Becky waged the old war.

—No one buys Philosophy, Phil.

—Yes, no one buys Philosophy from *us* because we have a terrible selection. Back in the day, we had awesome titles and it was an easy hand sell. Now there's nothing over there. Do you want *The Philosophy of Buffy the Vampire Slayer* or a copy of *The Idiot's Guide to Plato*? It's pathetic.

Jake The Rube then made a terrible mistake.

—What types of Philosophy do you like, Phil?

I advise that you never, under any circumstances, ask a bookseller what they like to read. You will not get an honest answer. It is their profession to talk about these things and they tend to be overly savvy. They take note of what types of people buy what types of books. They understand that reading different authors puts you in different social structures. And I'm not just talking about the difference between reading James Patterson versus James Joyce. A seasoned bookseller can take your measure and gauge whether they can garner more respect by favoring Tess Gerritsen over J.D. Robb, Patrick Rothfuss over George R.R. Martin, Roberto Bolaño over Gabriel Garcia Marquez. Let me tell you about Ludmilla. Every time a customer asked Ludmilla for a recommendation, she talked about Dostoyevsky and Tolstoy and anyone else she could think of with a Russian-sounding name. But during her breaks she could always be found in the back leafing through one particular science fiction series about pirates in outer space. The customer who asked her the question received a *CliffsNotes* description of *The Master and Margarita* and a full biography of Dostoyevsky's time spent in a Siberian prison. No mention of cosmic buccaneers, only a thin façade of Russophilia.

Phil was the worst offender. Did he actually read Philosophy books? Maybe. He usually kept his nose in a graphic novel during free time. But he would talk your ear off about being and nothingness if given the chance—not just to customers but to fellow employees as well. Phil was one of those curious people that could not read facial expressions, and without a vocal cue, could not tell when the conversation was over. Jake, with his thoughtless question, had unwittingly loosed a half-hour lecture upon himself.

I finished shelving my returns and regarded Jake. He was engaged with Phil, asking questions and nodding at the answers. Was he really that false or was he interested in what Phil had to say? I couldn't decide. I left the room. Even though Becky had given me a hard time about Ingram Paper, I felt bad that she had to sit through the history of Philosophy according to Phil. Again.

7.

Karen S and the Very Bad Customer Service

A LOT of the trouble began the week I trained a woman named Karen S. At this point in my career, I had trained so many shelvers that I was able to identify a good employee by the way they learned. When I had trained Chelsea, for instance, I found she had developed poor habits while working at her college library. That's fine. I had dealt with this issue before. She was a wounded arm that I could set, heal, and make stronger. Karen S was different. She was something more insidious, a cut that you just know will become infected.

Karen S was a smartass. She was old—not as old as me, but old—and she dressed like she was still young—tight white pants, a pink blouse, and a flowing, silver scarf. I eyed that scarf warily. I've never had much luck with scarf-wearing women. It quickly became clear that Karen didn't respect me or her new station. She smiled wryly when I told her that shelving was the most important job in the store. She was playing with her cell phone while I demonstrated proper usage of the shelving log. Every time I outlined the intricacies of the sections or the necessity of shifting the bays while shelving, she said *Oh, reeeeeeally*, dragging it out like a test of the emergency broadcasting system.

We finished shelving and returned the carts to receiving. Back on the sales floor, I walked Karen S through the computer's search engine while we waited for the mid-shift booksellers who would take over and begin a new portion of the training. A customer approached while we waited, big and burly. He had hard eyes and a jaw line disinclined to losing arguments. A tough cookie. I thought this would be a great opportunity for Karen S to witness the proper handling of a patron. I put on my customer service face.

—Hello, sir. What can I help you with today?

—Yeah.

One syllable is often all it takes to surmise a stranger's mood. He continued.

—I'm going to need a road map of Wyoming and a history book about Wyoming.

Nodding my head and typing.

—Now, I know we're not going to have a road map of Wyoming in the store, but maybe I can order one for you.

—What about the history book?

—I'll have to look that up.

—How do you know you don't have a map of Wyoming without looking it up?

—We only carry local street maps.

—I was in here a while ago and you had all kinds of maps.

—That's right. I'm sure we did. But we recently changed. We just have local, New York City maps now.

From left field, Karen S.

—What do you need a map for anyway?

The customer looked over my shoulder at Karen S, appalled that she had spoken out of turn. He enunciated as if she didn't speak English.

—I'm . . . going . . . to . . . Wyoming.

—Well, no crap. Use the computer.

The man didn't say anything now, just stonewalled Karen S with those hard eyes. He then looked to me for the customer service he required.

But Karen S would not be passed over.

—You don't know you can get maps on the internet? They're free.

—But I like to have them in the car.

—Print them out.

I should have intervened before this.

—Karen, please. Just observe for now.

She threw her hands in the air.

—All right.

Mortified. Completely mortified. Not only was she being rude to the customer, but she was actively trying to lose a sale with this internet talk. And she said *crap* to him. I mean, who in the hell acts like this? Insane. Karen S was clearly not going to work out. I would have to tell Don about her behavior. I ordered both a map and a history book on Wyoming for the customer and sent him on his way. My customer service was clean and fluid as surgery. He didn't seem quite angry enough to call the corporate number by the time he left.

I begged the clock to hurry, wishing that the next bookseller would arrive soon. I couldn't deal with Karen S any longer. I felt that the very sound of her voice might brush burn my skin. Just to kill some time we toured the front end of the store—the best sellers, the magazine bay, and the SwiftFoot counter. Karen S observed the best sellers and the magazines with mild interest, but she was particularly taken with the Color SwiftFoot. She picked it up and inspected the screen. She read the price aloud in a dubious tone and then whistled through her teeth.

—Tell me how this thing works.

I shrugged my shoulders.

—You buy books from the shop page and then the books show up in a library. Then you read the book.

—Huh. It does a lot of other things, though, right?

She pushed buttons willy-nilly. The SwiftFoot lit up like a pinball machine. I took the device from Karen S and set it back down on its pedestal.

—Don't mess around with it. It sells itself. You don't have to know everything.

Ludmilla mercifully appeared at the SwiftFoot counter. I was able to relax at customer service while Karen S was given a tour of the Music and DVD sections. I was on autopilot for the rest of the day, anxious over what I must do. I don't like to deliver bad news. I would never get another employee in trouble if it weren't completely inevitable. But with Karen S being so new, I figured if we nipped this in the bud right away it would be easier than waiting until she really screwed up later on. Don had me in charge of training because he trusted me and wanted me to be honest about the new employees. What would have happened if the district manager had witnessed the awful display that Karen S had just put on with the Wyoming customer? It'd be a shitstorm, that's what. I owed Don the truth. I was going to have to tattle on Karen S.

It was a shame to lose a brand-new employee, really, what with the difficulty of finding capable help. Miles of Book received tons of applications, but so few of them were good enough to consider hiring. There are many, many clowns out there who think it's a great idea to work at a bookstore. So many, in fact, that the management team often indulged the staff with some of the more ludicrous employment applications. They were funny, I'll admit it. We ate it up.

Any number of goofs will inspire a manager to pass an application around for purposes of ridicule. Some reasons are not so fair. Applicants have been mocked for misspelling a word. They've been scorned for attending a technical school instead of a college. Sometimes previous work experience makes us laugh, such as places of employment called *The Big Banana* or *Fudgey Wudgey*. I remember Michael P fake interviewing an imaginary applicant in the breakroom, speaking in a condescending baby voice: *Awwww, did you* wike *working at da Fudgey Wudgey? Did dey let you put sprinkles on da ice kweam*? Messy writing will always do it; we call it *serial killer writing*. And no one should ever admit to having a grade point average less than 3.0 or serving jail time. The opposite can be claimed without fear of investigation. I've seen people write that they are applying because their psychologist believes they are depressed and need more human contact, that they love Manga and want to have the employee discount to purchase more of it, or that they need a new job because their current employer is an asshole (this one is actually common). Miles of Books received about forty applications a week and hired maybe five or ten people a year. Many applications were never looked at. When people asked when they would hear from us, we said, *Soon, soon*. The real answer? Most likely never.

Of the applicants that are respectable (and they are rare, indeed), there is more luck involved than anything else in actually securing an interview. If the application is on top of the pile and it fits the general requirements, the applicant will be interviewed. The main requirement, the one that counts more than anything else, is that they are available to work at all hours. I've seen serial killer writers get hired due to their open availability.

Management didn't like to go through the hiring process. They avoided it when they could. But they'd have to go back to the starting line with this one—Karen S was not going to cut it. I mean, we might have another Terry Fernando on our hands here. There had been an industrious young girl with café experience that they waffled on hiring last month. Maybe they could call her back, if she hadn't already found something else.

I entered the breakroom and crept quietly near Don's office door. Becky was inside, talking with him. I moved into view, lingering in the doorway. Becky had smashed her girth into a swivel chair while Don drank an Americano and laughed at whatever she had been saying. Don's laughter is strange. He hums his laughter in vibrating waves. He hums his words too; he's heavy on the Ms and drags his feet where staccatos should be. All this humming blends together and his speech is often difficult to distinguish from his laughter. It's as if his laughter is not spontaneous, but a long, drawn-out word that he uses when he finds something amusing. Becky was clearly agitated, but Don looked on serenely, occasionally sipping his espresso drink. When Becky began to repeat some of the things she had already said, Don reached out and placed his hand on her knee. He looked her in the eye.

—It'll be fine, Becky. I promise. Please stop worrying about it.

—But the district manager will be here tomorrow and we're not ready.

—You really think he's coming tomorrow? Hmmmm. How many times has he canceled on us?

—He'll show up eventually, Don.

—And when he does, we'll be just fine.

He held her gaze for a moment with his big, tired eyes and then finally turned to me.

—Hello, Charlie

—Morning, Don.

—The new hire seems to like you.

—Really?

He hummed some more laughter and glanced toward Becky.

—Are you surprised? Hmmmm. Of *course* Karen liked you, Charlie.

—Did she leave already?

—Yes, she was done at eleven. We don't want to overload her on the first day.

Best to cut to the chase.

—I need to talk to you about the training.

Don shifted his slow eyes to Becky once more and then back to me.

—Was there a problem?

—Well . . .

Don arched his eyebrows. I looked over my shoulder into the breakroom. Don followed my gaze.

—You can close the door, Charlie.

I nodded, pulling shut the office door. The place became cluttered and cramped. Piles of papers that I hadn't noticed before now appeared particularly messy. The space that separated Don and me seemed much shorter than it had with the door open. Becky was impossibly huge in her chair in the corner, like a tree that had outgrown its planter plot. There was a small foldout chair in the corner where I could have sat, but Don did not offer it to me. I said my piece.

—I don't know that Karen S is going to work out.

—And what makes you think that?

—She wasn't very receptive to my training, for one thing. It's her first day and she didn't seem to care about learning.

—All right.

—But the main problem was with a customer we helped.

I relayed the story to Don and Becky. Becky was oddly quiet the whole time. I got the feeling I was making her uncomfortable. I described the scene with the Wyoming customer the best I could, but the story didn't have the impact it deserved. I didn't tell it right or something. They weren't appropriately shocked by her behavior. The office seemed even quieter and more cramped when I finished.

—Hmmm. Thank you for sharing that, Charlie. We'll wait and see how Karen does.

I nodded again. I don't know what I expected Don to say, but this was a disappointment. I suppose I expected swift justice. I suppose I wanted Don to pound his meaty hand on the desk, upsetting his coffee with his furious anguish. I suppose I wanted him to snatch up the phone and roughly dial Karen S on her cell and explain to her in tense, eloquent sentences that her use of the word *crap* and her suggestion that Mr. Wyoming use the internet instead of buy a map from Miles of Books were utterly revolting. He could tell her to forget about her next shift, and as a matter of fact, if she stepped foot in this or any other Miles of Books location again, the police would be alerted and charges would be pressed. You have ruined yourself over this, Karen S, do you understand? RUINED!

Or, maybe more realistically, he could at least speak with her privately. I mean, we wouldn't want her thinking that her behavior in the Wyoming Incident was acceptable, would we? This more cowed conversation could still happen, I figured. Maybe Don already knew that Karen S was a problem. Maybe Mr. Wyoming called to complain. I opened the door and stepped out into the breakroom. Don called me back.

—Oh, Charlie.

Don scribbled something down in his notebook and spoke without looking at me. His words had the manner of an afterthought.

—I think Michael M wanted to talk with you before you leave.

Oh, great. Michael M. That Rasputiny prick.

I nodded once more. I fetched my bag and drifted onto the sales floor. Michael M often spent mornings in the café working on schedules. I saw him typing away, a coffee steaming next to the laptop. I felt nervous but I didn't know why. I hadn't done anything wrong, Karen S had. But there was an uneasy feeling in my gut as I sat down across from him.

—How are you, Michael?

—I'm superb, Charlie. We need to talk.

—Of course. What do you want to talk about?

—Do you think you don't need to know about the SwiftFoot© because it will sell itself?

That sentence sounded hauntingly familiar.

—No.

I frowned and shook my head. He was silent, so I reaffirmed.

—No. What do you mean? I need to understand the SwiftFoot; I know that.

—It's just really disappointing, Charlie, after all the time you and I spent going over the SwiftFoot© to hear that something like that came out of your mouth. And especially to a trainee. You are supposed to be an example to the new employees, not someone who is going to instill bad habits. Does that make sense? Do you hear what I'm saying?

I sputtered, said the first thing that came to my mind.

—But she was rude to a customer. He wanted Wyoming maps—

—We're talking about you and the SwiftFoot© now, Charlie. It is a big enough issue on its own. There is no need to bring in other factors.

I opened my mouth once more, but Michael M wasn't even looking at me. He was back on the computer, back to the schedules. He was done conversing. Fine. I was defeated anyway. Shrugged.

—All right. I'm sorry.

He didn't look at me but started speaking again.

—I don't want you to be sorry; I want you to take the SwiftFoot© seriously. The future of Miles of Books and, honestly, the future of the book industry itself hinges on who has the most successful E-Reader. We can't have people working for us who aren't willing to sell it. Do you understand? Does that make sense?

—I understand.

I stood up from the table. Numb with anger, I threw my bag over my shoulder again and walked toward the door. I spotted Karen S browsing in the Cookbook section. She selected a book about fat-free desserts and spread it open on the table, taking pictures of each page with her cell phone. A woman walked through the front door—early forties, dressed bizarrely in a big sun hat pulled low and dark sunglasses. She joined Karen S at the table. They hugged and then continued paging through the book. *Ooh, get that one,* I heard the younger woman say. Karen S snapped a picture with her phone. I shook my head in disgust and left the bookstore. I pushed through the double doors and almost ran directly into our troubled regular, Bernie.

—You see them Yanks last night, Charlie?

—I can't talk right now, Bernie.

—Yeah, forget the Yankees. I hit the lottery yesterday.

—Gotta go.

—Million bucks. I don't even want it.

My head was in turmoil as I picked over every sentence offered up by Michael M. I riffed on different paths I could have taken the conversation down, like a Choose Your Own Adventure where every string led to the assistant manager apologizing for his condescension. I humped along the crowded sidewalk, my carrier bag thumping against my hip. The day was sunny and chill, rays squinted my eyes nearly shut. I grumbled to the subway stop, its dank stairs descending to the cool, foul dungeon under the city. I swiped my MetroCard through the turnstile. Moving thoughtlessly, I bumped my stomach into the metal bar as the computer beeped at me—no funds. I pushed away from the metal contraption and swore at it—swore at all metal contraptions all over the world. They could all go straight to hell, I thought, all the E-Readers and cell phones and computers and GPSes. Fuck 'em.

I bought my new MetroCard and cast the *Open Sesame* spell on the turnstile as the N Train thundered down the dark hole. I entered the train and crashed into a hard, orange seat. I reached into my bag and fingered my book, knowing I wouldn't be able to concentrate.

My mind was weak, worn out. And when I get like that—when my psyche begins to crack—that's when the ghosts seep in.

8.

The Philosophy Re-Org

IT was a difficult night of sleep. Obsessive thoughts cockroached into the room as I tried to drift off. I shined the light on the verminous meditations every half hour, saying to myself, *You're still thinking about that stupid conversation with Michael M? That's ridiculous. Go to sleep!* But I couldn't. Maybe I don't take criticism as well as others.

Shelving calms me. Becky is an admirable receiver, and the carts are always nicely organized. The books are set up in a sensible manner, and with a little work, they always fit. There is something fulfilling about rolling out a stacked cart of books from receiving and pushing it back empty. This Zen-work is good to wash a bad conversation from the mind. It's a good way to prove to yourself that you are, in fact, a useful employee. Shelving provides a moment when one can step back and admire the work that's been accomplished. Like the deep satisfaction of sitting on a chair you made yourself. I spent the next few minutes daydreaming that I had been a carpenter.

Phil was my shelving partner, but I hadn't seen him for much of the morning. This was not uncommon as we were naturally working in different parts of the store. But when I ambled into receiving after I finished a cart, I found that there were no fewer books left to shelve. Phil hadn't done anything. As I've said before, I didn't mind shelving, so I don't care if I end up doing more carts than my partner. But I had done four carts and Phil had only taken one. We weren't going to finish in time if he didn't speed up.

And it wasn't like Phil to slack. He might have had his own way of doing things, but he did them quickly. Phil was a hard worker and leaving something unfinished was not acceptable to him. He often railed against others who he thought weren't following store standard requirements. He could be a real prick about it. The management staff often held private conversations with him in the back office about curbing his intensity, so it was an oddity that I was shelving so much faster than Phil. It occurred to me that he might be sick or something. I worked a little quicker to make sure the shelving was completed. It was a light day, and even with the lack of help, I finished by ten o'clock.

The store opened for business. I moved on to customer service, feeling much better after my shelving. I was totally and completely cured of the conversation with Michael M. It was gone, in the rearview. That's what shelving does for me and that's why I love it. But as much as I love shelving, I love customer service even more. I am excellent at it. It might be my age, or maybe just the way I look, but people enjoy talking to me. They like asking me for help and I am good at helping them. I don't care if I sound like a teacher's pet or if I sound sappy. It's all true. And Michael M could go screw himself for thinking otherwise.

The phone started to ring, and I was swept up in the pace of the day. I retrieved a hardcover from our History section called *The Face of the Third Reich* for one of our regulars. I hadn't seen Michael M actually retrieve a book for a customer in months, he's so busy writing his mistake-laden schedules. I used the computer to help a customer remember the name of a book she had read as a child and now wanted to buy for a baby shower. It was *Miss Nelson Is Missing*, by Harry G. Allard. (By the way, do not buy this book for a newborn child. It is not age appropriate. Michael M wouldn't know that, but I do.) I led another customer back to the music section to find out what CD we were playing on the overhead speakers. It was a Herb Albert live concert. I didn't recognize the tune, but Michael M wouldn't have either. Michael R, the music seller, even had to check the player to make sure. This whole time I was working, Phil was nowhere to be found. I eventually grew concerned and walked back to the breakroom to look for him. I heard Don talking in the office, so I went to stand in the doorway. He was on the phone with someone.

—Right. Right. I understand *that* part.

I liked Don. Not everybody in the store did. I never understood why this was so. He was a charismatic guy in my opinion. Way better than Michael M. Don sat at his desk for most of the day and somehow managed to remain calm as he drank more espresso than a grad student pulling an all-nighter. He had a mustache, just like me, and he looked old behind his bifocals and salt and pepper hair. Sometimes it bothered me that Don looked old because I knew I was at least ten years his elder. What did that say about me?

I'm not sure what Don did all day besides support the café's Americano sales. Every time I walked past his desk, he was either clicking around on the computer or talking to one of the booksellers about something personal—their school work, a new book they'd read, a sick relative. He didn't discuss the store very often. If I didn't know any better, I'd say that Michael P and Michael M had more to say about the day-to-day operations than Don.

—Yes, but the sales are good. We're beating plan and LY.

He was apparently discussing the store's affairs now, though. He was silent again, nodding his head as the person on the other line answered him. I'm not sure he knew I was there. He kept talking.

—I've got to be honest here Ronald, that doesn't make a whole heckuva lot of sense. Memberships, gift cards, café upsells . . . how could those be more important than core sales?

Ronald. It was the district manager, Ronald Gephardt on the line.

—Right. Outside influences are affecting core sales. But if we *weren't* beating our sales plan or LY sales, then that probably *wouldn't* be outside influences. It would be the store's fault. No, I'm not being smart. That's how it is. If we beat plan, then plan is irrelevant. If we miss plan, then what the hell were we doing? Right?

Don held the phone away from his head for a moment and sighed. It occurred to me that I probably shouldn't be listening to this. I didn't move.

—No, I'm not angry. I'm not. Right. Ok, I'll see you then, Ronald.

Don hung up the phone and sat still for a few moments. Then he lifted his Americano to his mouth and rotated the chair, slowly. He saw me and lowered the cup. He hummed at me.

—Good morning, Charlie. How are things?
—Just fine.
—I heard they're raising the subway fare again.
—Yeah. I heard that too.
—Hmmm. It wouldn't be so bad if the service got better after you gave them more money.
—Right. But it's still cheaper than owning a car.

Don shook his head ruefully

—Don't I know it. Hmmm.

Don commuted from Staten Island. He was a wellspring of car and traffic woes. But I was here for a different purpose.

—Have you seen Phil?

I was not trying to get Phil in trouble by asking after him. Don never left the office, so if Phil were slacking somewhere reading a graphic novel, there was no way he would be caught in the act. I was beginning to wonder if Phil had gone home sick and they had forgotten to tell me.

—Mr. Miller was in here talking to me this morning. He was concerned about Philosophy. He thinks we don't sell philosophy books due to what he called *the turds* we keep in the section.

—What did you tell him?

—Oh, he's wrong. Hmmm. We *do* sell Philosophy. I looked at the numbers and we're doing just fine. As compared to the other stores in our district, anyway.

—Huh.

—Do you need any help out there?

—No, I'm all right. Thanks, Don.

I returned to the customer service counter and clicked around on the computer—checked some batting averages for the Mets and then scanned through headlines on CNN. Back in the music section, Michael R finished with the Herb Albert and spun an album of flamenco guitar by a Middle Eastern fellow called Armik. When I had exhausted CNN, I found a rag and a can of spray in one of the bottom drawers. I dusted the shelves close to the customer service desk. You wouldn't believe how dusty a bookstore can get.

Eventually a customer approached the customer service desk. I went over and said hello. He asked to see whatever we had by

Socrates, and I nodded in pleased surprise. *How about that?* I thought. *A Philosophy shopper. Don must be right.* I walked the customer to Philosophy and finally found Phil. He sat in front of the section working on the bottom shelf like a grease monkey under a car, fiddling with books, moving titles around fluidly. He scurried away when he saw me coming and quickly slinked beyond the Religion bays. Suddenly rife with suspicion, I watched him retreat. Weird. Phil usually liked to butt in and steal customer service opportunities—especially ones in his favorite subject areas. But he had disappeared around the corner and now hovered by the Bibles. He acted like he was straightening the King James Versions, but it was clear that he was watching us. I proceeded like everything was normal.

—Philosophy. Here we are.

I scanned down the bay, looking for the spot where we should have had seven or eight books written by Socrates. On the very first shelf I saw Jostein Gaarder followed by Aristotle and I knew something was wrong. B.F. Skinner was curiously close to Kierkegaard. I became confused. My face pruned. While I was pruning, Jake walked down the main aisle of the store. He waved when he saw me. Reading the concern in my body language, he stopped to help, even though he hadn't yet punched in for the day. He nodded to the customer.

—What are we looking for, Charlie?

—Socrates. But something's wrong. These are all out of order.

Jake stared for a few moments at the Philosophy section. The customer was patient but started to shift his feet. Jake eventually agreed with my assessment.

—Wow. You're right. This is a mess.

I leaned in so that only Jake could hear me.

—I think Phil might have done something. He's standing around the corner there.

Jake looked over his shoulder at Phil and then back at me.

—Phil, come here.

Phil slouched toward us, eyes watching his feet. His shirt was buttoned up all the way to his Adam's apple. I noticed that there was a small hole in the knee of his pants. Jake folded his arms.

—What's going on with the Philosophy section? Are you in the middle of a project or something?

Phil considered the question for a moment and then spoke quietly.

—No, it's in order.

—It's not in order. Look at it.

—It's in a different kind of order.

—What do you mean? What kind of order?

Phil mumbled something that sounded like *pin land.* Jake didn't understand him either.

—What?

—Pin land.

—What are you saying, Phil? Enunciate.

—PIG LATIN. It's alphabetized by the author's last name, but in Pig Latin.

There was a long pause during which we stared at Phil and wondered what the hell was wrong with him. The customer spoke up. We three had forgotten he was there.

—Can you just tell me where books by Socrates are?

Jake scanned the shelves.

—I don't think you did this right, Phil. Shouldn't Socrates be *Ocrates-say* in Pig Latin? Shouldn't it be next to *Oucault-fay*?

Phil turned a couple different shades of purple. He sighed heavily.

—He would be next to *Oucault-fay* if he ever wrote a book, I guess.

—What?

—Plato wrote the books. Not Socrates. Up there, next to *Meditations* by *Aurelius-way*.

The customer selected his book and walked to the cash registers. After he left, the three of us studied the Philosophy section with repulsive awe, like a renowned painting desecrated with a squiggly mustache. Next to me, Jake silently shook and then broke out in a full laugh.

—Wow, Phil. I mean, to alphabetize this many books based solely on vowels? That really is some attention to detail.

Phil looked at Jake nervously and began to laugh himself. I was too stunned to have a reaction. Just stood there with my mouth open. Jake spoke before I could think of anything to say.

—Why did you do this?

—Don insisted we didn't have a problem with the Philosophy section. He said the sales numbers were good and that people shopped it all the time. He's wrong about that.

—So, you changed the section to Pig Latin?

—Yeah. And you're right, it was really hard to alpha them. It took me way longer than I thought it would.

—I'm still not making the connection here. *Why* did you do this?

—I thought no one would notice. I was going to tell Don a month from now that the section had been in order by Pig Latin for all this time and no one noticed.

—But instead, we noticed within five minutes.

Phil looked at his work with an odd mixture of shame and pride. Jake shook his head.

—So, maybe Don was right?

—I don't think so. It was just bad luck. If we leave it like this and don't tell anyone, it will still work.

—No, Phil. We need to change this back right now. The Michaels will kill you if they find this.

I retreated to the customer service desk. It wasn't busy and I hadn't had a bad morning, so I didn't say anything to Phil about doing all the shelving myself. Part of me wanted to be angry, but I didn't feel angry. I don't know why. I checked the daily schedule posted at the customer service desk and saw that Jake didn't start for an hour. But he was laughing and working with Phil, helping to arrange the section back in order. Phil was a curmudgeon and didn't like anyone. But he liked Jake. And let's just say it; Jake had me too. I had gotten used to his oiliness, I guess. Or maybe I was starting to realize that Jake wasn't oily at all. He was just confident and friendly, and I was so far from those two things that I didn't have the capacity to understand them. Huh. And then I was down in the dumps again. It wasn't even Michael M's fault this time.

There were points in my life when I tried to be like Jake. I remember specifically in my early forties, when I was dead-set on dating and getting remarried—I tried to own a natural state of happiness, to talk to strangers as if they were my good friends, to have a kind and supporting word for everyone I met. I thought it might help cut down on anxiety, too, if I were like that. People who are always happy never worry, right? Nope. It doesn't work. I can fake it for a day or so, but I can't sustain. Eventually I turn wooden, then rude, then silent. Books are easy conversation, of course, but anything else causes me to grow quiet and sullen. I keep my head down when I ride the subway. Some people are like that, I guess. Stuck inside, for the most part. We can't all be Jake, and no amount of envy can change that.

9.

Charlie Dreams of Love

KAREN S constantly chapped my ass. I hoped that she would implode after a few weeks and either get fired or quit. Neither happened. To my complete and utter amazement, people liked her. The younger booksellers thought her funny because she was older but willing to cuss and be frank with them. The café memorized her drink, had it ready for her when she came in each day. And the Wyoming Man, whom she had spoken to so rudely, returned from his trip to Wyoming and become a regular of Karen S's, asking for her specifically.

On top of all that, no one was calling her Karen S. They just called her Karen. This was no good because Karen Arlett was a part-time worker on the weekends. She had been here much longer than Karen S. Karen Arlett, by rights, was Karen and Karen S—Schneider, was her last name—should carry the burden of the initial. The original kept the name and every other person with the same name had to use their initial. This rule was hard and fast and knew no titles. It even affected management. The Michaels had to go by Michael P and Michael M because Michael Reynolds had worked in the music section since before the two of them were hired. But within a few weeks everyone was calling Karen S, Karen. I rarely saw Karen Arlett because I didn't work many weekends. I could only imagine her smoldering outrage.

Karen S was scheduled early—retail managers tend to schedule the older workers early because they know we don't mind waking up—and so I dealt with her more than I cared to. She wasn't a terrible shelver once she got going. She was probably a little faster than me, though I question her accuracy. Her customer service was thoughtless and brutal. I winced every time I heard her talk. I did my best to avoid her.

Chelsea, on the other hand, was a sweetheart. She worked occasional mornings with me. If she wasn't the shelver, then she was the morning customer service worker or cashier. She wasn't particularly good at the job, if I'm being honest. She was smart—don't get me wrong—detail-oriented and knowledgeable. But she was so, so quiet. Her words just disappeared in the air, died in obscurity before they reached people's ears. Maybe she was embarrassed by her mush mouth.

It was a Wednesday, a tick past ten o'clock. Chelsea had just begun her shift. I was finishing the Religion cart as she talked on the phone to a customer. It had been a pleasant morning with only a few shoppers in the store. The Religion section had recently been zoned—meaning that the slower selling titles had been taken out and sent back to the publisher—and the books fit snuggly into their alphabetized destinations. I was moving along on the cart pretty well—T.D. Jakes, C.S. Lewis, Joyce Meyer—when I heard Chelsea raise her voice. This was odd because, as I said, Chelsea was very quiet. I thought maybe she had a customer who was hard of hearing on the line. Kept shelving—Stormie Omartian, Joel Osteen, Rick Warren. But Chelsea's voice continued to be louder than normal, and I started listening to the words.

—I'm not sure why you're seeing a different price online. But this is the price that my computer tells me.

I realized now that her voice was higher because she was upset. She nodded into the phone and spoke sternly.

—I understand what you mean; you don't have to talk like that.

I put a copy of *The Jesus I Never Knew* by Philip Yancey in its proper place on the bottom shelf. I abandoned the Religion cart and hurried to the customer service desk where Chelsea held the phone to her ear. Her googly eyes bulged out of their sockets as I got close.

—One moment please!

She punched the hold button and then slammed the receiver against the customer service desk. CRACK! My heart jumped at the sound. The man in the café looked up from his newspaper. It was such an unexpected and violent movement. Chelsea dropped the phone, letting it hang to the ground on its curled cord like a stranded bungee jumper. She threw both hands over her face, leaned against the counter. I thought she was crying.

—Is everything all right? Do you need help with something?

When she finally spoke, I could tell that she was extremely angry and doing her best to hold back. She spoke calmly, in her sweet, quiet voice.

—Charlie, there's an asshole on the phone.

I admit: her cursing surprised me. With a voice like that, the word *asshole* didn't carry the same meaning. It seemed like she might be referring to princesses or kitties or tea parties.

—It's about an order. He wants to get it shipped to the store, but he wants the online price.

—One of those …

—Yeah, but he really won't take no for an answer.

—I'll try, if you like.

I was good with customers, particularly angry customers. I don't know what it is, but I have a calming effect on shoppers. Plus, people who are cruel to young women are never cruel to old men. It's the flipside of misogyny. I was this customer's kryptonite. Chelsea pulled the receiver off the floor by the cord and handed it to me.

—Hello! This is Charlie speaking. I understand there's a problem with an order you'd like to place?

The stream of swear words that came through the receiver was unseemly. George Carlin might have blushed. How anyone could get that angry about a book was beyond me. I chalked it up to mental illness. I don't like to believe that the world had sane individuals who would treat another person to such profanity.

—You have a good day.

And then I hung up.

Chelsea and I observed a moment of silence as we regarded the phone.

—Did you just hang up on him?

I waved my hand.

—Come on.

I walked and she followed.

—Charlie, did you just hang up on him?

—It's no big deal.

I led her down the main aisle past my Religion cart and hung a left at the bathrooms. Punched the security code into the breakroom door and then headed straight to Don's office, Chelsea in tow. I stuck my head in the door.

—Are you free, Don?

He was typing on the manager's computer, an Americano steaming beside him, a potential avalanche of paper piles framing him in his seat. Staring at his computer a moment longer, he sighed. I read over his shoulder. I shouldn't have, I did. It said *Store Manager Action Plan*. He clicked the mouse and the page disappeared into the brain of the computer. He turned to us with his slow eyes and nodded.

—Chelsea had an irate customer on the phone.

Irate was the official word we used for an unreasonable asshole. On a few occasions I have been made to write up descriptions of irate customer interactions that were later forwarded to the corporate customer service office. For whatever reason, corporate wanted the moment described when the customer became irate. It was much like when CNN did bio-reporting on a terrorist and liked to point out the moment when they were radicalized. When Mohamed Atta saw his village destroyed by an errant US bomb strike, he became *radicalized*. When the customer was told that the BOGO deal on Sudoku had ended, he became *irate*. See?

Don hummed his question.

—Hmmm. Is he still on the phone?

Chelsea looked to me, terrified. I 'fessed up.

—I said goodbye and then hung up. He was cursing.

Don shifted his gaze to Chelsea. There was no humming this time.

—He was swearing at you?

—Yeah. A lot.

—You don't have to talk to someone who is using abusive language toward you, Chelsea. If he calls back transfer it to me.

—Ok. Thanks, Don.

—And could you close the door on your way out, Charlie? I'm working on something here.

—Sure, Don.

I closed the door and looked up at the clock. It was five past eleven, time for me to call it quits. Chelsea held the door for me to go back to the sales floor.

—No, I'm done for the day. But I didn't finish that Religion cart. Do you mind shelving the last couple of books and taking it back for me?

—No problem. I guess I owe you one, right?

Chelsea closed the door to the breakroom and doubled back to her locker, started turning the combination this way and that. I thought that she should probably get out to the floor since she was the only customer service person. I kept my opinion to myself. I went to retrieve my lunch from the fridge. She finally managed to get her locker open. She removed a sheet of paper.

—Charlie, I'd like you to come to this if you could.

She handed me a flyer. Black and white photo, brick wall, five young kids leaning against it. Their eyes were all fixed in different directions, none of them at the camera. Most of them appeared bored. One made a funny face, sticking out his tongue and crossing his eyes. Across the top of the photo were the words *Counting Cows*. Chelsea talked while I looked it over.

—It's a comedy show. Improv. It's only five dollars ...

—You want me to come see this? Do you have a friend in it or something?

She smiled, then. She was really beautiful when she smiled. She must have had a hell of a dentist back in Cincinnati.

—I'm in it. That's me.

I looked again at the flyer, and sure enough, there was Chelsea, standing in front of that brick wall in blue jeans and a white blouse. She was one of the bored-looking ones, with her arms crossed, her eyes concentrated somewhere to the left.

—You . . . you're a comedian?

She blushed scarlet.

—Well, I'm trying . . . it's sort of why I'm staying in New York for the summer. To really make a go at it.

I wanted to tell her that she was too quiet for this, too nice. That her audiences were going to be numb with uncomfortable silences and coughing. Once again, I kept it to myself.

—You should come see it. Ludmilla will be there and Rosa and Jon. Um. . .

She numbered the people off on her fingers.

—And I think Michael will be there—Reynolds, not M or P—and, oh yeah! Even Karen will be there.

Well, that settled it. I kept my eyes on the flyer as I shot her down.

—Thanks, I'll check my calendar. I'll try to make it.

I strolled home in the early afternoon and thought about Jake. He had certainly picked a great girl to be heartbroken over. Chelsea was something special. Too special for Jake to let slip away, I understood that now. He couldn't handle losing her. He was so young—hardly even a man yet. And at his age, the triumph of the future is clear on the horizon. You can just see it, like a helicopter whirling toward you. If something upsets that triumph, the whole world goes dark. Jake was so sure tomorrow was amazing that it made today shabby by comparison. I get it. Tomorrow can be tricky that way. I was never like that when I was Jake's age. I didn't get the chance to be like that. Good, I guess. Who needs the hassle?

If anything about the future amazed me, it was its resemblance to the past. I never lived in a Recreational Room of the Future, like the display at Fun Land that my father had been so taken with when I was a child. Far from it. My food was currently in a refrigerator that didn't even have the decency to link with a conveyer belt. I lived approximately three blocks from where my parents raised me. The building in which I grew up had been razed, replaced by a prosperous row of restaurants, bodegas, and clothing stores. Every day when I walked to the subway terminal, I passed the place where that building once stood. Nostalgia never occurred to me.

My current apartment had two rooms, three if bathrooms count. I had a bedroom and then a room that served as both the living room and the kitchen. It was just a touch smaller than the apartment in which I grew up, and I paid nearly five times the price in rent, I'm sure. The floors were hardwood, and my couch was blue, purchased in 1994 from a secondhand shop that offered free delivery. If there was anything odd about my apartment—something that set it apart from the place I grew up—it was the number of books that I owned. Maybe you saw that one coming.

I rarely bought books from my own bookstore. We received fifty percent off coffee and food and thirty percent off the price of books. This seems like a good deal, but it's not. It was still too expensive to shop there. I bought items on clearance and occasionally from the bargain section, but otherwise I perused the many thrift stores populating New York City. I spend a lot of my time in thrift stores. I'm primarily there for the books, but if truth be told, I buy my clothing there as well. And a piece of furniture every few years. And glassware. Movies. A watch, once. You simply can't beat the prices. But my purchases were mostly books. Old, used books. Used books are better than new books and anyone who says differently has a defect of the soul. Don't trust them.

Thrift shopping takes me back to the days when I worked at a bookstore called Geraldine's with my friend Dennis. Geraldine's was my first job after the law firm, after the divorce. My first bookstore. It was a wild place—dusty, disorganized, and populated by beautiful, bespectacled girls from the NYU campus. It's been closed for thirty years now. The thrift stores I frequent are usually messy like Geraldine's had been—organization as haphazard and mysterious as the slabs of Stonehenge. The thrift stores have the same smell as Geraldine's, too—a nutty fragrance of old book and salty somehow, like the very flesh of the writer emerged after a certain amount of time had passed, a certain wear and tear achieved. Sometimes I find classic covers on the older books, art from another age. The simple Rockwell-esque style of the fifties thrillers. Psychedelia on the covers of seventies sci-fi. There is often writing from a previous reader marking impressive lines, giving one the feeling of traveling a path well-worn and homey. But mostly it's the visceral aspect—the yellowed pages of old books give a sense of mysterious excitement. The smell turns me into an archeologist, a daring explorer sifting through forgotten catacombs or Gandalf researching the One Ring in the libraries of Gondor.

The smell is probably due to fungus. But, hey—cheap is cheap. I went to five different thrift stores regularly, and on weekends I often explored other parts of the city to widen the possibility that I might find something I wanted. The average going price for books at a thrift store was seventy-five cents for a mass market book, one dollar for a trade paperback, and between three and five dollars for a hardcover book. To put this in perspective, Miles of Books sold mass markets for $9.99, trades for $15.99, and hardcovers for upward of thirty dollars.

I don't ever throw books away after I read them (who would?), but I do lend books to people. Lending books, in many ways, is like conscientiously throwing them out. I used to huff and puff, lose friends in arguments about lost books I had lent. Let me tell you, it's no use. People rarely return borrowed books, there is no policing it. I hate making generational comparisons, but it's true—parents just aren't raising children to return property in a timely manner anymore.

I had approximately three and a half thousand books in my apartment, and I had read 1,958 of them. That number of finished books isn't as impressive as it sounds. I'm actually a slow reader. For the amount of time I spend with my nose in a book, it should be much higher. And not to be a downer, but it occurred to me in 2004, during a week when I was home sick with the flu staring feverishly at my stacks, that it was not possible to finish reading the books I had purchased. At the rate I read (in the ballpark of forty books a year), it required another twenty or twenty-five years of reading to accomplish the feat. I probably didn't have that long. And that calculation only held up if I stopped adding to the collection, which I knew I wouldn't. Honestly, I wish I had never done the math.

Was it difficult to fit three and a half thousand books in my apartment? Yes. Yes, it was. The day was soon coming when the cache would be impossible to store. I had no plan to deal with this crisis. The problem was a creeping dread in the back of my mind. As it stood, I had twelve bookcases that fit about two hundred books apiece. I had a closet stacked with books and there were books neatly piled under my bed and couch. They were almost all fiction, I am embarrassed to say. I have never been a good nonfiction reader. Sciences, histories, biographies; I like them in theory, but there is nothing like a good novel.

I woke up from an afternoon nap to find that the sun had set. Standing up and stretching my shoulders out, I selected *Middlesex* from a shelf in my bedroom and strolled into the kitchen area, my nose buried in the words as I wrestled a Miller Lite from the fridge. *Middlesex* was a Pulitzer winning novel by the author that Jake and I had discussed at the bagel place, Jeffrey Eugenides. Jake had had so many interesting things to say about the book, and every time I ruminated on Jake, it made me want to peruse *Middlesex* again. My copy was roughed up, but it was a first edition hardcover. Few people nowadays have even seen this cover, with the figure on the front blossoming out of a flower. It was far superior to the paperback cover art. I paid four dollars and seventy-five cents for it. I flipped around and read some passages at random, reacquainting myself with the plot and the style. *Middlesex* is a story of generations. In the novel, one decision affects a family for nearly one hundred years. I tried to imagine what a young man like Jake took away from this story. What did *Middlesex* mean to someone who was twenty-three years old? *God*, I thought, *twenty-three years old*. People were born when I was twenty-three who have now grown old themselves. Some of them are even dead. How did that happen?

I thought about Chelsea and the way that Jake couldn't shake her from his heart. I don't know if it was the beer I had opened or the beautiful passages I was reading, but I started to get sappy. I wondered briefly if I had been as in love with Teresa as Jake was with Chelsea. Did I hurt as badly when Teresa left?

But that didn't matter, did it? That was long gone. I shut the book and crossed my legs, staring out the window at the streetlight. Did the broken relationship of these two kids really have the power to upset me? No. I sipped my beer. *As a matter of fact*, I considered, *who can even say if Jake really loves her? He's only twenty-three!* At twenty-three, people are just in love with themselves. They project feelings of love to pretty objects around them. Come to think of it, the way Jake felt about Chelsea was a load of flowery bullshit! I opened another beer and things started to clear up. The whole matter began to settle before my eyes. Jake wasn't a spurned lover. Jake was an investor whose gamble on the stock market had crashed. He had done something big, made a passion play, put his comfort in jeopardy. Jake had had a crazy thought—he was going to drop everything to pursue a girl!—and he had the guts to follow through. Good for him! But it hurts when risks like that don't pay off. The pain comes less from the disappointment of being denied what you want and more from the embarrassment of trying and not getting it. There is embarrassment in an unsuccessful bid to improve your station. Grace makes its home in dormancy, buffoonery in hard work failed. A lot of people know that.

Now, with my clear thinking—and, what the hell, maybe one more Miller—the facts were remarkably ordered. Love, what young people call love, has nothing to do with a successful relationship. Love to them is the dizzying, sappy state achieved when chasing an object of affection. When young people say they want to be in love, that high is what they want. They want to have a target for their idolatry. And they can have it any time; all they need to do is pick someone.

Older people mean something a little different when they say love, a little more boring, perhaps. Old people want a consistent person to be their friend, to be on their side in most matters, and to split the costs of living. They want someone they get along with. Someone who they think is funny. Old people's love is just as valid as the other kind of love; it just doesn't play well in movies. If young people's love is an amphetamine, old people's love is decaffeinated tea. *Hmm*, I thought, now that my beer was gone, *a mug of decaf sure would hit the spot.* I set my book aside and carried the empty beer cans to the kitchen. I set them on the counter to be recycled and then retrieved a blackened kettle from underneath the counter. I placed the kettle on the stove and stopped, stood still. In that moment, it occurred to me that real love, the kind that defines your life, should start wild and youthful and grow into the slow and steady rock. Maybe neither is as good without the other. I would never have that.

And then I saw my wife, Teresa, in my mind's eye. My body grew very tired. All this thought of love had left a crack in my defenses and she and Kurt had slipped through without my noticing. There they were, Kurt in his crib, Teresa in our bed. The old nightmare back from the depths. I hadn't thought of them in quite a while. I let their memories torture me for a few moments. Then, I put them back where they belonged—deep, deep in a leafy forest in my heart. Deep in a place of nature where I hoped they were healthy and happy and breathing fresh air.

10.
The Accidental Invite

It had been a brittle and slogging winter, but the first gusts of spring were ushering the cold away and green buds donned the crest of every branch. The bookstore had undergone its normal cycles of promotion—diet books and new-you in January, relationship and Black History in February, Irish culture and baseball in March—and now we were building tables of Easter and Passover. It was the slowest time of the year. February, March, and April fall between two pillars of commerce: Christmas and the summer reading months, when children shop with long lists of books they must read before school begins again in the fall. There are some lesser holidays around this time—Valentine's Day, Easter, Mother's and Father's Days—and these generate small bursts of business. But otherwise, time drags like a Victor Hugo novel.

The booksellers bonded during these months. I tried to stay busy, but the deliveries were miniscule. Some days shelving was finished an hour after I got to work. On days such as this there was little to do but stand around and talk. Loafing, you might say. I hate to admit it, but sometimes when the circumstances compelled me, I loafed.

On a Wednesday, after my shelving was complete, I spent some time back in the receiving room loafing with Becky. Well, *I* was loafing. She was actually quite busy, incensed because the truck driver had lost three boxes of books the previous day. If Becky wasn't upset about something, then she was on the lookout for something to be upset about. One of *those* people. And the more upset she was, the more vulgar her insults became. It was fun to watch when there was nothing better to do. I took a gander at the return shelves while she worked the phone, cussing out everyone in the distribution center. It was amazing that Becky didn't lose her job with a temper like that.

I was skimming a memoir from a standup comedian whom I didn't recognize when Becky slammed the phone.

—Get me a goddamn American!

I looked up from my book.

—Excuse me?
—I'm talking with foreigners, here!

Becky yelled, a fury in her eye like the fires of Hades itself. Her eyebrows were a deep valley.

—The ass wart at the distribution center transferred me to the complaint department. They must outsource the calls or something. The fucktard barely spoke English.

So, you see Becky's problem—the ass wart had transferred her to the fucktard. Becky was not what you might call *politically correct* with her speech.

—So, what are you going to do about the missing boxes?

Becky pounded away at her computer as she spoke.

—Who the hell knows? We'll probably just eat it.

She finished typing and gingerly rose to her feet. She sized up the return shelves with loathing and spun a tape gun in her hand.

—Time to get some of these returns done. Charlie, either help me or get the hell out of here.

—There's not really anything to do on the floor.

—It's quarter till eleven. Why don't you just leave?

—There'd be a gap in floor coverage.

—There's a gap right now! You're back here talking to me. Besides, I saw Karen come in early. She's probably out there.

—Karen S?

—What? There's another Karen?

—Yeah. Karen Arlett? She's worked here for, like, three years.

—Oh, yeah. Karen Arlett. No. Other Karen. S. And she always clocks in early.

I read the clock. Ten minutes till. I was hungry anyway, so I left the receiving room and made for the breakroom. Crossing the salesfloor, I saw only two customers in the store, and they were both buying coffee. In the breakroom Karen S sat at the table staring deeply into a SwiftFoot. Becky was wrong, she hadn't clocked in early. I thought about heading back out to the floor, but my lunch was calling to me. Karen S looked up and we dipped our heads at each other.

I knew that Karen S had gotten me into trouble over the comment about the SwiftFoot, and she somehow knew I had tried to have her fired on her first day. At least, I *thought* she knew. We had gotten over these hurdles. We were on basic speaking terms but were by no means friendly. I retrieved my lunch from the refrigerator and sat down on the other side of the table. I carved off the lid of the tuna with my can opener and then scavenged through a Styrofoam cup filled with plasticware in the center of the table to find a fork.

—Do you eat that cat food every day?

She barely looked up from her E-Reader as she spoke. I regarded my tuna fish defensively.

—Every day for lunch. Pretty much. Yes.

—Don't you ever get sick of it?

I checked out the container in front of her. She was finished eating, but a few leaves of lettuce remained, a small pillow-like tangerine, balsamic residue. It was from Soho, the salad place down the street. Expensive stuff. That salad cost her nearly twelve dollars, I surmised.

—No, I don't get sick of it. As long as I'm hungry when I eat, I don't really care what it is.

—Hm.

—Do you think that's boring?

—Yup.

She swiped her finger across the screen, turning the page. But I wasn't done with the conversation just yet.

—Well, I don't care. That doesn't bother me.

She finally looked up from the screen.

—I know you don't care. You wouldn't have that mustache if you were worried about being boring.

I tried to let this pass without comment but failed. I unconsciously stroked my face.

—What's wrong with my mustache?

The small beeps of the security code buttons sounded on the breakroom door before Karen S could answer. The door swung open, and Phil burst in with his work shirt slung over his shoulder, his hair curly and wild from the warm wind. There was tension in the breakroom, but it was nothing Phil could pick up on. He wasn't good at things like that.

—Ladies and germs . . .

He threw his bag in the corner and collapsed boneless into the chair next to me, buffeting a breeze of cheap cologne and cigarette smoke.

—Our game is in one week.
—I know. I'm off tomorrow. I'll go down to the box office.

We held a tradition in the store of attending the second home game in the Mets season. Many fans went to the home opener, and so tickets were hard to come by and expensive. The second home game was usually quite empty. Many years ago, there was a crowd of booksellers that went to this game. It was an event. Back then I would go down to the box office with a pocket full of cash that my coworkers had entrusted me and buy ten, twelve tickets, a whole row just for us. Over the years our numbers had dwindled. That old crowd of booksellers got other jobs and moved on to other things. It was really just me and Phil now, and it had been for a few years. It was still fun.

Karen S.

—You two are going to the Yankees game?

Me.

—Mets.

Her question reminded Phil of something.

—Hey, I was telling Jake about the game. He wants to come with us.
—Good! The more the merrier.

I would soon come to realize that *the more the merrier* was an abhorrent choice of phrase. Karen S, with curious eyes.

—Is this a work thing?

She looked more at Phil than me.

—Can I come?

Excitement from Phil.

—That would be great!

My face must have turned a couple different shades of red at this suggestion. The trip had just gotten much better with the addition of Jake—Phil can be tiresome by himself—and then much, much worse. I couldn't fathom why Karen S would want to come to the Mets game. I didn't peg her for a baseball fan, she and Phil rarely talked, and she had a burning scorn for me. Why would she do this? Then I figured it out. Relief and disdain washed over me in alternating waves. She was messing with me. It was a threatening posture, a social cue from a silverback ape. A bluff. She wouldn't really go.

Karen S and Phil both had an eleven o'clock shift, so I was left in the breakroom by myself. I finished my tuna and got going on my cottage cheese. I tried to read my book while munching on some almonds. I was reading Barbara Kingsolver. *Animal Dreams*. People think Barbara Kingsolver is just for ladies, but they're all wrong. I sell her to skeptical men all the time and they come back to the bookstore raving. *Poisonwood Bible*? Come on. She's brilliant. But despite the brilliance, I found myself finishing pages without retaining the plot. I stood up and paced the breakroom, swishing the remains of my coffee in the paper cup. Some new notices were posted on the wall—a schedule for next week, a Loss Prevention flyer concerning internal theft. Michael P had written a note to the staff about our falling discount card sales. It begged a refocus. I saw myself in the breakroom mirror and stopped. My hand went to my mustache, my fingers smoothed down the white bristles.

I gathered my things and threw my bag over my shoulder. Checked my wallet to make sure I had my Metro Card. Bopped my head into the office and told Don to have a good day. Walked through the sales floor and thought about getting another small coffee for the ride home but decided against it. Phil was at the customer service desk helping a young man. Phil looked tired and annoyed. I was happy to be getting out of work for the day. The sun shone through the glass front doors like light into a cathedral. I thought about riding the N train all the way into Manhattan to check out a thrift store on the Lower East Side. Nothing but pleasantness awaited me.

Then Karen S intervened on my merrymaking. Waiting by the door, her money-filled hand lurched toward me.

—Here. For the Mets game.

I took the bills from her, dejected that she was following through with this, and counted.

—This is way too much.

—I need two.

—Who else is coming?

—I'm bringing Chelsea.

My body froze while my brain did the calculations. This was no good. Jake was coming to the game. And now Chelsea was coming to the game. How, I wondered, could I stop this from happening without making a big deal of it and embarrassing them both? I flubbed like a fish on the dock. Karen S was completely exasperated with me.

—Come outside.

—You're on the clock.

—It'll just be for a moment.

I looked over my shoulder to see if Don or the Michaels were on the floor as we exited through the double doors. Karen S didn't seem concerned. She pulled out a small handbook and removed a white cylinder from it.

—What is that?

—It's a smokeless cigarette.

As if this was the most obvious thing in the world.

—It's got nicotine in it. I'm quitting.

She sucked on the end of the cylinder and blew out a pale stream. Right in front of her place of employment. Like we worked at the fucking dollar store or something.

—You're going to get in trouble.

She didn't care to stick to the subject.

—You don't want Chelsea to come to the game.

—It worries me. There are some things you don't know.

—I know them.

—You know about Chelsea and Jake?

—Yeah.

—Then why would you do this?

—Because they should be together.

I couldn't believe we were having this conversation. Here we were, two old farts discussing the love lives of Jake and Chelsea like they were the stars of General Hospital. What a joke.

—Does Chelsea want to get back together with Jake?

She took a drag from her fake cigarette.

—She won't say it, but yes. She does.

—She won't say it? So, this is something you've deduced?

Karen looked at me as if I had said the F-word in front of her mother.

—*Deduced.* Yeah, sure.

—You shouldn't be doing this. Just let it go. If Chelsea wanted to be with Jake, she would at least talk to him. She doesn't even talk to him.

—Charlie, you don't understand anything.

—And you do?

Karen S put her white cylinder back into her handbag.

—Chelsea says that Jake broke her heart, and she wants nothing to do with him. But I know two things that point to the contrary. One, Chelsea broke up with her other boyfriend a month ago, and two, Chelsea *knew* that Jake was working here when she applied for the job.

Oh. Well, how about that? I was scandalized in spite of myself.

—She knew?

—Mmmhmm.

—I didn't know that.

—We'll take them to this game. They'll have to talk.

—I don't know. I'm not comfortable setting Jake up like this. I think I'll tell him beforehand.

She looked me in the eye with an intensity that made my bladder go numb.

—Charlie, don't tell him.

—Well . . .

She put her hand over my mouth. Actually reached out and put her hand to my lips, her index finger blanketing the broom of my mustache. That was the first time she touched me. The smokeless cigarette must really be smokeless because her hand smelled like perfumed bed sheets.

—No. Just don't tell him.

Karen S turned around and walked back into the store. I stood there for a moment in the gentle spring breeze with my jaw hanging open watching her walk away from me. Her scent lingered just under my nose. She swung her hips and turned dramatically through the double doors. I gathered my wits, clutched my bag to my side and walked toward the subway with a heavy mind.

11.

The Ballgame

THE days passed quickly, and I didn't tell Jake about the shanghai scheme. It wasn't easy. He was a really good kid, it turned out. The two of us had somehow grown friendlier. He would often sit with me in the breakroom after my shift and discuss different subjects of interest, subjects that he thought I could shed some light on, being, in the words of the teenage baristas, *old as hell*. Jake shared two interests close to my heart—baseball and literature—and one subject that shaped my life but I barely thought about—war.

Jake had an intense fascination in America's wars, especially World War II, and could often be found reading a book about Nazis, Churchill, stories from the Italian front. I didn't know much about World War II. No more than any other red-blooded American. I was only ten years old on D-Day. My father hadn't been involved with the war effort because of some delinquency that was never explained to me. But I was in Korea when that whole mess occurred. I didn't mind telling some tales.

When I was growing up, everyone had been to war. Talking about war was like telling a dentist's office story. No one wanted to hear it. We would never discuss a soldier getting shot or a landmine taking his leg. It was commonplace and therefore vulgar. But guys like Jake had never been to war and didn't really know anyone who had. Jake was raised with money and today only poor people fight wars. It makes sense, I guess. I wouldn't have gone to war if I didn't have to.

Jake didn't confide any more details about Chelsea, and I was thankful for that. If he started talking about their broken relationship again, I'd have to be honest with him. I'd blab the whole conspiracy, giving Karen S another reason to think I'm an asshole. Now and then, when Chelsea walked by and Jake was standing in proximity, he gave me a knowing look, as if to say, *There! There walks my heart's desire*! It was a little much. But even this didn't compel me to confess Karen's scheme. Really, when the moment finally came, my plan was to deny I ever knew about it. Just lie my ass off.

The second home game of the year took place on a beautiful day, sunny and calm, cool and perfect for watching baseball. A day like that magnifies the magic and wonderment of a baseball field. Baseball players, if we're being honest, are grown men specialized in a child's game. But on a day like that day, it felt like we had come to the park to watch legends in action. It felt like a tall tale, like Paul Bunyan might step into the batter's box and knock a dinger. What a shame that I was wired sick with nerves.

I deeply regretted the agreed-to plan. It was bungling and childish—the giddy stuff of summer camps. This setup wouldn't have its desired effect and would only succeed in forming a rift between Jake and me. I would be embarrassed; Jake would feel betrayed. And rightfully so, on both sides. Work would be a nightmare until I croaked or Jake quit.

Phil was there when I arrived, sitting in the seat with his legs spread wide and a plate of nachos resting on his groin.

—Hey, Charlie. What a day, huh?

—It's nice.

The stadium smelled like buttered popcorn or barbecue, depending on which way the breeze turned. The players stretched on the green grass down below, slowly throwing baseballs to each other, flexing their shoulders, jutting their knees to their chests. We weren't in the sun, and that's a good thing. You can get a nasty burn at an afternoon game if you buy the wrong tickets. I sat down next to Phil, scanned the stairs for either Jake or Chelsea. Instead, I saw Karen S making her way up to the folded seats. She wore a tank top and a long skirt. Her white-blonde hair was pulled back, sandals with straps climbing up her shins. She was dressed like a sixteen-year-old and it somehow didn't look bad. I judged my own outfit and found it wanting. Pleated khaki shorts and a thrift store golf shirt produced for a charity benefit I knew nothing about. I started to panic, wondering if Karen S would ask for the background of the shirt. What if she wanted to know what cause the Saint Benedict Annual Golf Tournament supported? I didn't even know how to golf. I bought it because it was fifty cents and because it was blue.

From five rows away she called.

—Hello, boys! What beautiful weather!

If my wardrobe ends up being the biggest problem of the afternoon, I thought, *then I will have gotten off lucky.* I dared hope that, perhaps, the Jake and Chelsea collision course had been derailed. Maybe Chelsea canceled on us. These kids are always canceling their plans, aren't they? I nodded to Karen S and made pleasantries as she gathered her purse and sat down. *How was your ride to the park*, I asked. *Did you work a shift this morning?* I tried to make it seem like nothing was on my mind. *Did you eat before you came?*

Because those hot dogs sure smell good. This was just a regular old day at the ballpark. Nothing to discuss, nothing to stress about.

When an appropriate amount of time passed.

—So, is Chelsea really coming? Because Jake should be here any moment.

Appropriateness is such a subjective thing. Karen S and Phil tilted their heads back and widened their eyes. I tried to ease into the topic, but what I had actually done was ask forty-seven seconds of rapid-fire questions, ending with the Chelsea/Jake query.

Karen S with her hand on my knee, in patronizing repose.

—Relax, Charlie. It will be all right.

As we talked, Chelsea wandered onto the scene, slowly scanning the seats for us. She wore a Reds shirt, her curly brown hair falling around her shoulders in the way curly hair often falls around the shoulders of beautiful young girls on perfect days. Phil whistled loudly between his fingers to get her attention. It worked and she climbed the stairs waving.

Infectiously exuberant mush mouth.

—Hey, everybody! Ready for some baseball?

Chelsea weaved down the aisle. I noted how Karen S blocked her way so that she had to take the second-to-last seat, forcing her to sit next to Jake when he arrived. She was a shrewd one, Karen S. But then she slipped up.

—Who's buying the first round?

Ballpark beers? Phil and I glanced at Karen S and then out to the field. Before Karen S could assume we were a pack of recovering alcoholics, Chelsea pointed out the obvious.

—None for me. I passed one of the stands on the way in. I can't afford ten-dollar beers.

Karen S blushed as she realized her faux pas. She looked down at her purse in worry. None of us could afford to drink beer at the stadium. I admit it; I reveled in her mistake. She persevered.

—Let's just do one round. I'm buying. Phil, come help me carry.

Phil licked some nacho cheese off the tips of his fingers and handed me his plastic boat.

—You can have one chip, Charlie. One.

I was left alone with Chelsea. After a short, awkward pause, she relayed a funny conversation she overheard on her subway ride from Astoria. The Mets were still warming up when she had finished, so I told her who the players were one by one, some facts about each of them. Once at a game in Cincinnati, she said, her father had taken her down to the field before the first inning to have a ball signed by Barry Larkin himself. I was impressed. We were having a nice time chatting and enjoying the sunshine. Then, the worst happened.

Jake spotted Chelsea before he approached. I watched over Chelsea's shoulder as he hemmed and hawed a few rows away. I repeatedly checked the rear entrance for the return of Karen S and Phil, hoping that they would run in to Jake, hoping it wouldn't be me, sitting here like Brutus, ditched by all his knife-wielding friends. My denial strategy had gone up in smoke. Chelsea's eyebrows curled at my expression; she must have thought I was having a seizure. I praised God for every second she didn't look over her shoulder and see Jake. Another minute passed and Phil and Karen S still did not arrive. Jake decided to face his doom and inched over to us.

Shoulders slumped, pale as a foul line.

—Hey.

Chelsea turned around to see who it was and then immediately turned back to me. She was furious, her cute face distorted in red anger. I scrunched into a rueful grimace as Karen S and Phil mercifully returned, bogged down with amber beers.

Karen S with a façade of cheerfulness.

—The whole party's here. Take this off my hands, Jake. We bought you a beer.

Chelsea looked around and saw the sham for what it was. She stood up, keeping her eyes on the peanut shell covered floor, brushed past everyone out to the exit. Jake glared back at me and then followed, leaving Phil, Karen S and myself with half a tub of nachos and plenty of beer.

—I told you we shouldn't have done this.

—Oh, shut up, Charlie. This could still work out.

Phil, literally and figuratively from left field.

—Is something going on?

Me.

—How is this going to work out? How?

Karen S.

—They're going to talk.

Phil.

—They didn't take their beers. Are they angry about something?

Karen S to Phil.

—They used to date.

Phil to Karen S.

—I thought they were cousins.

Karen S to Phil once more.

—No, Phil. Not cousins.

Phil, flustered, sat back and searched his mind for the inception of this misinformation. Me to Phil, but really directed at Karen S.

—They used to date. And *Karen here* thought it would be a good idea to meddle in their lives and put them in an uncomfortable situation, like we were in some sitcom where imbecilic plans like this might work.

—It *could* still work.

—Let's just watch the game and try to forget about this whole mess.

—If they're not coming back, we should drink their beers.

—Shut up, Phil.

The Mets took the field. Phil retrieved his nachos from me, inspecting them like a teenager's parent wondering at a low watermark on a liquor bottle. I had eaten four chips while he was gone. Whatever. I took a swig of the beer Karen S bought me, realizing that I hadn't properly thanked her, and that if I thanked her now, it would certainly have a sarcastic tone. I decided to remain quiet, even though she had spent a small fortune.

Jake and Chelsea were still absent come the sixth inning, but they were long forgotten. We were in for a hell of a game. The Mets had put up three runs and their pitcher, a fellow named Santana, had yet to give up a hit. This kid seemed to have every trick in the bag. He wasn't throwing with any particular heat, but his movement and control were extraordinary. Painting the edges of the plate. Baseball like a butterfly, moved out of reach by the slightest wind. Batters like paranoid men in the dark, swinging at ghosts. He had nine strikeouts already! When anyone managed to make contact with the ball, it popped straight into the air to fall inconsequently into the glove of a Met.

There were still no hits during the seventh inning stretch and no sign of Jake and Chelsea. Phil hopped from one foot to the other. He had had to use the bathroom for three innings but wouldn't miss a pitch.

—Can you believe this? Have you ever been to a no-hitter, Charlie?

—No. And you're not supposed to say it. It's a jinx.

Karen S clung to my arm in her excitement.

—This is great. I've never had this much fun at a ballgame.

—There is nothing like seeing a good game live.

I was having a great time too. The ballpark was electric with the tension of the no-hitter, and to my surprise, I was enjoying Karen S's company. She wasn't exactly different outside of work—she had the same surly attitude and excitability that put me on edge in the bookstore—but her boisterous manner was just the thing for a ballgame. She continually grabbed my arm when the game got hairy. Sometimes she squeezed so hard it hurt.

The crowd was howling like a pack of hungry dogs at the top of the ninth. Santana was still hitless and at this point Phil, Karen, and I were huddled together with our arms around each other's shoulders holding our breath every time a batter swung.

Karen S, screaming into my ear.

—Hey, look!

Jake and Chelsea climbed the steps toward our row. I thought Chelsea had tears in her eyes. Jake looked like he might have been crying as well. But to my astonishment, they were holding hands.

I looked at Karen. One of my arms was around her shoulder, the other around Phil. I tilted my head.

—You were right.

Karen S was the smartest, most clever woman in the world.

At that moment a loud crack sounded and struck the crowd mum. Santana turned on the pitcher's mound to watch his no-hitter sail over the right field wall. The whole world groaned, and Phil fell to his knees in agony. But Karen and I remained standing, my arm still around her, oddly looking into each other's eyes.

The moment ended quickly. The dreamlike aura deflated back to normalcy. Karen sighed.

—Do you believe that? In the ninth inning!

—It was a good run. And still fun to watch.

Phil picked himself up from the floor. The crowd gave Santana a standing ovation as the last batter popped out to right field and the Mets won the game 3-1. Jake and Chelsea stood with their arms around each other, emotional and smiling. Their happiness made the rest of us happy. Jake addressed us as if he'd just won a Golden Globe.

—We want to say thank you. We were angry at first, but it really worked out. Thanks so much.

The players shook hands on the field and the ballpark started to empty out. Karen and I were so pleased we could barely speak. There was a lump in my throat as I looked at the two lovebirds on that beautiful day just after that great game. It was too much. I guess my heart was melting or something. I had nothing to say in reply to Jake's word of thanks.

From Phil, just before dashing off to the bathroom.

—No problem, you guys.

12.
Upselling

—You can't match your own online prices?

—I'm sorry. I can give you the cheaper price if I ship it home to you, but in the store, it is $29.99.

I looked mournfully at the book dividing us on the counter. It was from the science section—cognitive science, to be exact. Concerning innovations for improving memory. The Miles of Books website had the price listed as $11.38, but I had to sell the book for nearly thirty dollars in the store. The price disparities between the digital Miles of Books and the brick-and-mortar locations were an ongoing issue.

The woman who was quickly losing her patience.

—How long will it take to ship the book?

—About a week. If you get a Miles of Books Membership, it would be cheaper . . .

—How cheap? Like $11.38 cheap?

—No. Ten percent cheaper.

—Off the thirty-dollar price?

—Well, $29.99. But the membership might be a good deal either way. Because if you opt for that $11.38 price, you'll get free shipping with the membership card.

—Ten percent off the $11.38 price, then?

—No. You'd pay the full price of $11.38, but the book would ship for free.

—Oh. Ok. I guess I'll do that. Do I fill out a form or something?

—You do that at the membership sign-up counter. There is a small queue and a twenty-five-dollar fee.

—A fee? For what?

—For the membership.

—I have to pay for the membership?

—Yes.

—So, it would cost, like, thirty-seven dollars to get the membership's *free* shipping? That's more than it would cost if I bought the book right now.

—Yes, but you would have the membership for a year and get ten percent off every time you shopped. Plus, great coupons.

—Have to be honest, I probably won't be shopping here again. Ok, so the cheapest way I can get the book is by shipping it home. That would only be $11.38, but it would take a week.

—Well, seven to ten business days. And there is a $3.99 shipping charge if you don't get that membership.

—All right. Let me get all of this straight. The cheapest price at which I can buy the book is almost *sixteen* dollars and close to two-weeks' wait for shipping. Right?

—Um, that's right.

—And you're telling me I could get the membership and ship it "for free" and that would be thirty-seven dollars and also two-weeks' wait.

—Yes. That's right.

—And, God knows why I would do this, but you seem to also be suggesting that I buy the membership and then purchase the book you have on the shelf right now. That would be, what, over fifty dollars?

—But you would get the book today. And, like I said, a year's worth of membership benefits.

—Good Lord. I just want the book today and I don't want to get ripped off.

—All right . . .

—But my only real option is to buy it today, with no membership and pay about seventy percent more than the cheapest available price.

Her math skills were blinding. I didn't reply. She kept up with the questions.

—Does that make any sense to you?

—I suppose you're paying for the services of the store? I'm sorry.

—Don't be sorry. You're right. I'm paying for the services of the store. For *lovely* conversations like this. Do you realize that your employers are suggesting that I *not use* your services anymore? By setting these prices, by structuring your membership program in this bizarre way, your bosses are telling me *not* to shop here. They are telling me that they would rather I stay home and order online. I sure hope you're looking for another job. . .

She squinted at my nametag.

—*Charlie*.

Again, I had no reply. She was angry, and I certainly understood that, but this conversation was turning toward unacceptable personal cruelty. Look, we wear nametags, but it is highly insulting for a customer to say our names unless we vocally introduce ourselves. Everyone knows that. Time to pass this one off.

—Would you like to speak to a manager?

—You know what? Yes. Yes, I would.

I paged overhead for a manager to come to customer service. The woman and I stood like Vladimir and Estragon anticipating a higher authority. She remained quiet, but I could see by the undulations of her lips that some nasty thoughts were brewing. I looked over my shoulder for one of the Michaels and was surprised to see Jake at my side.

—Hi, I'm Jake. What can I help you with?

I regarded Jake dubiously for a moment and then took a step away, folded my hands behind my back. I wasn't sure what he was doing. I worried that he thought I was in some type of trouble and trying to cover for me. One of the Michaels was sure to answer my page at any moment and then Jake would be caught impersonating a manager. What a silly thing to do! It didn't make sense, but I was powerless to stop it.

Jake listened to the woman's complaint nodding his head and saying *Right, right. I understand.* The woman kept talking and Jake kept understanding. It appeared that she was going to talk until Jake said he would match the online price. But the rub was, I knew that he would *never* match the price. There had recently been a companywide memo shared with both booksellers and management forbidding the matching of online prices. Jake's hands were tied here. So, he went into training-video mode.

—Do you have one of our SwiftFoots?

—No. And I don't want to buy one. I just want the book. I need it today.

—You don't need to buy a SwiftFoot to get the benefits. I notice you have a laptop with you. Have you heard of our SwiftFoot App?

Jake was basically repeating verbatim a training video that we had all been made to watch a few months ago. *Handselling in the Digital Age*, it was called. All well and good. But the trouble with training videos is that their techniques make booksellers sound wooden. They don't really work.

The woman, preparing to scalp Jake.

—There's an app? Like, an app I could put on my phone?

Hmm. Not exactly tomahawk-ish.

—Yup. Or your computer. Or both! And it's free. You download it from our website for free. And then you can buy an E-book that you'd have right away. It's almost like free, instantaneous shipping.

Jake had said the word *free* three times. The customer cracked a joke.

—I bet you pay for the book, though.

And then she laughed. This woman, who had said my name out loud because she was so angry, was yucking it up with Jake.

Jake with a chuckle of his own.

—Right, right. It's not unlimited free books. Let's see here...

Jake deftly typed the title of the book into our search engine.

—Huh. Look at that. The E-book is even cheaper than the ship-to-home price.

—All right. What do I do?

Jake went about setting up the SwiftFoot App then and there. The customer unveiled her laptop, he took her to the appropriate webpage, and within ten minutes she had the book on both her computer and her phone for around nine dollars. The woman paged through the E-book on her computer. She was so impressed with Jake's presentation that she bought a Color SwiftFoot, even though she said she wouldn't. For two hundred and fifty dollars!

Jake strutted back from the cash area after upselling the woman to the tune of three hundred dollars—what with the warranty and the cover and the screen saver and such (You have to have a screen-saving plastic film thing, apparently). Afterward, he leaned against the customer service desk with a smug air. *Well deserved*, I thought.

—That was ludicrous. She was ready to knock your head off at the beginning of that conversation. Nice job, son.

—It was nothing. I know the price matching stuff is difficult, but the company gives us outs. Look into the E-Reader, Charlie. Learn it. It will make life less difficult.

—Eh. I don't know. I tried. It's not for me.

This really worried Jake. He wore the face of a drug addiction sponsor. Christ, he loved the SwiftFoot.

—I'm not saying you should buy it. But you should learn how it works so you can sell it. You think of yourself as a good bookseller, don't you?

—Of course. I've been doing this for nearly forty years.

—So, think of the E-Readers as a change in bookselling. It's an innovation in your profession. Since you're such a great bookseller, you should be an expert in digital books. There must have been other changes to publishing in the forty years you've worked in bookstores.

He was right about that. I remembered back at the beginning of my career, wasting time at Geraldine's with Dennis. There was a period in the early sixties when a good chunk of the day was spent bemoaning Gold Medal Books. Dennis could swear a blue streak about Gold Medal Books. He hated them. Gold Medal Books was the first publishing house to put out real literature in the mass market format—the little paperback books. Before Gold Medal, there were romance, mysteries, and sci-fi that would be published as mass markets, but the good stuff was treated to the better printings. Now we were seeing the likes of Hemingway, Dickens, the Bronte sisters, all released as if they were pulp. At the time, we were sure this ratty, cheap format was going to be the end of the hardcover and therefore the end of the bookstore. I remember sneering at a tiny copy of Pearl Buck's *The Good Earth*, wondering why someone had taken the time to typeset a diamond inside a piece of shit.

The digital stuff evoked the same feeling, but it was much worse. This time around the book wasn't just being made smaller and cheaper, it was being made extinct. See, a book isn't just a story; it's a piece of art. I hate to be corny about it, but it's true. A book is greater than the sum of its parts. There's a cover and pages and black ink. The digital format assumes that the story is all that matters. And, sure, the story is the most important part. But you can't disregard the art form of bookmaking completely. You can't disregard the different properties of a book and how they intermingle. Every inch of the Sistine Chapel can be viewed on the internet, but people still form a line halfway across Vatican City. Why? Because real is better than digital. Real is sacred. I mean, what about cover art? What about the cut of the paper at the ends? People love to talk about the smell of books, don't they? A SwiftFoot smells like fucking plastic. What about the knit cover beneath the book jacket with the author's initials? What about the glue in the binding? What about bookmarks? What about licking your finger to turn a page? What about me?

I shook my head. Jake didn't want to hear all that.

—You're right. I should look into it more. Thanks for helping.

—No problem.

He began to walk away. Off to solve more problems, I suppose. I called to him.

—Hey, you should be careful. That woman asked to speak to a manager and I think she assumed you were one. You could get in trouble.

This turned him around.

—I didn't tell you?

I raised my eyebrows.

—I'm being promoted. I'm a manager-in-training.

13.

Charlie goes to Hell's Kitchen

I didn't think I was in the right place. It was a bar in Hell's Kitchen. And as far as bars in Hell's Kitchen go, I suppose it was serviceable. It was a large building; I'll give it that. High ceilings. The floors were constructed of a chipped hard wood, its abused state hidden by shadows due to the lack of windows. Lights hung down from the darkness to hover above the bar like the glowing tentacle of a predator in the Mariana Trench. Most places in New York had banned smoking at this point, but here, a thick scent of cigarette hung in the air. There weren't many patrons—six or seven—and those hirsute souls crouched at the bar, clutching mugs of dark beer. They were old—not as old as me, but old. This made me feel a bit more comfortable, except that they were also predominantly garbed in denim and leather. Bikers, I guess.

The bartender was fat, maybe in his fifties. He was bald on top but sported a long, auburn ponytail seesawed by a long auburn goatee waving from his chin like a matador's flag. He had wild blue eyes. Leaning over the bar, his great girth pressed up against the glass mugs that hung underneath, he spoke savage whispers into a customer's ear. The guy listening was an old gent in a leather hat, wolfish, with scraggly, gray facial hair. He howled at whatever the bartender said and then leaned back to down his drink. The bartender turned his wild blue eyes and swaying goatee toward me.

—Hey there, pal. What'll it be?

Nice enough, I guess.

—I think I'm in the wrong bar. Is there. . .some type of comedy show here tonight?

I was sure that I was about to be laughed out of the place, a foolish old fuck who wore khaki pants to a biker bar. Instead, the bartender's wild eyes lit with recognition.

—You're with the kids, then. Yeah, the show's downstairs. Buy your drinks from me, though.

—Fantastic.

I stepped up to the bar, next to the wolf with the leather hat.

—Whatever you have on tap.

—Guinness, Bud, Miller Lite, Brooklyn Lager.

—Miller Lite.

The wolf leaned in.

—Hey. Listen to this. Tracey just told me this one: E-flat walks into a bar and says, *Can I have a drink?* Bartender says, *Sorry, but we don't serve minors!*

The man finished the joke with a long, rasping laugh that grew into a coughing fit reminiscent of Mann's *Magic Mountain*. Tracey, the bartender, filled my beer at the tap, shaking his head and muttering, *we don't serve minors* . . .

—Good one.

I chuckled. I didn't really get it.

—I'll have to remember that.

I slid a five-dollar bill across the table.

—Down the stairs, you said?

I collected my drink and made my way toward the long rickety hole in the ground that Tracey had pointed out. One hand on the railing, I went step-by-step, carefully making my way in the dark. My knees clicked like a grandfather clock.

—Charlie?

The voice came from behind me, up the stairs.

—Hello!

I didn't look back, fearing a geriatric tumble down the rathole. When I hit the last step and turned around, Jake was in front of me, smiling—a rosy-cheeked cherub in the pits of hell. I could tell he'd had a few.

—I didn't know you were coming! Chelsea is going to be so happy!

—Good, good. Where is she?

—Backstage!

I took in the room bit by bit. What Jake had pointed out as *backstage* was a narrow, dark space between two walls. All the kids from the flyer, Chelsea included, stood in that dark, cramped nest, smoking cigarettes and drinking. Two of them were passing a marijuana joint. All right. On the other side of the wall was twenty feet of free space and then six rows of lined chairs. The area without chairs was the stage. A system of spotlights kept the stage bright-ish and the rest of the room a dusk-like gray. There was a bathroom toward the rear that had no door. I saw a young man standing at a urinal, peeing right there in plain view.

Jake and I came upon a large troll at the bottom of the stairs.

—Hey, Sydney.

Jake produced some bills from his wallet and shoved them into a jar tucked under Sydney's left arm. Sydney seemed pleased with this, so I did the same. I followed Jake to a corner of the room where I recognized some other employees—Sonia, Yesinia, Quinn, Rosa, Michael R. They laughed when they saw me; I don't know why. The girls hugged me politely and Michael R shook my hand, grabbing my elbow with his left like a politician. Heavy metal music blared over the sound system, so we couldn't really talk to each other. Jake held a shouting conversation with Quinn, but I'll be damned if I understood a word of it. Everyone was laughing a lot, so I smiled and tried to laugh with the crowd.

The place was really filling up. Young people poured down the steps, drinks in hand, cigarettes at their lips, tight jeans stretched across their thighs. A lot of people. I wondered if we should be finding our seats. I was about to shout this sentiment into Jake's ear when someone grabbed hold of my bicep.

—Take this.

It was Karen. She wore jeans and a green, flowing blouse. Black-rimmed glasses rested low on her nose. She looked over her shoulder and around the room like Hunter Thompson fearing a bat attack. In my hand I found a small squeeze bottle of antibacterial ointment. She turned back to me.

—Have you touched anything?

I thought back and was pretty sure my hands touched the bar when I ordered my drink. Plus, I held tightly to the railing while inching down the stairs. Now that I considered it, I most likely had a staph infection. I flipped the bottle open and covered my hands in liquid.

—Thanks!

Through this exchange, Karen and I realized that there was no way we could hear each other, not over this music. She waved me over to the fast-filling seats. We left the bookseller crew behind and found a pair of metal foldouts near an aisle, in case we needed to leave for any reason. Karen raised her eyebrows at me and shook her head, as if to say, *Do you believe this place?*

Now, as a younger man, I was something of a barfly. I had frequented some murky establishments—maybe not as gloriously befouled as this, but still, unsavory spots. I wondered if Karen had ever been to a beer and shot place like this. My guess was no. Sure, she was making just above the minimum at Miles of Books, but the way she dressed, the way she threw money around—she had spent some time on the Upper East Side, if you know what I mean.

The thunderous music shrank back to a reasonable decibel and I breathed a sigh of relief. It had almost given me a headache. I glanced at Karen and then looked at my shoes. We could hear each other now, if I could think of something to say. I scanned the stage to see if anything was going on yet. Looking back at Karen again, I raised my eyebrows in the same gesture she had made to me earlier. She patted both hands on her knees. So far, this wasn't exactly working out the way I had envisioned. Karen thought of something to say before I could.

—I'm so glad you came, Charlie. Chelsea told me she invited you, but you couldn't make it.

—I told her that I would try.

—Well, it's nice to have someone here my age. The kids at the store have really taken a shining to me, but sometimes they're . . . I don't know . . . tiring.

It was nice of Karen to call us the same age. In truth, I believe I was good deal older than her.

—Well, I had such a good time at the ballgame, I figured I'd come out again.

Karen turned quickly after I said this, looking me curiously in the eye. A warm feeling bubbled up in my chest. It was like I was scared, but in a good way, like watching a particularly silly horror movie. I became clumsy.

—What?

—Nothing. I had a good time at the game too.

—GOOD EVENING, LADIES AND GENTLEMEN!

Karen and I were interrupted by one of the young men from the group, standing in the center of the stage area, shouting. He had no microphone and was made to shout because the raucous group of young people dashed about like dogs at an ownerless dog park.

—I said, GOOD EVENING, LADIES AND GENTLEMEN!

The pups started to calm down. The folding chairs adjacent to us filled rapidly, a particularly drunken young woman crashing next to Karen, scrolling through her cell phone, giggling.

—THANKS FOR COMING TONIGHT FOR THE FIRST PERFORMANCE OF COUNTING COWS!

I peered over my shoulder at the lines of young people standing against the back wall. All the seats were filled, standing room only. There were some older people—a few bikers and a couple of gray-heads paired off that I imagined were parents of one of the performers. I bet the kids in the crowd thought Karen and I were someone's parents. Or grandparents.

—Tonight we will be performing a technique called The Harold. We will have one theme, run three separate storylines, and then tie all the storylines together in the final scene. And …

Dramatic pause.

—…we will be making it all up on the fly. First, I need a suggestion from the crowd!

Karen cupped her hands and called out like a cheerleader on the sidelines.

—BOOKSTORES! DO A BOOKSTORE!

I had never been to an improv show. In the seventies and eighties, everyone was doing standup comedy. Some of my friends gave it a go, and I was dragged to more than one of those performances. But I had never been to anything like this. Was it a trick? Were they really just going to make things up? This was going to be horrible. I checked in with Karen.

—What's going on?

Everyone around us was shouting and Karen kept her eye on the young man hoping that he would choose her bookstore suggestion.

—You call out a word that you want to be the theme for the night. And they'll use it to make all their sketches.

The ringleader picked up his signal.

—Concerts! I heard someone say *concerts*.

Karen deflated back to her seat.

—So, without further ado: COUNTING COWS!

The loud music picked up again and I resisted the temptation to cover my ears. Karen had changed her attitude, bopping to the music, excited about the show. I supposed she must have been to these types of things before. I made a solemn vow to myself that I would not ask her any more questions about how it worked, lest I embarrass myself.

Chelsea walked onto the stage area with a young man whose chest was shrouded in a ridiculously long beard. Like, ZZ Top-long. The kid was probably too young to know who ZZ Top was. He started bouncing his head to some imaginary music and Chelsea followed suit. The bearded gentleman spoke in a high, reedy, hippie impersonation.

—This is a cool concert, man.

Oh, good God. It was like *Laugh-In*, but rudderless and idiotic.

I gripped the sides of my foldout chair tightly and prepared to watch a couple of stoned twenty-somethings play a game of make-believe. I was artistically repelled by what was happening, my soul a hissing vampire under the glare of a crucifix. I began to dread seeing Chelsea at work, having to pass off some lame, positive opinion on the whole deal.

But then something strange happened. As the scene progressed, it turned out that Chelsea and the bearded one were at a show for children, a band called The Wiggles. I knew who The Wiggles were because there were picture books about them at Miles of Books. As Chelsea and the bearded one explained, they had no children themselves, but were on tour following The Wiggles from city to city, calling out requests, getting high with the band backstage. They were Wiggles groupies, basically. It was funny. People were laughing.

And Chelsea—my God!—she was foul-mouthed! Funny, yes—but crude as a construction worker. This was not the quiet girl from the bookstore. It was someone else entirely, someone with a wicked, sarcastic sense of humor. Someone who did not hold back. I was proud of her in a weird way, as I listened to her drop every word in the book in front of a crowd of laughing people. And I laughed, too, I'll admit it. The Counting Cows were damn funny.

When the show ended, it was as if Karen and I had just seen our child in a high school musical. We gushed at her. There was no helping it. Just gushed. Chelsea was pleased at our gushing and even teared up, hugging me, overcome that I had attended her performance and enjoyed it. She said I was the best, just totally the best. I don't know that I deserved all that.

The crowd exited the biker bar but didn't want to go home. A warm pack of cigarette-smoking loiterers hung for ten, twenty minutes, gossiping, telling jokes. Karen and I floated in their wake. A garbage-laden breeze bent around the city blocks, red neon lights flashed heatedly in my eyes, car horns blared their anger—but I was beach-combing-calm. I became brazen.

—We should go out more often. It's always a blast.

I don't know why I said that to Karen as we were standing outside the bar in Hell's Kitchen. The kids were a few feet away and no one could hear except the two of us. I was a little drunk, I guess.

—Really? You think we should go out again?

My own statement repeated back at me sounded overly forward. I thought too long about an appropriate answer. My brain iced over. I was at a loss. I mumbled something lame.

—Maybe. We'll see what the kids cook up for us next, I suppose.

Karen looked at me searchingly, as if she could read what I was thinking from the wrinkles on my forehead. I turned away and looked down the street toward the subway terminal. Just a minute before, Karen offered me a ride home and I had declined. I don't know why. It seemed like the polite thing to do, decline a ride. But now I was going to have to take the subway all the way back to Queens. I fuddled absently with my wallet, looking for my Metro Card, thinking how to make a graceful exit, wondering if there was an R Train I could catch or if I was going to have to transfer. I didn't know if my bladder would make it.

—Really, Charlie, let me drive you home. I'm parked in a garage just around the corner.

—No, no, no.

I waved off the suggestion.

—Nonsense, I'm fine.

I fully realized how ridiculous it was to turn down this ride, but I turned it down nonetheless. It would save me forty-five minutes and would put her out of her way by only a few blocks. And she clearly *wanted* to drive me home. But an ultra-polite puppet master had taken my strings and directed me away from common sense, toward absurdity.

—Don't trouble yourself. I'll see you at work tomorrow.

And with that, I waved to the kids and walked off into the darkness. I looked over my shoulder because I hoped Karen was watching me walk away. She was. I waved again to her.

I was in emergency mode by the time the R train rumbled down the track. My bladder was a painful rock and I was a stupid, old man who made stupid, old decisions. I held out till the Forest Hills stop, made it off the subway car doubled over, metro attendants asking if I was all right. Then a thing happened to me that has happened to aged men since the beginning of time. My organs betrayed me. A beautiful night ruined by senseless choices and a worn-out body.

14.

Mustache No More

WITH the electric trimmer positioned under my nose, I felt my courage wan. Just do it, Charlie! I took a deep breath and pushed through. White and black hairs (almost all white, to be honest) fell to the sink and stuck to the porcelain like leaves in a gutter. When half of my mustache was gone, I stopped, the hum of the trimmer buzzing in the echo of my bathroom. I smiled crazily. I mowed the rest down and clicked the trimmer off.

I ran hot water, wrapped the trimmer in its own cord, placed it back in the drawer of the sink. Removed a razor and a bottle of shaving cream, set them both on the sink as the water began to steam. The shaving cream was cool and hot at the same time, bizarre to have it under my nose. I held the razor under the water, carefully dragged it down my cheek, rinsed it, dragged it again. I saved the remaining stubble of my mustache for last, went over the skin a few times until everything was smooth. Hunkered over the sink, I splashed hot water on my face again and again.

Upon looking in the mirror, my first thought was *not bad*. I couldn't exactly remember the last time I was clean shaven. I started sporting the mustache sometime in the late eighties and before that I had a full beard. There were occasions—to attend weddings, for instance—when I was cleanly shaven. But I hadn't been to a wedding for a long, long time. Lots of funerals, not so many weddings.

I ran my hand over my smooth upper lip. It didn't feel like part of my body, but a transplant from a younger man. My face was much more serious, somehow. My eyes more piercing than they had been before, my chin more pronounced. I was good-looking. Like Clint Eastwood, almost.

I quit my vainglorious observations and got dressed for work. As I buttoned up my best pinstriped dress shirt, a seed of dread blossomed inside me. Everyone was going to be in my business today. I don't like people talking about how I look, even if it's complimentary. The polite harassing that Ludmilla endured over her pixie cut had lasted all of December. She said she couldn't sit in a bathroom stall without someone handing her a square of toilet paper and whispering that they liked her new style. I had called down the opinions with my grooming, released myself as open game. Being a man instead of a young woman, I figured it would all be over in a week. But still.

Michael P kicked off the jeering.

—Look at Clean Gene!

Good Lord. I tried to remain friendly.

—Yup. Shaved off the old push broom. Do you like it?

—No. I hate it. Kidding! Seriously, it's super.

—Thanks, Michael.

I placed my lunch in the breakroom refrigerator. I stayed in there a while, letting the cool air hide my head from the adoring public. I wished I could have stayed there forever. Or at least until my mustache grew back. I had been at work ten minutes and I already knew this had been a mistake.

Don poked his head out of the office to see me. His slow eyes studied my face, his own mustache protuberant over his mouth, shameful and sloppy in the contrasting absence of mine. Don's hangdog inflated to a warm smile. He hummed his laughter in my direction.

—Fantastic, Charlie.

He recoiled back into the depths of his office, like a crustacean into its nautilus.

—Fantastic. Hmmm . . .

More than anyone else, Becky was amazed at my transformation. I had been in the receiving room for over ten minutes placing my returns on their proper shelves. She stared at me the whole time. She sat on her impossibly small swivel chair, her head resting on her hand as she gazed in my direction. She had just received her delivery, but she wasn't touching it. In fact, she wasn't doing shit.

—Do the boxes just open themselves now?

For what must have been the fifth time.

—It's really amazing, Charlie. I can't believe it. You look like an old movie star.

—Thanks, I think.

—No, I mean you look like a handsome old man. This old . . . old, good-looking guy.

—I get it, Becky. Thank you.

As the day went on, I grew accustomed to the attention. If I'm being honest, I started to feed off it a bit. There was some strutting. I spoke to customers with more gusto than I had in quite a while. The shelving was finished in record time. Phil looked at me mysteriously when he came into work—as if he had had a case of déjà vu—but then said nothing about it. Blinking away his confusion, he pushed a mass market in my face as he was wont to do. The cover showed a moldy zombie limping about on a high-tech spaceship.

—I know you don't read a lot of Sci Fi, but you should really consider this one.

On the sales floor, I helped a woman find a gluten-free cookbook, a gentleman to the music books to see what we had in stock about Bob Dylan, and three young ladies to the teen section to find the latest in a series about a group of nasty, murderous high school girls. Before I knew it, my shift was over and it was time for lunch. I took out my apple, tuna fish, and cottage cheese. I was three bites into my can of tuna when I heard the beeps of the security buttons on the breakroom door. It was Karen. She stopped in her tracks when she saw me. She screamed.

—Ahhhhhh! Oh my God! Charlie, you finally did it!

You'd have thought I won a fucking marathon.

She walked over to me and ran her fingers over my upper lip. I sat there bug-eyed and stiff, as if I was Helen Keller's teacher, letting my student get a good look at me.

—It looks so, *so* good.

—Thanks.

She backed away, beaming, and opened her purse on the breakroom table. She took out her cell phone and placed it in her pocket before putting her purse in a locker. The attention dissipating, I continued working on the can of tuna. She wasn't done with me yet.

—So, when's the next Mets game?

—They play almost every day.

—Ha ha. When are *we* going again?

—I don't have any plans to go.

—They have a series with the Yankees coming up, don't they?

—They do. But it's probably already sold out.

—I'll get tickets.

I shrugged my shoulders, took a bite of tuna, and turned the page of my book. She kept going.

—When is the series?

—Two weeks? Three?

—Oh.

Karen paused to think. She was acting strangely. I couldn't possibly guess what was going through her head. It was like I was sitting in front of the sphinx. She came to life.

—What are you doing for dinner tonight?

—I'm making chicken and broccoli.

There was another pause here. Karen stared at me for a long while.

Look, I know I was being an idiot. But think about it this way: I hadn't dated anyone in nearly twenty years. Yes, I felt a certain way about Karen, but dating was hardly on my radar. Besides, my head was all spun around from the attention I was receiving over my stupid new look, and I had had four beers at Chelsea's show which, for me, constitutes a hangover. There were a lot of factors contributing to my blindness.

—Really? You're sure?

—Yup.

I turned another page.

—Chicken and broccoli. Maybe rice. What are you having?

—I don't know.

I finally looked up because her tone was unusually flat. Almost caustic. Karen turned abruptly and walked out onto the sales floor, her movements suddenly rough. I put my plastic fork down in consternation. I heard the wheels of Don's chair roll across the carpet and I knew—though my back was to his door—that he was looking at me. I turned around. There was a sly expression on his face.

—Charlie . . .

—What?

—I've been married a long time, so maybe I don't know what I'm talking about. But I'm almost certain that Karen just asked you to dinner.

I stared back at him, pensive. He finished the thought.

—And you just turned her down. Hmmmm.

Spot on. Phil must have been rubbing off on me. I was not Clint Eastwood at all, just another mustacheless fool. I didn't *want* to be a mustacheless fool. I set down my fork, pushed out my chair and left the breakroom. I posted up in the center of the sales floor where Karen typed at a computer with a phone pressed between her ear and shoulder. I stood in front of her and waited with nervous patience as she placed an order for the customer on the other end of the line. She glanced up while she was still on the phone, arched her eyebrows, silently asking what I needed.

—I'll wait till you're done.

She continued her conversation and I drummed my fingers on the customer service counter. Someone slapped me on the shoulder.

—How 'bout them Yanks, Charlie?

Shit. Bernie.

—Hey, Bernie. I'm actually sort of waiting for Karen to finish here…

—Whoa! No more snot catcher, huh?

—Oh. Yeah. I shaved.

—No more lip-caterpillar!

—Right.

—No more mustache rides for the ladies!

—Bernie, go away.

He paused, unsure of how to proceed. His mouth hung open until Ludmilla walked past with a cart of frontlist.

—Ludmilla! You still knittin' those sweaters?

I turned my attention back to Karen. She moved the phone away from her mouth, whispering.

—It's a long order. What are you waiting for?

To the customer.

—No, no. There's nothing wrong with the order. You can get as many books as you want.

—All right. Do you know Donatello's, the Italian place in Forest Hills?

—Yes.

I was about to continue, but Karen kept talking.

—It's available. I can get that one for you.

I frowned.

—Was that *yes* to me?

—Yes.

—You know the place? Donatello's?

—Yes. The book is in the warehouse.

Eyes on me.

—Yeah, I know the place, Charlie.

—Oh. Right. So, I was thinking more about dinner. And, there's Donatello's. And I know it's really good food. Anyway, do you want to go? There? With me?

—Yes.

I pointed to my chest inquisitively. Karen put her hand over the phone. She snapped.

—Yes, you! I want to go to dinner with you, Charlie. Seven o'clock. Now get out of here so I can place this order.

I was too shocked to move for a moment, so I didn't. Karen ignored me and continued to speak with her customer on the phone. Eventually, I turned around, blood rushing through my veins like a waterslide park, and nearly skipped back to the breakroom, still a fool, but for an entirely different reason.

15.

Charlie Goes on a Date

My apartment hadn't seen a visitor in some time. Years, perhaps. This might sound sad, but loneliness hadn't even occurred to me until Jake and Chelsea arrived. Then, suddenly, my apartment was a private area exposed, like they had walked in on me in the bathroom instead of the living room. Jake's eyes widened.

—Holy shit, Charlie. You have a lot of books.

Chelsea pinched him. I cringed.

—Yes . . .

I scanned the rows beyond rows of tattered paperbacks and cheap, black shelving.

—Do you think it's too much?

Chelsea told me what I wanted to hear, but Jake answered with innocent brutality.

—No! It's not too much.

—Well, I guess it depends on what you mean by *too much*.

—Do you think it's strange? Like someone might think I'm a degenerate if they saw all these books?

—Of course they wouldn't think that.

—A degenerate? What do you mean, *a degenerate*?

—Like a weirdo or a hoarder or something?

—Oh. *Weeeell* . . .

Jake considered this possibility. The necessity of consideration was damning enough.

—I guess it is a little weird.

—Jake!

He strolled down my stacks a pace or two while Chelsea stood patiently next to me.

—Why don't you get rid of some of them?

—I don't know.

—Because he likes them, Jake. Leave it alone.

Looking over some of the shelves myself, the old thought occurred to me.

—Which ones would I get rid of?

Jake paused and cocked his head to the side.

—Good point.

His eyes narrowed while standing near the D section.

—You could lose this one. *Great Expectations*. This book sucks. I had to read this in high school. I hate Dickens.

Normally, I would have ripped the young man's throat out for smearing the name of Dickens in my living room. But I was too worried and embarrassed to work up the fervor. Jake read more spines as he walked down a row of shelves. He stopped at every tenth book or so, pulled it out, and examined the cover. He opened a poetry book of John Berryman for a good while, reading the author's bio and flipping through to scan a poem or two. I fetched us three beers from the refrigerator, cracked them open, and handed them out. Chelsea smiled.

—Thanks.

Jake took the beer, made a funny face at the Berryman, and kept reading. Chelsea rolled her eyes at him and then cut to the chase.

—So, you're going to Donatello's with Karen?

—Yes. And you two aren't as surprised as I thought you might be. This is beyond strange, isn't it?

Jake kept scanning the bookshelves. Chelsea tilted her head to one side, put a finger next to her crooked witch's nose.

—*Weeeell* . . .

—What?

—We knew she liked you. Karen was hinting around that she wanted you to ask her out.

—Why didn't you tell me?

Jake, now perusing my copy of *Something Happened* by Heller.

—Why didn't you tell me Chelsea was going to be at the Mets game?

Now I rolled my eyes. I took a swallow of beer. This whole thing with Karen was driving me crazy. *How many people know about it,* I wondered. If these two knew she was angling toward me, and Don knew what had happened, what about everyone else? Did the entire store know we were going on a date? Jake disappeared behind a bookshelf and I turned to Chelsea.

—I don't understand how this happened.

—What don't you understand?

—Why would she want to go out with me?

—She likes you.

—But she doesn't. Not really. I just don't understand.

—Charlie . . .

Chelsea shook her curly head and turned her mush mouth into a matronly frown.

—You're being ridiculous. You're a handsome man. You know that.

—Oh, come on . . .

—And you're funny. Dry, sure. But people like that.

—She's just so much younger than me.

—Yeah, how old *are* you?

—Shut up, Jake! That doesn't matter. We're focusing on the wrong things. Have you thought about what you're going to wear? What you're going to talk about? Maybe some questions you might ask her?

—Shit, I haven't thought of any of those things. I have no idea.

Jake reappeared from the stacks.

—Do you want to do this? Do you want to go out with her?

I paused. Eventually I nodded, sheepishly.

—Yes. Sure, I do.

He clapped his hands like a football coach.

—Ok, then! Let's make a game plan.

And Chelsea ran with the ball. Her questions and recommendations were dizzying. The whole thing went on much longer than I expected. These two were genuinely concerned about my welfare on this date, and I truly didn't understand how this concern had been mustered. I tried to imagine myself as a young man helping out someone decades and decades older than me with something as ticklish as this situation. I failed. I *couldn't* imagine it. These two were a different breed. Chelsea talked and talked and I did my best to appreciate and heed her enthusiastic advice.

—Definitely talk about yourself a little bit. People say you shouldn't talk about yourself too much on dates, but I don't know. I think a little bit of your life story is good dinner conversation.

—All right. But I don't have much of a life story.

—And be sure to ask about her. What do you know about Karen?

—She reads romance novels. And she likes gadgets. She recently quit smoking.

—Good! That's plenty.

—But dinner is going to take two hours. That's not enough.

—One topic will lead to another. And Karen will hold up her end of the conversation, don't forget.

But forgetting was exactly what I was worried about. I wasn't going to remember all of Chelsea's details. If anything, stuffing my head with this date-strategy bullshit would only serve to trip up any natural conversation. Why was Chelsea doing this?

—Chelsea, why are you doing this?

—Doing what? Helping you?

—Yes.

—I owe you, Charlie. We both do. We're in debt to you and Karen.

She looked at me sideways for a moment.

—And maybe Phil?

—No.

—Right.

Jake stood next to Chelsea now and put his arm around her.

—If not for you and Karen, Jake and I wouldn't be together now. When I think of all the secret maneuverings you two had to do to get us to that game—HA!—it's crazy. We owe you this help. We *want* to help you.

I hadn't done all that much to make the ball game happen. If anything, I had tried to stop it. I *did* buy the tickets, I suppose. Jake put his free hand on my shoulder. He breathed in the dust of my books.

—You're going to do just fine, Charlie.

My last real date took place in the early eighties and it wasn't much to write home about. My first date ever had been with Teresa, way back in the fifties, and I had ended up marrying her. I had been back from Korea for about six months and was clerking at a law office where Teresa did the typing. We went on two dates, both to the same movie theater, and then were going steady. After we were officially together, we stopped going on dates and just hung out at bars and parties in the city. We were pretty wild for a handful of years there. We didn't get married until she was pregnant with Kurt. Then we settled down some, I guess.

I arrived at Donatello's and lingered outside the window. As I stood on the sidewalk, people moved past me at different paces—racing home from work, walking aimlessly while staring at a cell phone, a homeless man shuffling with his cardboard sign at his hip, lovers walking hand-in-hand. I was the only stationary thing, standing there like a dumb-dumb, arms crossed, gripping both my elbows. I was really early. Almost an hour. Why did I come this early? I slid my hands into my pockets and rocked back and forth on my shoes. I worried over silly things, wondering how old Karen was—I was over seventy. She could be as young as fifty by the looks of her. The concern over suitable conversation reared its ugly head again. And the money—I certainly worried that I was going to spend too much money on this dinner. I had a hundred-dollar bill in my pocket, for God's sake. But then my mind settled on Teresa and Kurt, as it often does in times of stress. I felt basically horrible.

—Hey, there.

Karen was a few steps behind me, her smokeless cigarette in her hand. She blew out a cloud of steam and placed the phony implement back in her purse. She looked beautiful, her hair down and brushed to the side, a flowery dress, blue and white. Again, I wondered why she wanted to have dinner with me. Despite Chelsea's prepping, I was sorely inadequate and underprepared.

—How are you doing, Charlie?

—Good!

Then, I burst into maniacal, cackling laughter. I don't know why. Karen looked at me curiously for a moment.

—Let's go inside.

Since we were both so early, our table wasn't ready. We bellied up at the bar, glancing at ourselves in the mirror and then quickly looking away. We had both eaten at the restaurant before. I had been here just over eight years ago when a coworker I was close with retired. Karen had eaten here last month. Donatello's was a popular place, with white cloths and carafes of wine on the table. It hadn't changed in the years since I'd eaten here. Hokey paintings depicting Italians of vastly differing importance—Da Vinci, Sophia Loren, Christopher Columbus, Pavarotti, Emeril Lagasse. Heaping plates of pasta smothered in marinara, alfredo, black truffle butter. Couples leaned over tables laughing, red-faced. I was going to order the black truffle because that's what I had eight years ago and I liked it. Plus, I saw on the chalkboard outside that it was on special.

Karen ordered a glass of wine at the bar and, though I am usually a beer drinker, I ordered the same. When in faux Rome. Not being used to wine, it went straight to my head. Halfway through the glass I found all my worries about conversation dissipating. *This isn't going to be difficult at all*, I thought. *I'm quite the witty fellow!* Shortly after we finished our first drink, they sat us at our table and we ordered another round. And what did we talk about? Work, of course. And the people we worked with. No shit, right? It was such an obvious subject that I couldn't believe Chelsea hadn't considered it. She and I were so worried about meaningful conversation that we overlooked gossip. Karen was a gossip specialist. Though I had been working at the store for many years and she for only a few months, she had the dope on everyone. Phil had been married three times—no children, thank heavens—the Michaels were definitely dating and hiding it from the company, and Don, the store manager, had spent his youth working on an oil rig. I wasn't aware of any of these things.

After hearing Karen's Page Six best.

—Get out of here!

I didn't usually like to get into other people's business, but I must admit these tidbits were fascinating. Karen's infectious grapevining riveted me.

Our appetizers came and we eventually talked about me. I didn't discuss my family, but I mentioned Korea, that I had been married. I talked about all the different bookstores I had worked in, a trip I had once taken to Croatia with a friend of mine.

—Did your wife die?

I guess she wanted to hear about that. Ok. I spoke while looking at my glass of wine.

—Not while I was with her. We separated a long time ago. She remarried. I did hear she passed away in 2002.

Karen nodded, knowing that the love life of a person old and single is destined to be wrought with some tragedies.

—I was married too. My husband died. Heart attack. While we were married.

—I'm sorry.

—It was twelve years ago. And, honestly, we didn't get along that well.

—Was he cruel?

—No, just busy. He made us a lot of money, though.

—That's some consolation, I guess.

—Yup.

She took a sip of her wine. She smirked.

—Do you want to know some gossip about me?

—Sure.

—The job at the bookstore is my first job. Ever.

—No, it's not. How old are you?

I regretted the question as soon as it escaped my mouth. Any blockhead knows you don't ask a lady her age. Especially on a date. Look at this fucking idiot. Besides, what age could she possibly report that would explain not yet having a job? Twelve?

But she wasn't bothered at all by my blunder.

—Sixty-eight. And never worked.

I was relieved to hear she was so old. What's eight years? Nothing. She continued.

—I never worked growing up, my father wouldn't let me. I went to college and got a degree in communications and then married Jerry my senior year.

—What did you do all day?

—I had kids, Charlie, what do you think?

—Oh.

The waiter appeared and placed our entrées in front of us, removing the appetizer plates and refilling our waters, topping off our wines. It had grown dark outside. The candle on the table threw a sphere around us, our own warm bubble of soft light, buoyant with food and drink. The black truffle sauce was in front of me and Karen had squash ravioli. I was jealous of her food.

She dug in.

—Three children. Two boys and a girl.

—And they're all in New York?

—Just Kate. Both boys live in California.

—It must have been hard after your husband died. Once you get used to a certain lifestyle it's difficult to change. Did you have to move?

—Oh, no. I still live in the same place. And we have an apartment in the Upper East Side if I'm staying in the city.

She popped an orange cut of ravioli in her mouth.

—Mmmmm. This is wonderful! Do you want to try?

I didn't understand. I could have sworn Karen just told me that the bookstore was the first time she had to work for her money. How did she have an extra apartment on the Upper East Side? She saw me pondering and lowered her fork.

—Jerry left me with money after he died. I guess I wasn't clear about that.

—So, you're working . . . why? For fun?

My attitude began to sour. I never had much of a taste for wealthy people. She paused for a moment and set down her fork.

—You could say that . . .

The pause dragged on. I didn't know what she was doing. She sniffed loudly and then I realized she had become emotional. Her voice leaped an octave.

—I'm sorry.

She wiped tears from her cheeks.

—I promised myself I wasn't going to talk about my problems.

She pointed to her wet eyes.

—And this is why.

She shook her head. Dabbed her eyes with the cloth napkin.

—Silly.

I hadn't said anything in a while. I was becoming desperate to think of something to say.

—Are you sad about your husband?

She laughed that terrible, chortling laughter that people do when they're in the middle of a good cry and trying to play it off. Like a car-hit dog wagging her tail at her owner before she dies. Horrible stuff.

—No, Charlie.

She sniffed loudly once more.

—No. It's my daughter. It's Kate. She's sick.

—Oh.

—Ovarian cancer.

—Right.

—And I was trying to help her; I was going over to her apartment every day to help with the kids and to make sure she was taking her medicine, to make sure she went to her doctor's appointments on time.

—Sure.

—Well, I think I started to bug her.

Karen was calmed now. Took a healthy sip of her wine. This was dangerous territory for me, but I thought I was faring well so far.

—I stopped visiting so often, but it was driving me nuts. I needed something to do.

—So, the bookstore.

—So, the bookstore. And it's been great. I love everyone there. I love working there. I wish I had worked there my whole life.

—Well, you're good at it.

And I meant it. I didn't agree with her style, but customers loved her.

—Especially for someone who has never worked before.

She raised her glass and tilted it toward me.

—Thanks. That means a lot coming from you. You're picky, Charlie.

—And how is your daughter doing?

She drank her wine.

—Oh, better and worse. Mostly worse, I guess. It seems like she's not trying to get better. Like she's just letting it happen.

But I can't say that to her. She's so tired all the time. But it feels like she quit, you know? Like she gave up?

—Hmm.

She shook her head. Looked back at her plate.

—I don't think I could take it, Charlie. A parent should never outlive their child.

And then, it was as if someone pressed a button on the back of my neck. I powered down. Dropped off, staring at a far-away place beyond where Karen sat. She kept talking about her daughter I suppose, but I was gone. Zoned out. I revived at one point and realized Karen was asking me if I was all right. I said I was fine and then stood up. There was blackness around the edges of my vision and I couldn't hear very well. Muffled. I had sense enough to put my hundred-dollar bill on the table.

—I have to leave. I'm so sorry.

16.
Kurt and Teresa

LONG time ago, after Korea and before the bookstores.

The fan was broken. I had done my best to fix it, but it was still broken. I was clerking at the law office but Teresa had quit to raise the baby. We were living on one small income, but neither of us was used to having money anyway, so it wasn't much of a struggle. The point is we couldn't buy a new fan. I had to fix it.

Teresa and I hadn't been sleeping on account of the heat and because of little Kurt. He was five months old and our doctor suspected his teeth were coming in early. We let him suck on ice before bed—Teresa wouldn't let me rub whiskey on his gums—and we borrowed an old fan from Teresa's grandmother. With the ice numbing his mouth and the fan directly on him, he slept all right. We had finally managed to get caught up on our rest, at least a little bit. But now the fan was broken and we were nearly hysterical about its repair.

I worked on it for about an hour before giving up. I was never any good with motors. I told Teresa I was sorry. We each drank a beer while watching Kurt roll around on the rug, divining the horrors he would subject us to for the next ten hours. It was a Monday, so if I were up all night it would ruin my entire week. I wouldn't have a chance to catch up until Saturday. This was no good. There was something going on at work, a chance for promotion, perhaps? I don't even remember. One of those inconsequential work scenarios that the world hinged on for a moment and which was instantly forgotten afterward. Anyhow, I was concerned with something that seemed personally important. Isn't that the thing about being young, though? Everything seemed so personal and so important. I was easily offended back then. I couldn't stand any criticism or any extra burden. I was the center of the universe when I was young, and how *dare* you hinder the universe? How *dare* you stop its progress with your feeble needs? Age, and the events that go along with it, change that perspective. Instead of the center of the universe, you become a string of planets in the solar system, then one planet in a galaxy, then one island out of infinite galaxies. As the years pass, you become a speck in the vastness. You become like I am now. You don't matter.

But that night, when Kurt began crying at one o'clock in the morning, it was a catastrophe. It was a personal attack on my well-being. I *had* to sleep. I had to get my rest to be one hundred percent ready for work. Billows of frustration puffed in my chest each time we rocked him back to sleep only to hear his piercing cry moments later. There were literally tears in my eyes, I felt so sorry for myself. *Tears.* Good God, the shame I have at remembering that.

Then, miraculously, at three in the morning, we set him down and he stayed down. This broke with tradition, since once Kurt got going, he was usually not subdued until the sun came up. In those hours, I had a sleep like I hadn't had in the past five months, in the past five years even. Total black out, no dreams, no waking, for three hours. And then when I did wake up, around six-thirty,

I snuggled in the covers with Teresa and was lazy and warm and content with my eyes closed. I pulled myself out of bed at seven-thirty, stood under a steaming shower for twenty minutes. Got dressed, made myself oatmeal. Packed a lunch for the day. I did all those ordinary things without yet knowing.

I walked to his nursery, trying to move lightly so that my shoes didn't upset the creaky floors. Poked my head through the door and saw him lying in the crib. I don't know why, but I went in. Normally I would be too terrified of waking him to enter the room while he was down, but something propelled me. Maybe I suspected. I stood over his crib, my briefcase in one hand, a sack lunch in the other. Morning sun shone through at such an angle as to send long shadows off every object. Set down my briefcase on our changing table and my lunch on top of it. Hovered over Kurt, mindless. I bent down and touched his cheek. I touched his cheek again, this time pressing harder. *Kurt*, I whispered. *Kurt, time to wake up* . . . Reaching down with both arms, I picked him up. His head bent sharply, his mouth open. I pushed his head upright. He felt heavier than he had before. I pressed his limp body against mine, as if maybe he was just too cold. I immediately thought of medical attention, ambulances, CPR. But he was so cold, a forgotten cup of tea left forever steeping on the kitchen counter. His lips were blue, his chest, lungs—still. I was immobilized, crouched down and sat on the floor, Kurt in my lap. I kept whispering to him, imploring him to wake up like I never had before.

I should have woken Teresa, I know this. I just couldn't do it. I couldn't tell her. She was asleep, in that warm bed. I had just been there myself; I had just been comfortable and ignorant of this cold, little person. I couldn't call out; I couldn't wake her. But the time would come when I would have to wake her, when I would have to ruin her life. We would have to tell our friends, I realized. And our family. Teresa's grandmother, Christ! We couldn't tell Teresa's grandmother about this. Everyone at work. How would they deal with this? What would they think about us?

My mind raged out of control as I sat there. *You did this!* I screamed at myself. *You did this! You wished for it and here it is!* I had fantasized last night, and how many other nights, about what life would be like if Kurt were not around. I mean, we didn't have him on purpose, did we? It was never said aloud, but we thought of him as a burden. So, I asked for this, I wished for it and now I had it. I felt such revulsion for myself. I realized some mistakes at that moment. I realized that I was not the center of the universe and my selfishness was so dark as to be dangerous. Kurt's death was my Copernicus, my Galileo, and I never thought of life the same after it. I am a speck, I knew then. I am nothing.

Teresa and I stayed together for a couple years after Kurt's death, but it wasn't the same. We were ghosts floating around the apartment, finding rooms in that small place where we wouldn't have to see each other. Teresa started waking up with a red face and puffy eyes. I told her it was probably allergies or something. That was a lie. I knew why she looked like that in the mornings, but I didn't want to tell her. She was crying in her sleep.

We didn't talk about Kurt much after his funeral which was probably our final undoing. We needed to discuss his absence, but we didn't. His death festered in our hearts, and we bore the pain alone while standing right next to each other. I could see the problems between Teresa and me, but just like that fan, I was helpless to fix anything. The motor that ran our love had gone cold. Our separation could not have gone differently, I know that. I was underwater, unhearing and moving slow. I imagine Teresa was the same. She found a new job and fell in love with a coworker there. We split right around Christmas, 1961.

I quit my clerking job that next year. I had become a magnet for condolences. Everyone at the office knew my plight. They regaled me with stories about people they knew who were also going through hard times. I didn't care. I didn't want to hear it. I didn't want to hear my own story told to me again and again through other people's sympathy. I left. The company had been paying for night classes in law school and, of course, cut the money off when I quit. I couldn't afford school myself and wasn't sure that I wanted to be a lawyer anyway. I dropped out and took my first job at a bookstore, at Geraldine's with Dennis.

I became someone new at the bookstore. It saved me. Or, at least, it made me something after I had become nothing. Dennis was aware of my troubles, but he wasn't the kind of person who would bring them up. He wasn't the kind of person who would tell other people your business. I really liked Dennis. He died in 1992. What did Geraldine's do for me? It gave me the license to act like an artist though I had never practiced an art. I used the atmosphere to fashion myself a new personality. I took the perceived IQ points from working in a place of literature and made the most of them. I became young again, frisky with women, greased with booze, and I read and read and read. I became a young bookseller, and this job became the fulcrum that pivoted me to a new life. As long as I could keep my mind in the right place, it was a nice way to spend a decade or three.

But that's the thing: I couldn't always keep my mind in the right place. There were days when I couldn't get out of bed. I told myself I felt fine, time would heal even these wounds. But the years passed and the symptoms set a dogged pace by my side. Why was I still exhausted after I had just slept for twelve hours? Why does my face feel numb for days at a time? Why can't I stop crying in the mornings? I never saw a doctor or anything. Dennis told me I was clinically depressed, but I knew better. I *always* knew better. It wasn't a sickness, I would say. I was actually sad. Something bad had happened and I was still sad. No pill was going to bring Kurt back. That's what I said to Dennis, anyway. Dennis' uncle owned Geraldine's and Dennis talked to him about me. After that, I was allowed to call off whenever I needed. His uncle was a nice man. Generous.

So, the years have passed and here I am, once again, alone in my bed, frantic, unable to control my galloping mind. Maybe I should have let Dennis take me to that doctor. Maybe I should have nipped this thing in the bud when I was younger. It just never seemed like the right thing to do. And it still didn't seem like the right thing to do after my dinner with Karen. I mean, it was already too late, right? It's too late to be free from this. It's too late to be happy. How did death transform that small child into this heavy, black monster? I don't know. The thing is, when you let yourself become this, when you don't do anything about it, you affect other people. I had upset Karen tonight. Karen, who was reaching out, confiding in me about her daughter's illness. I didn't want to make her unhappy. I didn't want to be cold to people at work because my body and mind had gone into a deep freeze. I didn't want to walk around the store with that fake grimace-of-a-smile while my mind begged me to rush home and bury my face in a pillow. Avoiding your problems is a selfish act, anyone knows that if they think about it. Your problems are contagious, just like the flu. I should do something about it, see someone maybe, drag myself out of this hell once and for all.

But not today. Not right now. It was morning and I hadn't slept. Head on pillow, I gazed out the window as the streetlights shut off one by one and the sun peaked through the haze over the Upper East Side.

17.

The Yearly Review

I went in to work the next day even though I hadn't slept the night before. I didn't like to call out. I worked sick all the time, unless I thought I was going to vomit or something. One time, I did vomit at work. I made it to the toilet, but just in time. Everyone had been disgusted and I was humiliated.

Karen was not scheduled to be in. I dreaded seeing her. I would have liked to call her to apologize but we never exchanged phone numbers. Shell-shocked, I shuffled around the sales floor like the last man on Earth, doomed to die alone.

Jake found me at the front of the store.

—Well?

He posed in front of the counter where the SwiftFoot was displayed. He tapped one of the units repeatedly, checking his email. He was dressing nicer these days, often donning a tie like Michael M. Some of the other employees made fun of him for this behind his back. I noticed he was carrying the manager's mobile phone.

—It didn't go well.

Jake looked up quickly from the screen. His tie was a wreck. The knot looked like a scrambled Slinky. His face fell, his shoulders slumped. He took a step towards me and put his hand on my arm.

—Charlie, what happened? You look terrible.

—I didn't sleep.

—Tell me about the date.

—It was going fine.

I paused and thought for a moment. What to say about the date?

—And then I suddenly didn't feel well and had to leave.

I paused again and tried to think of something to add.

—Actually, something happened and I had to leave.

—Did you guys fight or something?

—No. I can't talk about it right now. I still don't feel very well.

Jake's face twisted with concern.

—I'll tell you what, the shelving is light today. I would say you should go home right now, but I know the Michaels want to get your review out of the way.

—Review?

—Yeah, it's review season. You're one of the last ones they still need to hit.

—Oh.

—That's why I was looking for you; they're waiting in the office. Why don't you go sit with them and split right after? I'll cover for you.

—That's probably for the best. Thanks, Jake.

Reviews. I hadn't even realized it was time for reviews. Every year I sat down with a couple managers to participate in a hopelessly banal conversation about my work performance. They handed me a numbered sheet of paper and mumbled about store standard requirements and membership discount card conversion rates. They usually judged me to exceed standards in some respects and fall below in others. The marks were a throwing knife balanced to make sure I hit the target of Meets Standard. Average raise and a pat on the back. The increase worked out to ten dollars or so a week which was just fine with me. I could use another ten bucks. I hoped that the Michaels would be quick with me. I needed to leave. I shouldn't have come in, really. I thought I might vomit.

I squirreled my belongings in a breakroom locker then found Michael M and Michael P waiting for me in the back office as Jake had promised. Michael P sat with his back to me typing on the computer. I tapped on the door lightly to let them know I was here.

—We don't want any! Just kidding. Come on in, Charlie.

Michael P's head, as large as a basketball, tilted back and forth as he filled in the daily assignment sheet with capital letters that represented what employees should be doing during each hour of their shifts. Michael M toiled next to him, rewriting what I realized was my review. I saw my name on the top of it. I also noticed that their feet were touching under the table.

Michael M spoke without looking up from my review.

—Come in, Charlie. And close the door.

I obliged. Michael P spun around in his chair, smiling.

—Take a seat.

He indicated a metal folding chair, the clear inferior of the Michaels' cushioned swiveling rockers. I settled in and folded my hands in my lap. Bring on the drivel.

—Here you are.

Michael M handed me a copy of my review. They each held a copy as well and their eyes were cast down to the paper as I looked it over. There was a sinking feeling in my stomach as I scanned the review. The balance wasn't right. I read faster. Something was certainly off. Too many not-at-standards and not enough exceeds. I skimmed quicker. I turned the next page. Below standard, I saw. Raise: not applicable.

I flipped the paper back to the first page and went through methodically.

—I'm not at standard for *any* of the competencies.

Michael P leaned forward.

—That's not true. Look, the section titled Merchandizing and Physical Tasks. You have a Meets Standard rating for that.

—But, as a whole, I'm below standards.

Silence. Michael P flipped from the first to the second page of his copy of my review wearing a studious expression. I looked from one Michael to the other waiting for one of them to say something. They didn't say a word.

—I'm a good bookseller.

Michael M looked at Michael P with a questioning expression. Michael P nodded, giving some concession that I didn't understand. Michael M turned to me with a masochistic gleam in his eyes.

—Actually, Charlie, you're not.

—What?

He enunciated each syllable.

—You are not a very good bookseller.

That fucking prick. I gaped wordlessly at him. I turned to Michael P but he would not look me in the eye.

—What do you mean?

There must be some mistake here. This was absurd.

Michael M.

—There are five categories in your review. And underneath those categories there are descriptions of what a bookseller needs to do to be at standard. Do you understand how the review process works? Does that make sense? Read those descriptions and tell me which of those illustrates your daily routine—which one do you successfully accomplish on a day-to-day basis.

I was so angry I could barely see. My vision blurred like I was reading through a fish tank. I scanned the passages but couldn't make sense of them. *Pushes himself and others to not only accomplish tasks, but exceed expectations*, it read. *Takes initiative sans external motivation and remains goal-oriented*, it read. *Follows company directives and supports company policies.* I tore through the writing trying to find something I could point to, find somewhere that I was on solid ground, discover something they had overlooked to validate and prove the injustice of the review. But everything was so esoteric, so vague. This stuff could mean whatever you wanted it to mean. Bullshit. I stopped turning the pages, let the review go limp in my lap.

Michael M once again.

—We have asked you time and time again to train and become proficient with the SwiftFoot©. Haven't we?

—Yes.

—Does this make sense to you? Do you understand? You are one of the worst sellers of digital merchandise in the store.

He let that hang in the air while I waited, red-faced and flustered.

—You shelve books, Charlie. And occasionally you use a cash register. That's not bookselling.

—But I'm a great hand-seller. Name a book and I can upsell to a similar title. I know a lot about literature. A lot! And even if I don't know as much about the nonfiction, I can speak to it. I know the titles, I know what the books are about, and I can get the right customer the right book.

—That's not bookselling, Charlie.

Selling books is not bookselling? Honestly, how do you argue with that?

—Your discount card sales are subpar, you're no good as a trainer, you know nothing about our toys and games section, and I'm not sure you could name even *one line* of Jonathan Adler handbags from the gift section. Could you? Name one pattern of the Jonathan Adler handbags. Go ahead.

I couldn't. I couldn't name one line of the Jonathan Adler handbags. My will broke during that silence. I was defeated. Michael P looked up from my review.

—Gilded Drip. Talitha Sunburst. Camel Bargello. The whole Jaipur Linens line . . .

Michael M nodded sagely.

—You see? You understand? You're being a bookseller the way *you* think you should be a bookseller. Not the way *Miles of Books* wants you to be a bookseller.

—Oh! The Stepped Chevron.

—That's enough, Michael. Do you get it, Charlie? Does this make sense?

—I understand.

But I didn't. I was a tortured interrogate voicing a false confession, just wanting the end to come. Michael P mercifully handed me a photocopied booklet.

—This is all the information about the SwiftFoot© and some suggested selling tactics.

I eyed the leaflet. There was a black-and-white picture of the SwiftFoot on the cover and the phrase *Go the Extra Mile with Miles of Books* written underneath it.

—Every employee who received less than a Meets Standard on the digital section of the review is going to get SwiftFoot© Certified.

—A test?

—That's right. It will be good for you. It's an opportunity to start over. You have a month to prepare. Study the guide and come back to us with any questions. All right, Charlie?

I nodded but didn't say anything. I rolled the leaflet into a cylinder and walked out of the office. I put the leaflet in my bag and threw my bag over my shoulder. Michael P and Michael M whispered in the office and I heard Michael M giggle. Michael P said something with his deep voice and then started typing on the computer again. I made sure the book I was reading was still in my bag and I shuffled through the breakroom door. Darkness crept in at the corners of my vision. I was at the bottom now with little room to descend further. I wanted to go home and sleep off the sludge, but I knew I would wake up in a worse state. I'd been here before, I'd been here many times, in fact. On the precipice of something bad. There was only one activity that could help me edge away from that precipice; I just had to work up the energy to do it.

I needed to go book shopping.

18.
Retail Therapy

I won the mental battle and did not go home. I rode the subway two stops further than usual, getting off at Queens Plaza. The raised platform where I exited the car was hot and windy. As I trudged down the gridded, metal steps, the elevated trains exploded back into action, knocked bowling pins above me. At the bottom of the stairs, the street-level smelled sour with still-wet piss and solidified milk. The urban tumbleweeds of balled up paper scraps rolled across the street on the breeze. I turned into Second Lives, a thrift store in the lower part of Queens. The door was heavy and I was careful not to let it bang behind me. The sudden absence of wind left a ringing in my ears. Spoiled smells of city corners disappeared, replaced by an aura of moth balls and sweet, chloroform air conditioning. I was immediately comforted by the brown-red leathers, the tartan pants, the racks of old spectacles, musty children's toys, hideous neck ties. A place where the old and broken were treated like treasures. I felt at home.

Let me say first that I loved Second Lives; it was one of my favorite thrift stores. But—and this comes from a place of positivity—it had a serious problem with organization. It was as if an alien being had been tasked with making layout decisions for the store and, not comprehending the functionality of the products, made some guesses based on shape. Measuring cups and glassware might be on the same shelf. Dog leashes with shoelaces. Porcelain figurines and Barbie dolls. The first section of the store comprised movies, music, and shoes. The Entertainment and Footwear section, you might say. In the center of an area dotted with brightly colored plastic movie boxes and thin, hard-edged CD cases grew half a dozen shoe trees—each branch blossoming with red high heels, penny-loafers, Wolverine work boots.

Not to be a weirdo, but stuff like this really bothers me. I remember once, back in the seventies, I went to a party with my friend Dennis. The apartment belonged to one of Dennis's friends whom I didn't know very well. The front door of that apartment led right into the kitchen. Dennis and I met some people, got some drinks, smoked some grass, all in the kitchen. We were having a really good time. There was a girl named Catherine in that kitchen. Catherine was interested in me, and she was also writing a college dissertation on Toni Morrison. Catherine and I decided to get more comfortable, so we moved into the living room. That's when I saw it. The owner of the apartment had his books arranged by the color of the book cover rather than by the author's last name. *Nope*, I thought, as I looked over the perfect rainbow spread of the shelves. *No way*. I left the apartment. Walked right out through the kitchen, left Catherine in the middle of a sentence about the metaphoric structure of *Sula*. Fuck that guy. Fuck that whole apartment. Dennis found me outside on the sidewalk smoking one cigarette after another. He tried to get me to come back in, but I wouldn't. *Ask that stupid motherfucker if you can borrow his copy of Rabbit Run*, I told Dennis. *Just ask him and see how long it takes him to find it*. I guess I used to be a hothead.

I once asked Mohammad, the owner of Second Lives, why he didn't put the shoes back with the other clothing. I mean, maybe it just never occurred to him, right? Wrong. He said, *There is space. I put the shoes there. Mind your own business.* Fine. That's his prerogative. I've mellowed over the years; I can deal with it now. The adjacent media was on the wall, no order kept whatsoever. VHS tapes were placed with DVDs and the occasional Blu-ray that Mohammad was able to scrounge up. Music items were mixed in as well—old model iPods, records, cassette tapes, and even a few different 8-tracks that I presumed had been there since 1975. Move on, Charlie.

The next section was my favorite—board games, sun glasses, and (you guessed it) books. Second Lives had seven cases of used books that remained in constant fluctuation. We'll get back to this section in a moment, you can best believe.

The third section was clothing, men's on one side, women's on the other, and coats in the middle. There were also large children's items such as a spring-loaded rocking horse and battery powered scooters in the aisles. But the coats were the big deal, the main attraction. Second Lives was famous for its coats. Mohammad had a knack for finding furs, specifically. He had furs of every different animal, every different shade, every different size. It never failed that there was some immigrant from the Eastern Block perusing Mohammad's wares, haggling for their purchases. I often wondered if there was something illegal going on with those fur coats. But I didn't wonder too much. I was just here to mind my own business.

Mohammad, as I walked in and the doorbell sounded over my head.

—There is my friend, once again. Shakespeare of Queens.

Mohammad often called me Shakespeare of Queens. I don't know why. I suppose it's because I buy so many books. I told him my real name, but to this day he persists with the Shakespeare thing.

He is a tall man, Arab, bald with an intelligent look in his eyes. He had lived in New York City for many years and spoke with only a slight accent. He wore small golden glasses that sat at the edge of his nose. They reminded me of the kind of glasses a wizard from a fantasy story would wear, or maybe a machinist from a steampunk novel. I always wanted to ask where he bought them but could never work up the courage. I spent all my political capital on the shoe-placement question.

—Hello. How are you today?
—Good, good.

He wrote something in his ledger.

—We have some new deliveries in the back for you, Shakespeare.

The phone rang and he answered brusquely. He spoke in Farsi to the person on the other line as I walked back to the second section. Mohammad didn't keep his books much better than he kept his music and movies. They weren't alphabetized, of course, not by author, not by title, not even by color. That was fine. Second Lives was not a bookstore. But, like the music and movies, the books weren't even separated by *format*. Hardcovers were right next to mass markets, shoved next to trades and children's board books. There were even crinkled magazines wedged in with the used books. I once offered to organize the section for Mohammad. I didn't ask for money or anything; I told him I just wanted to do it. He laughed as if I had made a joke. When he realized I wasn't joking, his expression turned dour and he said no.

I could tell just by glancing that there were many new titles in stock. Good. I flexed my shoulders until the joint popped and then set to work. The hardest part for me was scanning the bottom parts of the bookcases and then standing up to see the next row. I'm not complaining; I've been lucky with my knees. There are people my age that can barely walk. At work, I had to crouch down and stand up constantly. It's certainly not a comfortable movement for me, but if I go slowly, I'm all right. However, since I didn't have to be professional at the thrift store, I took it easy. No deep knee bends here. I sat on the ground cross-legged to search the bottom two rows. After I'd completed the rows, I scooted over to the next bookcase and scanned the two bottom rows on that one. There were often hidden gems on the bottom rows because people would not bend over to look. I scuttled all the way across the floor and picked out *Jamaica Inn* by Daphne Du Maurier and an old copy of *I Am Legend* with Charlton Heston on the cover. I already owned a short story collection with *I Am Legend* included, but I did not have one with Charlton Heston on the cover. Good find.

I stood up with my books and gripped the wall while the dizzies went away. Now that the hard work of the bottom rows was finished, I could leisurely scour the top four rows without being too physical. I tilted my head to the side, adjusted my glasses, and focused on one spine after another, registering each title, each author, judging whether I would be interested in the book and then checking my mental inventory to make sure I didn't already own it.

I snatched up a few Agatha Christie novels. Those were always plentiful in thrift stores. Old ladies tend not to give them away before they die. I saw a copy of the third Harry Potter book and realized it had been here ten days ago when I was last in. I was surprised to see it, as that series was usually a hot commodity in the used book community. Naturally, I owned all seven. I was even able to find all but number six in hardcover. I was on the lookout for that one, let me tell you.

I was halfway through the bays, humming along now at a pretty good pace, the different colors and drawings that adorned the books lulling my mind into a meditative focus. I picked out a book called

Frog by an author named Stephen Dixon whom I had read before. There was a series called *Mistborn* by a writer that Phil had recommended. I slid the first in the series reluctantly off the shelf and added it to my pile. There was a small collection of Kurt Vonnegut. I wished that I didn't own all of them so that I could buy them again. I was starting to tire, so I lifted my stack and prepared to head to the register. But then I stopped. *Mother Night.*

Kurt Vonnegut meant a lot to me when I was younger. I felt akin to Vonnegut, like maybe he too would feel at home among the old and broken treasures of a thrift store. I usually wasn't one to reread books. There are so many books to get to that rereading always seems like a colossal waste of time. *What new thing could I be reading instead of rehashing this?* I always wondered. But, *Mother Night.* Maybe I should reread that. I slid the copy off the shelf and read the back cover. I nodded my head remembering the story of the man who had pretended to be something he was not for so long that no one believed he was pretending anymore. Kurt was named for Kurt Vonnegut. My little Kurt. *No, I should not reread this book*, I decided.

But a thought struck me: maybe Karen would like it. Sure, it wasn't what she usually read, but who *wouldn't* like this book? It was nearly perfect. I added it to my pile and trudged forward to the register with a plan to apologize to Karen set in my mind, my awful review with the Michaels forgotten altogether.

Looking back, this plan made little sense. If Karen was angry with me, this gift was not going to solve anything. I can't know everything with the power of hindsight, but I can guess at past-Charlie's motivations. He was wound tight, that one. He wanted people to find him, to sleuth out his whereabouts, to enter the leafy place hidden in his heart. But he couldn't just take them there. He couldn't hold their hand and walk them through the rusty gates. Wound up so tightly in himself, he could only leave clues, tattered maps, messages of invisible ink. At the time, he didn't know what he was doing with this odd gift. *Mother Night* had dragged him out of a dark place before and he hoped it had one more trick up its sleeve. Maybe it could be a map for Karen, maybe it could be a key. Maybe there was writing in invisible ink palimpsest in this used copy that would appear while Karen read and tell her all the yearnings of Charlie's heart. Maybe that old Charlie put too much stock in books.

Out the heavy door of Second Lives, back into the garbage-scape of taciturn Queens city blocks, up the iron-grid stairs to the platform of Queens Plaza to head back in the direction from which I had just come, armed now with a fortified mind, literature, and a questionable plan.

19.

Charlie and the Great, Glass Vestibule

KAREN had mentioned where she lived during our dinner and I remembered because it was the ritziest place in Forest Hills. I stood outside the apartment chewing on the crust of a pizza that I had bought just around the corner. My plan had seemed solid during the subway ride from Second Lives to her apartment and now, of course, I was losing my nerve. So it goes with me. Up and down more than the stock market. She would be very angry, of course. I imagined there were some embarrassing moments at Donatello's after I left. She must have waited for the check by herself.

My helium leaked and I deflated back to timid, old Charlie. I shoved my grease-stained plate from the pizza into a nearby garbage can and strode toward the place, *Mother Night* in my hand, bag around my shoulder, stretched tight and heavy with my new books, willing myself into the fray. I walked the spiraling pathway past all the intricate gardening of the apartment complex and through the glass double doors into the vestibule. I wiped my mouth one more time to make sure that I didn't have any pizza sauce hiding in the corners. That was one nice thing about not having a mustache:

the food only had so many places to hide. Finally, I geared myself up and pressed the button that said K Schneider.

A good amount of time passed while I stood there holding my breath, waiting for something to happen. I started to think she wasn't home. Then, an eerie buzzing sound filled the small, glass room. A voice spoke over the buzzing.

—Yes?

Leaning toward the intercom.

—Hello. Is Karen home?

There was a long pause on the other end. I stood still, leaning with my ear forward, listening to the static sound and waiting for it to form into words.

—Is this Charlie?

—Uh, yes?

—I'm coming down.

She was coming down. I paced the little glass room a few times and then leaned against the wall. I switched *Mother Night* from one hand to the other and then back again. My bag was heavy and hurting on my shoulder with all the new book purchases. I couldn't decide whether to keep holding it or unstrap and set it down. I kept holding it. It was taking a long time for her to come downstairs, I thought. A young woman passed through the first set of glass doors and I nodded to her on her way out of the building. But she didn't leave the building.

The young woman.

—Are you Charlie?

I realized that this was the voice from intercom.

—Oh. Yes, I am.

I noticed that the young woman's eyebrows were thin and wispy, her face drawn, her hair composed of the tough stuff of wigs. Karen's daughter.

—Are you Kate?

—Yeah.

We leaned against opposite walls in the tiny glass room and looked at each other. She was obviously sick and so it was hard to guess her age. She might have been close to forty but something about her eyes made her seem much, much younger. The more I looked at her the more I could see Karen. I figured I should ask how she felt.

Before I could talk, Kate.

—So, what happened?

—I'm sorry?

—At the restaurant, what happened?

—Is Karen upset with me?

—*I'm* upset with you.

I stared at Kate, wide-eyed. She kept talking.

—Why did you run out on her like that?

—I didn't feel well.

—Really?

I didn't like how this was going. I thought of leaving. Would that be appropriate?

—Of *course* you would be like this. Of *course*. You are the only person mom has shown interest in, so of *course* this is how you'd behave.

Her skin was smooth and blushed red. Her blue eyes were coy, but also hypnotic. I tried to catch her blinking and couldn't.

—What do you mean?

—She's been talking about you for two months. You're the only man she has ever liked, as far as I can tell. Ever.

—Surely your father—

—Ever.

She was quite insistent about that. There was an aggressive desperation in her manner that was off-putting. I could see the seeds of Karen's personality in there, but it was mangled by disease and heartache.

—We used to think she was a secret lesbian.

—Oh.

—She's not.

—Ok. Well, I like her, too.

—You should.

I nodded and then looked at my book.

—Is she upstairs? I bought this for her and I wanted to apologize.

—The cover is ripped.

—It's used.

—Nice. A ripped up, used book. Great gift.

We both looked at my sorry book.

—She's not here. She's in the city. At the other apartment.

—Oh.

I crumpled back against the wall.

—Could I call her? Do you think she's too angry for me to apologize?

—She's not angry at all. In fact, she thinks she needs to apologize to you.

—What?

—She almost went into the bookstore today to find you.

—I don't understand.

—Did you have someone die? Did someone die of cancer?

This situation had gotten completely out of control. Standing in this glass room, I felt very transparent.

—Mom thinks she talked about me too much. About my cancer. She thinks it's her fault you left, like you couldn't take the real-talk.

No one likes to feel transparent.

—Is that what happened?

—In a manner of speaking.

—So, someone in your life died of cancer. Who was it?

—No one. I lost a child. Not cancer. Kurt. His name was Kurt.

The words sounded hollow in the little glass room. I turned the book around so the cover faced my chest, hiding the author's name. I hadn't talked about Kurt out loud in such a long time that his death didn't even seem true. I felt like a liar. But it was true. Kurt died.

—How old?

—Five months.

Kate's eyes became wet. The swing in her emotions from anger to sorrow was seamless. She wiped the corner of her eye.

—You need to get over it, Charlie.

Something broke in my chest when she said that. Like she had thrown a fist-sized rock through the crust of a frozen-over lake. No one talked to me like that. But she kept talking.

—How old are you? This must have happened a long, long time ago.

I didn't answer her. She was over-stepping her bounds dramatically. I had just met this woman three minutes ago.

She didn't stop.

—My mom needs you and she needs you now. You can't just pause at one moment in your life and let that moment rule you forever.

—Uh, look. I really like your mother, and I don't want to seem rude—

—By all means, Charlie, feel free to be rude.

—. . . *and I don't want to seem rude*, but that's none of your business. I'm not comfortable talking about that part of my life. Especially not with someone I just met.

—Ok. Well, you need to get comfortable. Find a way.

—No. That's just not who I am.

—Then that's what you need to change.

—You want me to change who I am?

—Yes.

— I don't think I understand.

—Charlie. Of *course* you understand.

She shook her head.

—Ugh. One moment.

Kate pulled her wig from her head and then snapped off the little cap underneath. She folded the items up and shoved them in her pocket like they were change from the bus. The wig was too large and poked its head out of her pocket like a pet mouse.

—No matter how much money we spend, these wigs all look like shit and make my head sweat.

Kate ran her hand across her scalp and wiped the condensation on her shirt.

—Gross.

We stood there in silence for a moment. Her head was obscene.

—Who's comfortable now? Ha. I hate wearing wigs, but I've been wearing them on and off for over two years. You know why, right?

I nodded.

—Sure.

She pointed to her head.

—No one wants to see this every day. I have three kids. You think they're comfortable with this? They're not. No one is. But we got comfortable being uncomfortable.

—I see.

—'Cause I'm part of the deal, Charlie. Me and mom are a package, apparently. I mean, she won't leave me alone.

Kate was too much for me. The hyper-aggressiveness made me want to flee. But I stayed there and took it. Her pushiness, her insensitivity, her loudness were all periphery to one fact: Karen still wanted to be with me. This information sent me sailing to the top, nervous and jittery. I managed a smile which Kate probably mistook for approval or submission to her surly attitude. I didn't care. We each leaned against the glass walls of the corridor waiting for the other to finish the conversation. Someone walked through the front door, a young man in a suit with polished shoes and a briefcase. His hair was gelled and he held a cell phone to his ear. He looked from Kate to me and then back at Kate's bald head.

Kate, slick as a standup in front of a brick wall.

—Don't stare. He's my barber. You might hurt his feelings.

The man pulled a key card out of his wallet and quickly slipped through the interior doors. We watched as it slammed behind him. I turned to Kate and raised my eyebrows.

—So, how are you feeling?

20.

Charlie's on the List

THE next few weeks of my life were like nothing else. Magical, you might say. Karen was by no means my first relationship since my marriage ended. There were plenty, let me assure you. I dated one lady for nearly five years when I was in my early thirties. But there were so many other factors to deal with back then. Those liaisons were messy and unreal. I was drinking a lot in those days, and let's just admit it, smoking too much pot. I ran with some questionable characters. I didn't tell anyone about my past and no one really cared. They would have been shocked to know that I had been married with a child. It was as if I had appeared from the primordial ooze to drink beer, flirt with girls, and sell books.

Don't get me wrong, I think this derelict lifestyle is fine for a young man. There are plenty of well-adjusted people who spent their youths in a haze. But it wasn't fine for me. I had moments of real anger back then, a lot of uncontrolled, spiraling frustration. There was a general sense of outrage about the cards I had been dealt. Now that I look back, I was probably one accidental pregnancy away from being exactly like my father. How upsetting.

I learned to put a cap on those wild emotions as I grew older. They were still there, still turbulent inside me, but I stopped bothering people with them. I became the drunken bookseller. All I talked about was literature in those days. I did my best to be easy-going. If something personal came up, I related it to the book I was reading. The friends I had, the women I dated—they weren't with me, they were with my character. That lady, the one I dated for five years—I think she loved the drunken bookseller. And maybe he loved her. I remember one night at four or five in the morning, I told her about Kurt. Just spilled it all out there. She was gone before I woke up the next afternoon and I didn't see her until months later when we ran into each other at a party. I didn't ask what happened. Just said *hello* and kept on moving.

Things were certainly different with Karen. And I won't pretend that it had nothing to do with the fact that she knew about Kurt; it did. But also, we were sober most of the time. People don't talk about this to young folks, but as you get older, your hangovers get worse. When I was young, I assumed there was an age—thirty-five, let's say—when someone at the party walked over to the record player and lifted the needle. In the silence, they turned to their friends and said, *Hey, look, we're thirty-five now. It's time to grow up and stop drinking so much. Arden, put down that joint. Bruce, you need to go to bed. We're the adults now.* But that's not how it happens at all. Nature forces temperance with queasiness and terrible headaches.

But it's for the best. The truth is, my ten-drink-nights were never any more fun than my two-drink-nights. It was nice to remember things. It was especially nice to remember things Karen said because she had led an interesting life. Admittedly, parts of her stories were difficult for me to take, due to her wealthy lifestyle. It's hard to keep jealousy and self-pity at bay when someone casually mentions first-class seating and month-long vacations. I know my snide, silver-spoon comments upset Karen on some level, but I couldn't always keep them to myself. Perhaps I should have been more diligent about that. Because whether life was fair or not, Karen had done extraordinary things with her good fortune. She had been everywhere! The Caribbean, Argentina, Paris, London. Even strange places, like Russia and Thailand. Can you imagine?

I had always wanted to travel but never had the money. I took one trip to Croatia, once, with a friend who paid the way, and I once drove across the United States with another friend just after we had each read Kerouac. Both trips held a special place in my heart. When my mind has nowhere to wander, I will often wander there.

I listened to the stories of Karen's life and I told the stories of my life. Mine were about the bookstore, mostly. I was surprised to find that my tales were not as trite as I thought they might be. There are minor cultural events, the kind that come and go during one news cycle, that are far richer and intriguing in the bookstore life. There was the whole thing with *Naked Lunch*, for instance, and there was the outrage over *Holy Blood, Holy Grail*. There was the run on *The Satanic Bible* during that foolishness with Rushdie, and there was Oprah's shaming of James Frey. Oh! And ask any bookseller who isn't wet behind the ears about poor John Kerry and that book written by his Swift Boat team. That book was difficult to keep in stock, and I was called liberal scum and threatened when we were sold out—really threatened with physical violence. Over John Kerry! Jesus.

Karen and I went on a lot of dates for two or three weeks—almost every night if I'm being honest—and three ballgames. Karen managed to get tickets to the entire Mets/Yankees subway series. The Yanks swept, damn them.

There was one problem, though. One small grease fire in paradise. I was going broke. As I said before, my budget could not handle drastic fluctuations. I made almost exactly what I needed plus a little extra that I saved for emergencies. I kept about five grand in a savings account which I would dip into occasionally if an unexpected bill popped up. I'd been dipping into it with jarring frequency these last few weeks for gluttonous excuses: movies, wine, take-out Chinese. I had a mini panic attack when my savings dipped below three thousand dollars. Karen, God bless her, knew what was happening. Her empathy was a sixth sense, bent on rooting out stress and malcontent.

Karen, as we sat over eight-dollar sandwiches.

—I've got this.

My wallet half out of my back pocket, I paused like a diamond thief under a spotlight.

—Why?

—You've been paying for too much.

—We're on a date. I should pay.

Karen, chewing a bite of bread, tomato and salami.

—Are you ready to have this conversation?

—I don't know what you're talking about.

Karen put her sandwich down. She folded her arms. She looked at me sideways. She didn't like when I made fun of her posh upbringing, but she really detested when I played obtuse.

—I have more money than you, Charlie. A lot more.

My mind wheeled trying to think of a winning argument that would result in me paying for lunch. I couldn't formulate a strong strategy quick enough.

—We'll split it.

Karen, basically ignoring me while brandishing her black Amex card.

—I'll pay for it all. And for the movie. And the ball game next week.

She shrugged her shoulders.

—Look, I'm just going to pay from now on. For everything.

—No. We should split things. I mean you have two homes to pay for . . .

—They're paid off.

—The grandkids . . .

—. . . have trust funds coming their way.

—But Kate's medical bills alone . . .

—Charlie, they're not even making a dent. I promise you. I can afford to spend a couple hundred dollars a month on you.

—But I feel like such a cheapskate . . .

—Get over it.

People sure were saying that to me a lot nowadays. She tossed her credit card on top of the bill like a winning ace of spades. That was it. I had to get over the money thing.

I couldn't get over it. I tried, believe me. But every time a bill arrived at our table, I drowned in shame. I couldn't help it, that's just the way I felt. There were a frantic few days where I thought my inability to let a woman pay my way was going to spoil our relationship. But, once again, Karen sensed my discomfort. Suddenly, she was suggesting movie rentals instead of movie theaters, cooking-in instead of restaurants, walks in the park instead of through MoMA. We started staying home together, which, as most people know, is how real lovers set their foundations.

Going back to Miles of Books was strange. I didn't know how to have a work girlfriend. In the past, I had found that even having a regular friend at the bookstore birthed wearisome episodes. Work, though it's performed in the public, is a very personal thing. How each person works is an involuntary expression of their personality. And while there may be a friend whose company is enjoyable at a bar or a ballpark, it might not be right for the workplace. It is possible to grow very close to someone and still be at odds with how they approach professionalism. Of course, I had this problem with Karen. But I had had it before we were together, too. Now, instead of bottling up rage when she pointed to a section of the store rather than walking the customer to the book, I somehow thought it was cute. When she answered the phone without using her name, I turned a deaf ear. When she read a gossip magazine at the cash counter instead of calling customer orders, I asked her what Brad Pitt was up to. In short, I was going soft. These things happen.

Everyone knew we were dating. Everyone. I mean, even Sandra, who smelled like Windex and talked to herself in the breakroom, knew. If I were told six months earlier that I would be in a public relationship with a workmate, I would have ended my life right there. Plunged off the Tri-borough Bridge. But, living in the moment, it didn't bother me. Everyone at the store liked Karen. Everyone thought she was smart and funny and they were all correct. Normally, people like me—shy people—find people like Karen frightening. She barged her way into personal information. She kicked in the doorway of your mind like a swat team with a warrant. The trick was, most people were *happy* to talk about personal issues with Karen. Go figure.

Jake asked me this question every day:

—So, how are things going?

He was thrilled that Karen and I were together and seemed to take pleasure in my squirming to answer this question. It wasn't a bad squirm, though. I liked that he asked. I usually gave him some detail about the previous night and then asked how he and Chelsea were getting along.

Jake's roommate had flaked out on him a few weeks ago leaving him a whole month's rent to cover. Chelsea got out of her apartment contract and moved in. This was a problem because, unlike Karen and me, Jake's relationship with Chelsea was a secret. Karen and I knew about them, and Phil. And Becky knew, too, because Becky knew everything. But beyond that, it was air-tight. Jake was now a manager and should not be dating his employees. As if we all didn't have bigger things to worry about. I talked with Jake at the customer service desk about a movie he had seen the night before and then I made my way back to the breakroom to prepare for the day.

Jake, as I walked away.

—Oh, Charlie. Take a look on the bulletin board. Michael M posted when the certification tests are going to be.

—Certification?

—For the SwiftFoot? Your name is on the list.

I had forgotten all about the certification bother. I had forgotten, really, about my bad review with the Michaels altogether. I had lost the booklet of pointers they had given me. Threw it away, really. Perhaps I shouldn't have done that. A seed of dread took root in my chest and it began to bloom like a plant in those time-lapsed sequences from the nature shows. Fretful and desperate, I made my way to the breakroom and read Michael M's posting.

Attention Miles of Books Employees,

Some of you were informed during your review that you are found lacking in digital sales. The selling of the Miles of Books SwiftFoot© is a major component this year when considering how the store is to accomplish its monetary plan. We need to have all booksellers fully qualified to give a sales pitch for the SwiftFoot©, to answer in-depth, technical questions, and to troubleshoot problem devices.

For those of you who were alerted to a deficiency in these areas, there will be a certification test. The test will be in three parts:

1. *A written multiple-choice test.*
2. *A role-playing sales pitch*
3. *Troubleshooting a problem SwiftFoot©. The troubleshooting will be done with a live customer under the observation of a manager.*

The following people will be subject to the certification beginning this week:

Rosa D'Elia

Phillip Miller

Charlie Mueller

Amber Tipton

Arion Toles

Margaret Vasquez

Thank you,

Management

I read the note again, wallowing in cool rage. My face felt prickly and numb. I couldn't believe they posted our names. It was unnecessary cruelty. We knew who we were. I went down the list and, as I suspected, everyone on it was over fifty years old. There was only one surprise.

Phillip Miller.

It didn't seem possible that Phil had failed the digital part of his review. He often worked the SwiftFoot counter and we all respected him as one of the best troubleshooters in the store. Any time I had someone on the phone who was complaining that their SwiftFoot wouldn't work, Phil was the first person I paged. If he wasn't good enough for the Michaels, how was I ever going to be up to snuff?

I journeyed to the sales floor and began my shelving, already dreading the process that was to come. I finished the shelving early and, noticing that there were no managers on the floor, I wandered up to the SwiftFoot counter to give the thing a poke. It sprang to life, full of colors and advertisements. I wasn't totally ignorant to its workings. I surfed around the shop mode looking for a book to download. The demo SwiftFoots that we had in-store were set up so that we could buy whatever we wanted. Everything was free and the items simply disappeared the next day. I tapped a picture of the newest James Patterson book and within a minute it was in the library. I hit the home button and then the library button and opened up the book by clicking on an image of its cover. I messed around trying to change the text size. It was possible to change the text size, but I didn't know how to do it. At one point, the whole screen was black and the letters were white. I sort of freaked out. Phil walked through the front doors and stopped when he saw me punching my index finger against the screen with what might have been bad intentions. Dark patches of sweat had developed under my arms and I glared at the machine as if it were a lottery ticket off by one number. Phil cocked his head to the side. He didn't say anything, so I spoke first.

—I'm learning.

—Are you worried about the certification?

He leaned against the glass counter, his cigarette-stained fingers smudging up the place.

—Yeah. And I guess you should be, too. How did you get a Needs Improvement on digital?

Phil grinned. It was unsettling.

—You know how a couple weeks ago the Michaels told us that we weren't allowed to let a customer pass the counter without telling them at least one thing about the SwiftFoot?

—Yeah, the customer engagement initiative …

—I told everyone that it costs two-hundred and fifty dollars.

—But it does.

—Yeah. But that was the only thing I was telling people. I engaged the hell out of them. Every customer that strolled through the door, I grabbed by the elbow, pointed, and said, *That thing is two-hundred and fifty dollars!* People complained about me. Lotta people. Michael M didn't think it was a very good selling point. He said I was being spiteful and incompetent.

—Well, I might have to agree with him.

Phil held up his palm.

—Spiteful, yes. But not incompetent. I was being *anti*-competent. That's much worse.

—So, you have to get certified?

—Yeah. I'm going to ace the thing. Right in Michael M's face.

Phil nodded after he said this as if he had made some daring point. Then he walked to the breakroom.

Karen was the other shelver that morning. I waved to her on my way back to the breakroom around eleven o'clock. She tracked me down; a small stack of books tucked in the crook of her arm. She blocked the doorway.

—You're on the list.

—I know. It's no big deal.

—Are you sure? Are you going to be all right to take the test?

—I'll be fine. It's a test.

I mean, part of that statement was true. Karen stood very still. She pursed her lips. Maybe I should have confessed my dread. I considered this for a moment. Nope.

—Don't worry. It's not a problem. I don't care much for the E-Reader, so I don't work with it often. That's why I received a Needs Improvement on my review. But I can pass the test. I can do this.

21.

A Disagreement Over Bagels

As it turned out, I could not do it. I answered only seven out of thirty questions correctly on the multiple-choice test. There were two more sections still to take: the role-playing and the live customer troubleshoot. I hadn't performed the troubleshoot with a live customer yet but the role-playing ... well, the role-playing didn't go well.

I have always found role-playing to be an entirely worthless practice. I don't think a sane, self-respecting person can suspend disbelief enough so that the process is enlightening. Never, in my opinion, has someone become better at their job by pretending to do their job. Everyone involved feels hokey and idiotic and the process is rushed to lessen the pain. Just go out and do it, I think; mess up with a customer and the next time you'll be better. It was probably this attitude that caused me to crash and burn in my role-playing sketch. Pretending to be a mother who might potentially buy a SwiftFoot for her child, Michael P wanted to know what types of books were available for a five-year-old girl. He was really hamming it up, too. He made effeminate facial mannerisms and once, I swear, even batted his eyes at me. I guess it was supposed to be a joke. I stuttered for nearly thirty seconds and then inquired whether her daughter enjoyed the *American Girl* series. I was then informed by Michael P (who stayed in character while he corrected me) that *American Girl* was not appropriate for the age range and, besides, none of the books were available in the E-format. I said if she knew this much about the SwiftFoot catalogue, that I should be the one asking *her* questions. This did not get a good reaction from Michael P. Apparently, he was the only one allowed to make jokes.

I was hoping, since I had already failed two thirds of the test, that the observed troubleshooting would dwindle to irrelevance, canceled. It wasn't to be. Michael P informed me at the end of my test that I was still expected to do the troubleshooting. It had to be with an actual customer. One day during my shift, I would be paged to the SwiftFoot counter and asked to tend to a problem device while a manager looked on. *Great*, I said, nodding my head good-naturedly. *Can't wait*. Now *that* was some top-notch role-playing.

I met Karen and her daughter Kate for lunch later that day at the Israeli bagel place. Karen asked me to pick the restaurant, and I like to go places I've already been. I knew what to order that way. Kate often ate with us at Karen's place and occasionally came out to restaurants with us, too. I didn't mind one bit. We had a rough go of it during our first meeting, but Kate grew on me quickly. She was good company. She had not been feeling well a few weeks ago and finally let Karen hire a nanny to help with her three children. Kate split with her husband about a year back after some ugliness. Kate had discovered she had cancer after the delivery of her youngest child, and six or seven months into her treatment she also discovered that her husband was having an affair with a woman at work. I shook my head. Cheating on a wife with cancer. With three children at home, no less. I was shocked at the story, but Kate assured me that it happened more often than I would believe. People can't handle the pressure of illness, she says, and they do evil things to get out of the situation. Huh. I don't know. I didn't like the idea that something like this was commonplace and therefore not as ghoulish. Kate can spin the story any way she likes, but as far as I'm concerned, a single piece of shit still stinks even if there are many pieces of shit.

Anyway, the nanny was a big help. Her name was Sissy and she was a battleax of a woman. Short on patience, I thought, but capable enough. She was certainly necessary. The latest round of chemo hurt Kate in ways it hadn't before. She was tired and sick and not able to keep up with the three little ones. Bill was seven, Emma four, and Drew just two years old. I never had to deal with toddlers, but I imagine having that much nonsense in a house when you aren't feeling well couldn't be easy.

We balanced our trays back from the pickup counter and arranged our food across the four-top. Karen had lox and clear soda, Kate a bagel with plain cream cheese and to drink, a tea. I had the tuna and a coffee. Once we were set, Kate took *Mother Night* by Kurt Vonnegut, my copy with the ripped cover, out of her bag and slapped it onto the only space left on the orange table. It shook the surface and all of our food. Kate was prone to dramatic movements like this.

—Loved it. I thought it was hilarious.

I couldn't hide my pleasure.

—Oh. I didn't know you were going to read it.

—Yeah. I did. Mom loved it, too.

Karen nodded.

—I did. But I didn't think it was *hilarious*.

I agreed.

—Sort of bittersweet, right?

—Melancholy.

We talked about *Mother Night* for some time. I had underestimated Karen. Yes, she devoured romance novels, but she had experience in other genres too. *I'm not reading classics anymore,* she once said to me. *I read all that shit when I was younger. If I don't enjoy a book right away, I throw it aside. I don't have time for anything else*. Fair enough. Karen really enjoyed romance novels. Nothing wrong with that. She was currently reading a book called *The Accidental Rake*.

There are a multitude of genres within the romance genre. People who don't read romance are ignorant to this fact, but it's true. There is the whole Jane-Austen-rip-off-romance—*The Accidental Rake* was one of these—and there is the Scottish highlander type of romance book. There is bondage erotica that warns on the cover: *Caution: this book is hot!,* and there are cozy romance books where nice people have nice conversations. There is science fiction and fantasy romance, believe it or not. Vampires had been popular a few years back, but now it's all werewolves and shape shifters. There are romance books specifically for black people and there are romance books for gay people, too. There are Christian romance books that often take place within an Amish community. There are romance series that tend to be even more specific than that, in which the books, month after month, always involve baseball players or pirates or astronauts. There was once a series that told one particular story over and over again. It went like this: A woman became pregnant with her husband who then left her. While pregnant, she was swept off her feet by a new man (who happened to be a billionaire) and ended up marrying him only days before the baby arrived. There were twelve books in the series, all with this plot. The oddest and most inconceivable title I have ever come across is *Hot-tubbing at Casa Dracula*. That's actually a real title that, I assume, has a corresponding plot and characters. Karen read it.

But she genuinely liked the book I had given her, and this made me happy because Kurt Vonnegut held a place close to my heart.

Karen, changing the subject.

—How did your certification go?

I put down my tuna bagel and set my hands on the table.

—Oh, fine.

—Charlie? Did it not go well?

—I guess I failed. I still have the observed troubleshooting to do, but I already failed. A lot of the information has changed. I knew all about the first SwiftFoot, but this color one confuses me. Oh, well.

I lifted my bagel once more, but Karen wasn't going to let me off the hook that easily.

—The color one has been out for a long time. You'll have to catch up.

—Well, it doesn't matter now anyway. The test is over and I didn't do well.

Karen and Kate exchanged a look.

—What?

Kate spoke first.

—Do you think the managers are going to leave you alone about it?

—I imagine they won't have me work at the SwiftFoot counter. And good. I don't want to.

—You have to at least make an attempt on the troubleshooting. What if they fire you?

—They won't fire me.

I looked at Karen.

—You *know* they won't fire me.

Karen looked like she was puzzling something out. She had finished her lox and wiped her hands clean with a napkin.

—I own a Color SwiftFoot.

I raised my eyebrows.

—I know. I have no idea why you bought it.

Kate couldn't contain herself. She was an eye-roll in human form.

—Because it's *awesome*, Charlie. If you knew how to work one, you'd know how awesome it is. You can have, like, a million books in your hand at one time.

—Great. I tend to just read one book at a time, but whatever floats your boat.

Karen was gentler, but she was still against me.

—What's your problem with E-Readers, Charlie?

—I like *books*.

—These *are* books. And it doesn't matter what you like. You can't stop it.

I shook my head. I don't lose my temper easily anymore, but I don't like people telling me my business. I know books. E-Readers aren't books. They're machines. But Karen was persistent.

—I know what you think, Charlie.

—No, you don't.

—You think that maybe bookstores will go away because of this. And you might be right.

—So, why would you support that?

—Imagine if Miles of Books *didn't* build the SwiftFoot. Imagine if they decided that they were morally above the technology or something. They would be out of business by now.

—Right. So, instead, they will continue to make money online and everyone who works in a bookstore will be out on their ass.

—What would you have them do? You can't go back.

She was right and I knew it. People just want to press a button. I stood up, half my tuna bagel remaining on the table.

—Look, I'm going to go.

Karen, giving me the look.

—Charlie, come on. Are you mad at us?

—No. There's a Mets game on television. I want to watch it.

Kate, chewing her bagel.

—You should really go down to the ballpark. Watching the game on TV puts the ticket-takers out of a job.

Never mind what I said before. Kate was *not* good company. I frowned at her and left.

22.
The Lesson

THE Mets played a doubleheader because of a rainout the previous day. I was just settling in to watch the second game when my door buzzer rang. I wasn't expecting anybody. The only person to ever visit was Karen, but she never dropped by without first calling. My cell phone had been silent by my side through the whole first game. I checked it just to make sure there were no messages.

Descending the stairs of my apartment, I saw Karen's blonde head bobbing outside the window. My stomach nosedived as I approached the door. This couldn't be good. I said hello and asked if everything was all right. She assured me all was well, curt as a busy bank teller. We trudged up the stairs together, and I told her how the Mets were doing. Not so good. I asked her if she wanted anything to drink as we entered my apartment—a Coke, a beer, water. She said she didn't need anything and sat on the couch. Our repartee was completely wooden. *Why didn't she call before coming over?* I wondered. At the bagel shop just now, I had done the thing she didn't like. Again. I walked away from a conversation I didn't want to have. Was that it? Was that the straw that broke the camel's back? Was this the end of our relationship? If so, I knew I would not take the blow admirably.

Karen, in her serious voice.

—Charlie, sit down.

She patted her hand on the couch and picked up the remote control from the end table. She put the Mets game on mute. I walked over, quiet as the television, and sat. I kept my head lowered waiting for the axe to fall. She picked up her purse from the floor and removed something, so I raised my head to see. Was she going to Mace me? No. It was her SwiftFoot.

—You're going to learn how to use this, Charlie. I'm going to teach you.

I laughed.

—Oh, thank God. I thought you were breaking up with me.

There was a pregnant pause here and I thought, again, that I had done something wrong. Karen took hold of my hand, her face flushed red.

—Charlie, no. Don't think that.

I chuckled again.

—It just seemed strange. You were acting so serious, that's all.

—Listen, I know it's only been a short time, but I would never break up with you.

Karen looked a lot like her daughter in that moment. Intense. Desperate to be understood. Something was happening in my chest. It was almost like worry, but it felt good. I honestly don't know what to call it. Positive anxiety? Is that a thing?

—I know we haven't been together long, but this stays as it is until the end, right?

Her demeanor was on the borderland between frightening and endearing. But I agreed with her.

—Right. I wouldn't have it any other way.

We agreed on this. We said it out loud.

We kissed then and it was the best kiss of my entire life. It was the most romantic moment of my life, too. I think the Mets turned a double play while we kissed. There was a tender aura as we leaned our foreheads together, our hands on the cheeks of the other. It could have gone on forever. *Put us on a Nicholas Sparks cover*, I thought.

Karen, with a sledgehammer to a stained-glass window.

—Ok, no bullshit. You have to learn how to use the SwiftFoot.

Had she learned nothing from all those romance novels? Christ.

Karen sure knew a lot about the SwiftFoot. I asked how she learned it all and she wasn't sure. It just made sense to her. As it turned out, the Miles of Books SwiftFoot worked on some of the same concepts as Karen's smartphone. And her iPad. And her computer and her Kindle and all the other electronic junk she had spent her money on over the years. There was one point where Karen held her index finger and thumb together, placed it against the screen, and then pulled them apart thereby enlarging that section of the internet. I was duly impressed.

I don't know how I fell behind. I was always one to keep up with things, always one to be in with the general trends. I remember when the bookstores switched to electronic categorization. At that time, I had never used a computer mouse. This is how long ago that was: The word *mouse* was funny to us. We called it Mickey while the manager was trying to train us and thought we were a riot. It took me a lot of time and practice to get used to the mouse. And now here I was, mouse-less, manipulating a bright, little screen with my fingers, like a Philip K. Dick character.

I supposed I should have purchased a smartphone last year when I had to replace my cell. Karen demonstrated how the smartphone was a smaller version of the Color SwiftFoot. It could have been like training wheels for me, and I wouldn't be in the mess I was in now. Instead, I had insisted on a gray screen with physical buttons for the numbers. The salesclerk had looked at me like I was a fool. I had said I didn't want a camera on the phone either, but the harried young man at Verizon couldn't find a camera-less phone. Even so, I had never taken a picture with the thing.

Karen went through the whole rigmarole. She showed me how to play games, what an *app* was and how to buy it, how to subscribe to magazines and newspapers, the ins and outs of the SwiftFoot battery, how to do a factory reset when the machine was acting funny, how to update the software, and thankfully, how to change the text size of the E-books. A lot of the lesson stuck, too. Karen made me hold the SwiftFoot and tap the screen myself. She verbally instructed me but made me do all the work. This wasn't how the Michaels trained people. With the Michaels, I was handed a sheet of paper with some details on how the thing functioned. Then, they held it in front of me and worked magic. I couldn't learn like that. I needed to do it myself. *Wow*, I thought, *Karen should be a manager*. We focused on the SwiftFoot for about an hour and then watched the last inning of the Mets game together, holding hands, Karen's head resting on my shoulder.

Karen spent the night. A younger couple probably would have moved faster, but this was our first time. We had been together for almost two months. There are some uncomfortable things to discuss when you are as old as us, and I supposed these tidbits slowed us down. But that night, Karen stayed over at my apartment and it was very pleasant, like a cozy romance novel where nice people have nice conversations. And that's all I'll tell about it. What kind of weirdo wants to hear the details anyhow, right?

A weirdo like Karen, probably.

23.

The Store Visit

THE district manager visited the next day and the store was consumed by terror. Ronald Gephardt. Holy. Shit. The day of reckoning had finally come. Arion, all the way back in the music section had spotted him first, like a dorsal fin at a public beach, and paged, hyperventilating to the MOD. Balding head of auburn hair, a well-kept goatee, his patented red dress shirt with a black tie. He looked like he was dressed up as the devil for a Halloween party. I could almost smell brimstone. How Gephardt had gotten past the cash counter without a bookseller noticing was beyond me. Who knows how long he had been in our store, judging our merchandising, and listening in on selling conversations? The store was compromised. No one would ever know the slipups he witnessed.

Though the threat was ever-looming, Ronald Gephardt rarely visited our store. He was charged with the operations of six locations—three in Queens, two in Staten Island, and one Upstate. I'm not sure if he popped in at the other stores more often than ours. Honestly, it wasn't clear to me what he did on the days that he was not in our store. When present, he said little and smiled never. If he ever spoke to a bookseller it went like this: In an incredibly quiet voice, he asked questions such as, *What was the thought process behind setting up the display in this location?* or, *Do you have any new selling strategies that have moved the needle on membership sign-ups?* Then he tilted his head and listened with the concentration of a high-level chess player. When the bookseller finished speaking, Gephardt would wordlessly nod and find the next person. I don't know why he acted like this. I have heard theories about management types and the *Authoritative Management Style* that is supposedly written about in business books. I never read those books, but I don't think I need to. If your *management style* consists of acting like an asshole, it's probably not an act.

Anyway.

He was in the store roving from bookseller to bookseller until Michael M finally caught up with him. I shelved the History cart as they stood on the cusp of the café, where the tiled floor meets the carpet. I moved as efficiently as I could, imagining the whole time that the two of them were judging me for store standard requirements.

Ronald Gephardt, pin-drop quiet.

—Michael. How are you?

—Excuse me?

—I said, *How are you*?

—Oh! Good! Good, Ronald. It's nice to see you.

—How's business?

—Good! Good.

—Beating plan for the week? LY?

—No . . . neither. Down twenty-seven percent to LY.

—That's awful.

—We'll have a strong weekend, though.

—There's an empty spot in the bestseller bay.

—Oh . . . we'll get it.

They stood in silence for a few beats while I shelved. Michael M spoke again.

—I didn't know you had a visit planned.

—Today's the day, Michael.

—Oh.

—It's gone on long enough.

—Right.

—Are you ready?

—Sure. Yes! Definitely.

I could tell that this was bad news for somebody. Someone was getting canned, it sounded like. And the district manager didn't come in to fire regular employees. Was Sheryl, the café manager in trouble? Michael P?

—He's a mid, right? In at eleven?

—Yes.

I did my mental checklist of the day's schedule. It clicked in my mind. Oh shit.

It was five minutes to eleven. As Gephardt and Michael M talked, I heard Don's humming laugh reverberate across the store. I peered down the aisle, my arms numbly holding a stack of books. Don talked to Ludmilla by the customer service desk, humming at something she said, holding his steaming Americano in his left hand, his black briefcase in his right. He was tired and grumpy, like a lovable curmudgeon on a children's cartoon. Gephardt and Michael M were silent now, assassins waiting on the rooftop. A wave of loathing rose in my chest.

Don spotted Gephardt and his face fell for a moment. He recovered quickly, replacing his shock with a smug smirk. I've always admired Don for that smirk. He knew what was coming, I think. He strolled toward the two as I remained still. I didn't even pretend to work now, just planted there and watched this drama of the immortals play out in front of me.

—Ron, nice of you to finally join us in Forest Hills. When is the last time you were here?
—Good to see you, Don.

Gephardt reached out to shake but Don shrugged his shoulders. He looked at his Americano and his briefcase.

—Sorry, I don't have a hand.
—We need to talk, Don.
—Do we?
—Yes, we do. Can we use your office?
—I don't see why not. Is this one coming with us?

Michael M's eyes grew large, his face blushed red.

—Yes. Michael is coming with us.
—Superb.

And then he shook his head, hummed, and laughed. Don sure was good at whistling in the dark. I'll say that about him. They walked back to the office and around the corner. I held a copy of *Devil in the White City* to my chest, watching the corner where they had disappeared for some time and then put the book back on the H-cart. I couldn't concentrate anymore. Besides, it was past eleven now and I was supposed to go home.

I wheeled the cart to the receiving room. Becky had the whole staff back there with her, whispering, wide-eyed. Mike and Susan

M, Ludmilla, Melanie, and Desiree. *Seriously*, I thought, *is there anyone on the salesfloor right now*?

Becky from her swivel chair.

—Did you hear, Charlie? Don's getting fired.

—Certainly seems that way.

I didn't want to be a part of this. Something about their whispers seemed celebratory. Like I've said before, not everyone liked Don. I didn't understand then and I still don't now, but there was a contingent against him. Maybe it's always that way with store managers. I thought Becky had been his confidant, but she was crowing just as loudly as the rest.

—I told him this would happen. I told him! You don't just run the store how you *think* you should run the store. You run it the way the company *tells you to*. Our digital sales are terrible. And why? Do you ever see anyone working the digital counter? Do you ever hear conversations on the floor about the SwiftFoot? Have you ever seen Don even *touch* a SwiftFoot? I told him this would happen, so he can't blame me!

I wandered out of receiving and back toward the breakroom. I hesitated before going in. I didn't want to see Don's shameful walk out of the building. He would probably have to be accompanied by Michael M or Gephardt. What if he tried to talk to me? What if he said mean things to the employees who were against him on his way out the door? What if he fell to the ground and wept at the injustices of life? But I was spared this discomfort. The door to the manager's office was closed. Only indecipherable murmurings pushed their way through to the breakroom. A café kid named Ricky thumbed through his phone while eating a bowl of what looked like quinoa and vegetables at the break table, unaware of the movings and shakings happening just a few feet away.

—Morning, Ricky.

—Oh, hey, Charlie. How are you?

—Good, good . . .

I wasn't going to fill him in. He'd hear some version of it soon enough. Anyway, he seemed pretty intent on staring at his phone.

—How's MySpace today?

—MySpace? I'm not on MySpace. MySpace is for creepers.

—Oh. Ok.

—I use Facebook, if that's what you mean.

—Right. I've heard of that.

I peered across the table at his phone.

—What do you do with Facebook?

—Oh, I'm not on Facebook *right now*. Facebook's phone app sucks.

—Then what are you looking at?

—I'm reading Kerouac.

—With your phone?

—Yeah.

—*On the Road*?

—*Dharma Bums*.

—Wow.

Seeing Ricky with his phone, I retrieved mine from my locker along with a gray cap and my house keys. Still worried about an awkward moment with Don, I decided to take my lunch home and eat there. I took one step toward the fridge when a strange sensation buzzed through my body.

—What in the hell?

Ricky looked up from his bowl.

—It's your phone.

I looked at him, then at my phone.

—You're right. It's shaking.

—It's *vibrating*. You're getting a call. Have you *never* gotten a phone call before?

—It used to ring. Karen's been messing with my stuff.

And it was Karen calling. I saw her name on the screen. I pressed the button that said talk.

—Hello.

—Hello.

—What did you do to my phone? It's shaking.

—Charlie, Kate's sick. I need to take her to the emergency room.

—Oh.

Karen sounded so calm. So routine. They could have been out of milk.

—Are you on your way home yet?

—I was just leaving.

—Would you mind coming here, instead, to the apartment?

—Um, sure.

—It's Sissy's day off. She would come over, but it takes her an hour to get here.

—I'll be there in fifteen minutes.

Karen was dressed and ready to go by the time I got there. They had a bag packed with Kate's toothbrush, a book, her glasses, everything. It looked like she was going away for the weekend.

—Do you think you'll be there a while?

Karen shrugged her shoulders.

—You never know. She was admitted right away the last time we went to the emergency room. Don't want to be without a book, right Kate?
—Ha. Yeah.

Kate tried to laugh. It didn't really work out. I could tell they had put on this act several times before. Karen made a few more attempts to make light of the situation, but Kate dropped off. She was pale. She smiled, but there was real worry behind her eyes.

—No matter what, I'll be back by three to pick up Bill and Emma from school.
—Ok.
—Drew's in his room right now napping. He'll probably wake up in twenty minutes or so. Give him mac and cheese. It's in the fridge, just heat it up. Give him water, too, and if he's upset that we aren't here, give him chocolate milk.
—And then . . . what do we do?
—Play. Build a puzzle. Draw. Whatever.
—All right.
—He can watch a show if things are going poorly but try not to do that. He's watched three shows already today.
—Right.

And they left.

I stood for a long while. Like ten minutes, just standing there in the hallway leading toward the door. I normally wouldn't stand that long when alone. I didn't know what to do. I thought about checking on Drew. I knew they still kept him in a crib, just two years old. It was quiet in the condo, peaceful like that morning long ago with another baby in another crib in another apartment. I shook my head. No sense in letting the ghosts have their way. I ducked my head in Drew's door. He was on the little mattress, a fan spinning over him, arms splayed above his head like an Ali knock-out. I didn't think I would be affected, but I have to say, this scene made me dizzy and sick. It felt like the room was tipping sideways. The most peaceful thing in the world—a child sleeping—upset my stomach. Hell. I closed the door quietly behind me.

Back in the living room, I made tea and retrieved my book from my bag. I was reading Graham Greene for the first time, *The Quiet American*. I was really enjoying it, and I considered maybe reading the whole Graham Greene cannon. After a few pages and a few sips of tea, I set the book in my lap and thought about Don, imagining what he might be doing right now. I had neglected to tell Karen about the goings-on. There hadn't been an appropriate moment to bring it up, what with Kate heading to the hospital. I was sitting on a piece of information that Karen wasn't privy to. She would be furious. I shook my head, frowning. I chastised myself for taking pleasure in Don's pain.

—I'm allowed to climb out of my crib.

—Christ!

I jolted in the recliner, splashing a blip of hot tea on my chest. Drew lurked, bleary-eyed, in the hallway clutching a tattered, green blanket. He smiled mischievously.

—Christ.

—Don't say that. It's a bad word.

—No. It's God.

—I shouldn't have said it. Please don't say it again.

He waddled into the living room. He looked at Karen's massive, black television set. He sat down in front of it, spreading the blanket at his feet.

—Show?

—Are you hungry?

—No. Show?

—I have mac and cheese.

He stood up, collected his blanket, and exited the living room for the dining room. I followed at a jog.

—Now, hold on. I'll have to heat it up.

A whole Crock-Pot of macaroni waited in the fridge. I set the heavy tub on the counter and scooped a bowl's worth out with a ladle. It looked good, so I scooped myself a bowl too. I popped Drew's in the microwave for a minute; I ate mine cold while it spun. I poured Drew a glass of water and carried the lunch to the dining room table where he loitered with a small, plastic doll of Sponge Bob.

—I have chocolate milk?

—How about *thank you?*

—Thank you.

—Yeah, I'll get the milk. One second.

Drew hadn't asked where his mother was, where his grandmother was, why I was here. I wondered how often events like this happened. I wondered how often he was blown in the wind, the chaos of illness governing his life. I sat down with Drew and ate the mac and cheese. It was good. Salty. The kind of food a kid should have when he's growing up. Not for nutrition or anything like that, just because he *should.* He looked at me when he had finished. I nodded.

—Why don't you and I watch some shows?

I imagined Karen sitting on the cracked leather of a waiting room chair, Kate on the crinkling paper of a reclining stretcher. I imagined Don in the bucket seat of his car, driving back to Staten Island with his briefcase on the passenger side, a phone to his ear talking to his wife. Such life, such drama. I sat on the floor and watched a cartoon. It was about a pirate named Jake. Repetitive, but not too bad, really.

24.

Better to Receive

So, Don was really out. Fired, axed, ousted, shitcanned. A large contingency of the store claimed to have seen it coming. I was blindsided, I'll admit. I mean, Karen didn't know, so how would I? And now, on top of my worries over the digital troubleshooting, I was on the outs with the new manager. At least, that's the way it felt. Either permanently or to fill a gap—this was never made clear to the staff—Michael M was the acting store manager. I kept my head low.

I clocked in and out of work for a week, always waiting for the fire alarm of the troubleshoot to sound, always waiting to hear my name over the intercom, *Charlie to the SwiftFoot© counter, please. Charlie to the SwiftFoot© counter*. Each day that it didn't happen I felt an immense relief, as if a bad headache had immediately dissipated. But this relief was tainted with the dread that tomorrow would probably be the day. On the other hand, I was becoming a more adept digital user. The issue that sent Kate to the emergency room had eventually put her back in the hospital. Something to do with her port, the doctors said. No one seemed particularly worried, which once again reinforced the quotidian nature of her medical emergencies. She was released after a few days of observation. Karen needed something to think about other than her daughter, so the SwiftFoot lessons continued. We spent nearly half an hour a night covering different problems that could overtake the device and deciding the best way to fix them. I was getting pretty good, if I do say so myself. I spent each shift in agony, anticipating that call, but each evening I grew more confident that when that call finally came, I would be prepared.

The ripples from Don's firing were still undulating in wider and wider circles throughout the store. It was announced, or rather, it was gossiped, that Becky had put in her two weeks as receiving manager. Whether this was because Becky *wanted* to put in her two weeks or whether Becky was *forced* to put in her two weeks was a matter of wild speculation. It was known that she had been part of Don's inner circle, even though she tried her damnedest to disavow him on his way out. Becky had been with the company for seven years, if I remember correctly. There was a man named Jason before her, covered in tattoos and stinking of cigarettes, who didn't stay long. Before Jason was Frank, who opened the store as receiving manager and later became an assistant manager of another location. Frank was my favorite. He really liked baseball, that guy.

Unlike her predecessors, Becky did not look the part of a traditional receiving manager. The receiving room was everything she was not. Becky was round and rollie and the receiving room was all parallels. Even after lifting boxes for seven years, Becky's arms looked weak and flabby in contrast with the sturdy receiving area. There were shelves fastened to the walls around the entire room, gray in color and so reliable that I once saw them hold Becky as she climbed up to reach a book.

Whoever took up the reins as receiving manager would benefit from Becky's work. Becky's abhorrence of physical labor drove her to unheard of efficiencies. She had relentlessly designed the layout of the room to use as few steps as possible, so that she could find anything at a moment's notice and without exertion. Each area was destined to have one type of product, and if a bookseller tampered with this system in any way, God help him.

The receiving manager, unlike anyone else in the store, worked a "normal" schedule. Meaning, she worked nine to five Monday through Friday. The receiving manager was allowed to work these hours because of the truck deliveries. Normally, Becky sauntered in a little after nine and processed some of the books off the return shelves. She stacked the boxes and left them for UPS to pick up. The delivery arrived between ten and eleven and, if it wasn't holiday season, consisted of anywhere from seventy to one-hundred and twenty boxes. Becky, and usually one helper, unpacked the boxes and separated them into backlist—books we always carry such as *To Kill a Mockingbird* or *Mastering the Art of French Cooking*—and frontlist—the newest books or those that had been slated for promotional displays and customer orders. Becky made sure all these items traveled to their correct destinations, kept her room organized, and left at five whether the sales floor was a chaotic hellscape or not. She never talked to a customer; she never closed the store at night, she did not work on Memorial Day, Presidents Day, or the day after Thanksgiving because the trucks did not deliver on these days. Must be nice. It was a tantalizing position for the bookselling lifers who were burdened with laboring all hours of the day and dealing with the public psychosis. Once you learned how to lift a box without hurting your back (it was all about the legs, I'm told) you were home free.

I hadn't heard who was getting the position. Karen usually informed me of these things, but she had been out of the rumor mill while Kate was in the hospital. So, I thought I'd go back and see what Becky had to say. I always thought that Becky and I had a good relationship. She was a nice enough girl, loud and obnoxious, but nice enough. She was even nicer now that she knew she was done working at Miles of Books. Becky held up three fingers.

—Three weeks. I have three weeks of vacation between when I leave here and when I start my new job.

—Wow. That will be good. Are you going anywhere for vacation?

—No.

—Just relaxing?

—You got that right.

She smiled greedily and screeched a tape gun across a box, sealing it shut.

—I'm not going to do anything.

—Where is your new job?

—You don't know? I'm going to be working with Larry.

I looked at her blankly. She made an incredulous grunt.

—Larry? The UPS guy?

Becky assumed everyone in the store was on a first-name basis with the truck drivers.

—Oh, *Larry* Larry.

—Yup. I'm going to be a dispatcher.

—Hey, that's great.

—I know. No more picking up boxes. I just sit on the phone and tell other people where to pick up boxes. Ha!

—Good for you.

—Are you looking for another job, Charlie?

—Me? No.

—Are you going to retire soon?

—I don't think I have enough money to retire.

—Don't you have army checks or something like that?

—Something like that.

—And what about Social Security?

—It wouldn't be enough. New York is too expensive.

—So leave.

—Eh, where would I go? Besides, I like this job.

She shook her head at my sad Stockholm Syndrome. People leaving a place of employment like to think they're escaping something awful. It's offensive to them if you don't hate the job with proper fury. Almost like you're judging their decision to move on. I understand.

—Well, the thing is, Charlie, there might not be a job to work at much longer.

I knew exactly what she was getting at, but I played along. It was her last week.

—What do you mean?

—Bookstores are closing everywhere. Read the paper. Five years from now bookstores will go the way of music stores. People will be downloading everything at home and there won't be any need for Miles of Books.

—Damn. A lot of people have been telling me that lately.

—Because everyone knows it. You better make a plan, Charlie. I did.

—I'll ride it out. If the store is open for five or ten more years, that's probably all I'll need.

—There will be layoffs before there are closings. And, I hate to say this to you, but the old people will go first.

—I've worked here forever.

—You think they give a shit? There is nothing nastier than a company going out of business. You've worked here for a long time and so you make a lot more money an hour than some kid they just hired. You're an expense is what you are.

We heard a soft footstep by the receiving room door.

—Becky, could I have a word?

Michael M in the doorway. One eyebrow slightly higher than the other, clipboard in his hand, pen behind his ear. Becky scoffed.

—What? What's the matter?

—In my office, please.

He didn't even look at me. I stood frozen in the receiving room for a few moments after she left with the feeling that I had done something wrong. I replayed the conversation I had had with Becky in my head trying to remember anything that Michael M could have heard that should concern me. I couldn't recall anything. But you never know with that one.

My shift was over and I cautiously sneaked into the breakroom. I opened the fridge to get my lunch. Again, the office door was closed with a contentious conversation being waged on the other side. What was this place coming to? As I was closing the refrigerator, the office door swung open and Becky lumbered out. Her face was red, defiant. I sat down and began working the can opener over my tuna. I kept peeking at Becky out of the corner of my eye while she gathered her things. I ventured forward with a question.

—Are you leaving?

I knew Michael M could hear me, but I was too curious. It was only eleven o'clock. Becky still had five hours of receiving to do. She worked her coat over her shoulders.

—Apparently.

She grabbed a plastic shopping bag full of Tupperware.

—It was nice knowing you, Charlie. Good luck working with these dickshits.

And those were the final words of Becky the receiving manager. As Phil later told me, Becky had been doing very little since she put in her two weeks. She had not finished processing the delivery four days in a row and the return shelves were overflowing with books. The receiving manager position, coveted though it was, was not a place where one could slack undetected.

The main gripe that management had, Phil was sure, was her mutinous talk with any employee that would engage her. Becky had it in her head that Miles of Books was going under or, at least, that they were going to close all their stores and become an online business. She told anyone who would listen that they should run out and get another job. This, Phil told me, was why she had to leave without working out her two weeks.

I was glad that Phil relayed all this gossip. *I really got the dope on this one*, I thought. *Karen will be so impressed with me.* With Kate home and our normal lives back on track, Karen yearned for updates on the political environment at Miles of Books. As I was about to walk out the door and go home, I thought of something.

—Phil, how do you know all this?

Phil was usually clueless about the social happenings in the store.

—Michael P told me. Right after he asked me to be the receiving manager.

—Wow. Congratulations. Are you starting immediately?

Phil smirked.

—I'm not starting at all. I don't want that job.

—What? Why not?

—You don't get to talk books with customers.

Phil scrunched up his forehead like this last statement was a no-brainer. He walked off twirling a copy of *The Little Engine that Could* in his hand.

Hmm, I thought, *at least* someone *still has their head on straight.*

25.

The Troubleshoot

LIKE a power outage during extra innings, my troubleshooting day came at the worst possible time. Jake was the MOD from open until 10:30. This covered most of my shift. I was more relaxed on days that Jake was the MOD because he would be the one observing me if I were called for troubleshooting. Of course, the customer with the SwiftFoot problem arrived at 10:45. So, not only was the problem likely to keep me past my allotted schedule, but my observer was mister-acting-store-manager himself, Michael M.

My face grew numb when I heard my name over the intercom. CHARLIE TO THE DIGITAL COUNTER, PLEASE. CHARLIE TO THE DIGITAL COUNTER. This was it. I had dreaded this moment for nearly three weeks, and it was finally here. I was infinitely more prepared to handle the troubleshooting since Karen's nightly lessons, but I still felt inadequate. *This person will think I am a fool*, I thought. *They will take one look at me and ask to speak to someone who knows what they are doing.*

I walked onto the scene and thanked God that at least it was an old person. A gray-haired lady with some dental issues. Michael M stood next to her with his hands behind his back, nodding as the old girl described her problems.

Michael M, in training video mode.

—Ok, so this is Charlie. He's going to be helping you with the SwiftFoot©.

—Hello, ma'am.

She looked at me and then back at Michael M. I could see the ageist and racist wheels of opinion churning in her head. Old and bespectacled or young and Asian—who will better assist me? It was obvious, but she wasn't given a choice. She turned to me with her device.

—So, what seems to be the problem?

I took the machine from her. It was a black-and-white SwiftFoot. One of the old ones. I had been practicing these few weeks with a color version. I had some experience with the older model from when they first came out, but it had been a while. My heart began to race.

—It keeps freezing.

There was some anger not far under the surface. When you've worked customer service long enough, you can sense anger, even when it's being suppressed. Like a mailman with an unchained dog, I would have to tread carefully here. This woman was looking for someone to yell at. This was nothing new; customers often came in half-cocked, ready to be rude and nasty to the first person who offered them help. The trick is to be polite and friendly. Personal without crossing a line. The dissidence of tones made them realize the nature of their silly behavior. Usually. It didn't always work.

—It's freezing, huh?

—That's what I already said! I'm in the middle of my Debbie Macomber book and when I try to turn the page it won't move. I press the button again and again and it *won't move*. I have to turn it off and turn it back on to get it to work. And I wouldn't even know to do *that* if my son hadn't shown me! I thought this thing was supposed to be easier, but it's not. You have to be a rocket surgeon to work it.

I glanced at Michael M out of the corner of my eye. I'm sure he was enjoying this massacre. He rocked back and forth on his feet and kept a serious demeanor, but I could see the smile at the edge of his lips. The little twerp. He thought I was about to catch hell.

—Well, let's see if your software is up to date.

I hit the settings button and then clicked on *device info*. I moved slowly, ensuring that my fingers hit the correct spots on the screen, doing my best to appear fluid and knowledgeable. I didn't want to look up at Michael M for fear of making a mistake, but I wish someone had taken a picture of his expression when I said the term *software*. That must have been good.

—Oh, look at this. You're at version 1.4 and we're up to 1.6 now.

—What does that mean?

—You need a software update. The SwiftFoot starts to act a little funny if you don't update it regularly. I can do it for you.

—And how much is that going to cost me?

—Nothing. Totally free. And you'll get new games.

—Games? I don't want any games. I just want the Debbie Macomber book.

—All right.

I went about getting the software update for the woman. It was an easy enough procedure, but two weeks ago it would have been like spontaneously singing the *Star-Spangled Banner* in Japanese. Karen was a magician. I felt so smart. Michael M hovered by in shocked observation. He scrunched his eyes and looked over his shoulder—trying to spot a Cyrano De Bergerac behind the best-seller bays, whispering secret advice. After my test results and after reports of my role-playing, I'm sure he was eagerly anticipating a colossal failure. *In his face*, I thought.

The software update completed. The SwiftFoot shut down and restarted. I made some casual conversation with the lady, asking her where she grew up, what Queens high school she attended. Michael M was originally from Florida and was completely left out of the conversation. It took about five minutes, but the SwiftFoot responded well to the updates. I opened a book on the machine and paged through for the woman. She was satisfied that I had fixed the problem. I told her that if she had any other questions, she should come back and ask. We were always here for her. Maybe I laid it on a little thick. She was about to put her SwiftFoot in her bag. She paused.

—Oh, and one more question.

—Yes?

—How do you change the text size in the books?

—Oh.

I looked at Michael M with my best confused-old-man eyes. He put his pen to his clipboard, ready to take scathing notes on my gap in knowledge.

—I believe you go to *special options*, then hit *font*, then hit *text size*. Is that right, Michael?

Michael M lowered his pen to his side. I think he had an *Aha* moment.

—Yes. That's right.

Michael M and I talked in the back office about the troubleshooting. I could tell that he had nothing written on the clipboard he kept referencing. He suggested that next time I should try to upsell the customer on accessories. He said, for instance, that the woman didn't have a screen saver and I should have suggested that she buy one to protect from scratches. He said I should have asked if she had the warranty. If she only had the SwiftFoot for a month or less, then she could still add the warranty for just $24.99. Grasping at straws was what this was. The latter suggestion was completely irrelevant as it was a first edition SwiftFoot. We had stopped selling them a year ago. There was no possible way that the machine was still eligible for the warranty. So there!

I leaned back in my chair and flashed a cavalier smirk at Michael M.

—So. Did I pass?

—No, you failed the certification.

—But I passed the troubleshooting. I know I did.

—Yes. But that is only a third of the test. Overall, you failed.

Fine. Fair enough.

—Where do we go from here? I'll take that test again. And I'll do better this time.

—We'll see.

—What do you mean?

With finality.

—We'll see.

26.
Charlie takes a Victory Lap

I was too jazzed up to go home. I was supposed to do something with Karen that night, but she didn't get off until six. After eating lunch in the breakroom, I took the subway all the way down to St. Mark's to check out the thrift store there. This thrift store was called Yesterday's News. It carried the hippest, most post-modern used books in the city. Not always what I wanted, but it was fun to look around. I browsed for about an hour and bought three books: *A Bowl of Cherries*, from the McSweeney's publishing house, *Kafka on the Shore* by Haruki Murakami, a Japanese master whom I had read several times before, and a book called *The House of Leaves*, a David Foster Wallace-esque take on the haunted house trope. Yesterday's News was a little more expensive than the other thrift stores. These three books totaled twelve dollars, which sort of gutted me. A slice of lukewarm pizza made me feel better. I bought a coffee at a sandwich place before hopping back on the subway. Started reading *The House of Leaves* and found it a little silly. Four bucks down the tube.

I had planned on going back to my apartment to read, but it was still so early, and besides, there was cause for celebration. I threw caution and frugality to the wind, hopping off the subway at Queen's Plaza to hit Mohammad's store, Second Lives. Mohammad was yelling at someone on the phone in Farsi but waved to me just the same. He switched to English and quietly said *I love you* to the person on the other line before hanging up. He shook his head and widened his eyes behind his golden glasses.

—Ah, Shakespeare, it's one of those days . . .

I strolled over to the bookcases, my plastic bag from Yesterday's News swinging at my knees, and started to page through the stacks. Second Lives was a better store for classics and mysteries. It was clear that while Yesterday's News was supplied by young people moving out of the city or selling their books for beer money, Second Lives filled its bookcases with inheritances from the dead. My books would end up here, I guessed. I selected two books from Mohammad's: *Perfume* by Patrick Suskind and *The Complete Poetry of Stephen Crane*. I didn't even know Stephen Crane wrote poetry. How about that?

I finally made it home, opened my window to the light summer breeze, and read like crazy. I don't remember, but I must have fallen asleep around four or four-thirty, a book on my chest, the sun warming my arms, and visions of digital screens dancing in my head. It was twilight when I woke to my cell phone buzzing. I slid the poetry off my chest and sat up. I freed the shaking phone from my pocket and saw Karen's number.

—Charlie, where are you?

Groggily rubbing my eyes with my free hand.

—I'm at home.

—Come down to Piper's. All the kids are here.

—Kids? What are you talking about?

—All the kids from the bookstore. Come on down!

—You're out partying with the kids from the bookstore?

—Kate and I were here getting dinner and they all showed up. I heard about your troubleshooting with Michael M. Come down and get a drink!

I could tell she had had a few and it made me smile. I told her I would be right there and twenty minutes later I walked through the door. Piper's was just down the street from Karen's apartment. They specialized in the boxty, corned beef, beer, and whiskey. It was a good place to go if you wanted to get drunk. And there were a lot of drunk people in the bar at nine o'clock. Jake caught me first, slapping his arm around my shoulder.

—There's the man!

Chelsea was with him and she mouthed congratulations to me over the music. I hadn't realized that my defeat of Michael M had been so public. And I wasn't sure why it was such a big deal. I was just doing my job.

Jake, shouting over *Whiskey in a Jar*.

—I shouldn't be here! I'm not supposed to hang out with the employees anymore!

—All right.

—So, don't tell Michael M or I'll get in trouble!

—Got it.

—But these are my friends!

Damn. Jake was really drunk.

—These are my friends! What am I supposed to do? Go out and find all new friends because I got promoted?

—That doesn't seem fair.

—You're my friend, Charlie!

—Very good. Thank you.

—Chelsea likes you too.

—That's nice.

—Tell Chelsea your stories. Tell her about when you were in World War II!

—Korea.

—Tell her!

—Maybe some other time when it's quieter.

I nodded at Chelsea. She smiled knowingly at Jake's buffoonish babble and took a sip of her beer. Then Jake mumbled something disturbing.

—Man. I'm sure glad you aren't going to get fired.

—Excuse me?

—You're my friend! I don't want to see you get fired. I'm glad you did well on the troubleshooting.

I nodded to Jake and moved on with a hollow feeling. I wasn't sure if Jake knew what he was saying. He made it seem like my job had depended on that test. Was I really that close to ruin? No way. I couldn't believe that. Sure, Michael M would love to see me go, the cruel son of a bitch. But I had worked at Miles of Books for seventeen years. Michael M wasn't top of the heap; he couldn't do whatever he wanted. Ronald Gephardt was still in charge of our new interim store manager. And Gephardt had a boss over him, too, I'm sure. There were too many people involved for them to fire a veteran of my tenure over a silly certification test. With a command chain that long, common sense would prevail. What's right is right. Or so I thought at the time. I went to the bar and ordered myself a dark beer.

I heard my name.

—Charlie! Over here!

Karen and Kate sat at a high top in the corner. Karen was still in her work clothes, a V-neck blouse and a long khaki skirt, and Kate perched next to her looking tired but smiling. I noticed she was drinking a beer and I raised my glass to her as I walked towards them. I kissed Kate on the cheek and asked how she felt, then sat down next to Karen. She shouted at me when I was close enough.

—Do you want anything to eat?

She waved her hand over the table at the cornucopia of fried foods they had ordered. I selected a breaded zucchini and munched away. They stared at me while I ate. I felt compelled to say something.

—How was work?

Karen guffawed and then mimicked me.

—*How was work.* Look at him, Mr. Troubleshooter—so blasé.

The bar was loud with shouting people and a blaring version of *The Merry Ploughman* slamming through the sound system, but we managed to talk and eat just the same. Jake ventured over sometime later, subdued but still drunk. We had a meandering conversation about Hemingway. He was a good kid. He and Chelsea were both good kids. They weren't making much sense, but we humored them and nodded our heads at their heartfelt exclamations. I think we were jealous that they were so young. I certainly was.

We stayed at Piper's late—Kate, Karen, and I. Most of the booksellers had left hours ago. I didn't have to work the next day and neither did Karen so we let the time drift by like leaves on a river. Karen and I had a few more drinks than we were accustomed to, and Kate had to tell us it was time to leave. During the walk home Karen told me she needed to show me something, something in the city. I felt fine and I didn't want the night to end, so I agreed. Normally I would have asked more questions, but the tide of my success at work and the confidence granted me by the beers made everything less exact, less dire, soft around the borders, and I didn't have to know where we were going or what we intended to do. I just agreed.

We walked Kate to the apartment and hailed a cab. It was a bumpy ride and I thought I might become carsick at first. But we began to talk, and the focus cured me. We told stories about adventurous cab rides we had experienced, swapping them back and forth like baseball cards. Karen had the best ones, like always. She sure could tell a tale. We drove over the Queensborough Bridge and cut across Manhattan until we hit Central Park. Up the boundary of the park, into the Upper East Side. I stared out the window like a tourist; I was not used to the clean parts of the city. Trees kept in portioned-off little corners of cement, petrified demons on the ledges of buildings, everything wild frozen in its secured place. Stores all closed up, street corners with no bodegas, the sidewalks eerily absent of homeless. A perfect picture of wealthy New York, the one from *Sex in the City*, the one from *Wall Street*, the one Southerners expected to see. Stopped at Seventy-Fourth Street. Once I got out of the cab and Karen paid the bill, I started to wonder what we were doing here.

—My apartment is right around the corner.

—Oh. Right.

—Do you want to stay here tonight?

—Sure.

Walked down the street, freewheeling in the night air like a couple of hooligans. I hadn't been out this late in years. I hadn't been *awake* this late in years.

—Right here.

Looked up at the tall, beige building, buoyed by floodlights, a million stories tall. I still had trouble imagining what it would be like to have enough money. We stood in front of the swanky place while Karen smoked her smokeless cigarette. We were silent for a while, her exhalations the only sound in this quiet, tree-spotted corner of New York City.

—Look at that old building across the street.

She pointed. Dark storefront of a beautiful building. Ornate architecture, real stonework from the early twenties. Large window in the front with an empty display, like an attractive woman with missing teeth. A large white sign that read *Out of Business*. Awning covered the door. Empty display window littered with holders and cases that—obvious to a trained eye like mine—were meant to hold books.

—An old bookstore?

—Old as of last week. They just closed.

—Oh.

—I applied for a job there before I applied to Miles of Books. They weren't hiring.

—Ok.

—That was always my bookstore. I went there for years. They had a great Romance section.

—It looks like a nice store.

—It was. And that *Out of Business* sign breaks my heart.

—I understand.

—Do you?

She sucked on her fake cigarette and looked at me in the darkness.

—I was reading in my apartment while the movers loaded up everything from the store. I looked up occasionally, swiping through pages on my SwiftFoot while they emptied everything out. I hadn't bought a book from them in months.

—I guess, maybe, they should have started selling E-Readers.

—No. No, they shouldn't have to. They sell books. That's what they do.

I didn't know how to reply. I have never been good at winning an argument. Karen put her cigarette away and we stood next to each other holding hands and looking at the closed bookstore. It started to drizzle and I turned to go. Karen remained standing for a moment.

—Damn. I'm going to miss that store.

27.

A Breakfast Proposal

I woke up among soft pillows and softer sunlight, unsure where I was. Karen slept next to me. I pondered the previous night. My head hurt and I was thirsty. I sat up, rubbed my eyes, and retrieved my glasses from a bedside table.

I got out of bed and dressed while Karen remained asleep. The apartment was amazing. It was the first time I'd been to Karen's city apartment, and I hadn't really looked around last night. Walls a tasteful gray. A Monet print—might have been an original for all I know—hung over a dark red leather couch. Appliances—refrigerator, dishwater—all stainless steel with black trim. Hardwood flooring of light blond in every room. Floor-to-ceiling windows in the living area. We were high up enough that it was possible to see Central Park off in the distance, a green paradise, wild and squiggly in the middle of all those gray right angles.

I went into the kitchen and drank two glasses of water while looking through the cabinets for coffee. There was a little bag of gourmet stuff. I scooped it into a coffee pot and set it brewing.

I took the liberty of going through her refrigerator. She had the basics—milk, eggs, orange juice, parmesan cheese, butter, and a bag of salad. *She must come here often*, I thought, *to keep such perishables.* I checked the expiration dates on everything then set to work. Broke four eggs into a bowl and mixed them up with a fork. Found a grater in the drawer and went about shredding some of the cheese into the raw eggs until there was a nice white pyramid floating in the bowl. Folded the cheese into the eggs while butter melted in a pan, threw the whole concoction in with a sizzle.

Karen appeared from the bedroom just as the eggs were starting to firm up. She wore a robe, her hair tied up with a string. Karen wore glasses in the morning, too, and I thought they looked nice on her. She hated them. The coffee had finished brewing. I poured her a cup, adding a heavy dose of milk. I popped two pieces of bread into the toaster and flipped my scrambled eggs one more time.

Karen sat on a stool at the island in the center of the kitchen. I stood on the other side, cutting an apple into thin slices, separating the eggs equally onto white plates. I buttered each of our toasts, pushed Karen's plate towards her, and poured myself a cup of coffee.

—Thank you.

We ate in silence for a few moments. The kerfuffle of car horns and shouting pedestrians began to pick up outside. The distracting sounds made it particularly peaceful in the muted kitchen. I told Karen about some of the books I had purchased at the thrift stores the previous day, but she didn't seem to be listening to me. I quieted down again after I said my piece and finished my breakfast. I understood. It was a slow morning. We didn't need to talk. I went to pour myself another cup of coffee.

—Charlie …

Her voice sounded strange.

—Do you want to marry me?

I had my back turned to her when she said this and a coffee pot in my hand. I finished pouring, set the steaming pot down safely, and turned to address her.

—It hadn't occurred to me.

And it really hadn't. That was the most honest answer I could give. What I meant was that I was enjoying myself so much that I never felt the need to look further into the future. Now was so good. But, at the same time, it was clear to me that this could be construed as an insult. I followed up quickly.

—Of course, I would marry you. Yes.

—I'm not sure that's what I want.

—Hm.

What if I had said yes in that moment? No hedging, no wishy-washiness. Just yes. What would have happened? Did she really mean to marry me? I don't like to even think about it. I sipped my coffee and waited for her to continue. She didn't say anything, so I spoke up again.

—Don't fuss over it. If you don't want to, we won't. It doesn't matter much to me.

She stared hard out the window.

—I guess I feel the same way. I don't see the need to go through the whole process.

—Maybe we're too old.

—I don't think that's it.

A good portion of her breakfast remained, but she had stopped eating. I followed her eyes out the window. There was a pair of joggers running in matching sweat suits down Seventy-Fourth

Street. I had to look almost straight down to see them. I took another sip of my coffee. It was extraordinarily good coffee. I normally buy the cheap stuff.

—Did you love your first wife?

I paused before I answered. I gave the question some thought.

—I guess I did. But it's hard to remember anything except the end.

—And what was that like?

—Frustrating. I was angry at her, of course, for leaving me. But I was also disappointed in myself for giving her reason to leave. She handled Kurt's passing really well. Much better than I did. I didn't like that about her. It didn't seem right to me.

—You think she wasn't as sad as you were?

—Yeah. I guess I *did* think that. At the time. Looking back, I . . . it's ridiculous. Of course she was sad. Her baby . . .

I was surprised to find that a lump had grown in my throat.

—Her baby . . .

I didn't finish the sentence; my voice was haywire and cracking. My nose had become stuffed. I took my glasses off to dab my eyes. Karen had only asked three questions and I had gone from calm to stormy. Was I always this close to panic? Were memories of Kurt always this close to the surface?

—The young years with Teresa, they're gone.

I waved my hand.

—I don't remember much about that at all. Maybe we were in love.

—You're still upset about Kurt? Do you think about him a lot?

—No. Not a lot. The thing is, there was this fan. Teresa's grandmother, Barbara, gave us this fan for Kurt's room. But it broke.

I was shuddering now, but hurtled forward, like I was running down a very steep hill, and if I stopped, I would fall and tumble.

—Sometimes, I wonder how much that had to do with it. I didn't put as much effort into fixing the fan as I could have. If I had that night to do over, I would make sure to get it running, or I would call someone to fix it, or I would just go out and buy a new one. I was so damn *cheap*. I don't know why I didn't just go out and buy a new one.

My throat contracted; my words became one long moan. Karen stood up and took my coffee from my hand. I closed my eyes tightly, squeezing out a series of tears. She wrapped her arms around me and whispered some sense into my ear. Her whispers were things that I already knew, but it was good to hear them. It wasn't my fault, and I knew it. But no one ever told me it wasn't my fault. No one ever said that to me, really. Anyway, it was nice to hear.

—We shouldn't get married. You and I have had enough marriage.

She was probably right about that.

28.

Out of Print

THE summer reading months were upon us. The store filled with sun-crazed children and their pestering mothers, all wanting the same books. Each year our store tried to obtain the reading lists from local schools so that we could prepare and stock appropriately, and each year we failed on one title or another. This summer the failure was *The Yearling*, by Marjorie Rawlings. Yes, *The Yearling*. Some masochistic, swimming-pool-hating teacher had assigned the poor children of Queens to read *The Yearling*. Christ.

The business generated by summer reading was welcome, I could tell you that. The months between February and May were the slowest and could be excruciating with tedium. Some booksellers liked it when the store was slow, but not me. Give me a busy shift any day of the week. I would much rather help customers than shoot the breeze with other employees or do busy-work projects.

It had only been a handful of days since my troubleshooting with Michael M and the glow hadn't yet worn off. Despite my moral misgivings about selling the SwiftFoot, I found myself becoming a regular at the digital counter. Before, if I saw a customer waiting for help at the counter, I would hightail it the other direction and hope that somebody else was waylaid with the problem. I didn't want to touch it. But now, with my new digital confidence, I went looking for trouble. I brought up the SwiftFoot in conversations. I even sold a couple, I'm embarrassed to say. My only defense of my new SwiftFoot attitude was this: Look, I'm no rebel and I'm no Luddite. I like working in the bookstore. If this is the direction the business is going, I'm on board. What else can I do? It's not like I'm a soldier in Nazi Germany here. The stakes are low, and I will gladly fall into rank. I'll sell the damn things and I'll fix them, too, if that's what the company wants. Least, that's what I thought at the time. Maybe it would have been more honorable to refuse to sell it, like Phil. Really go out on my shield.

I was at the SwiftFoot counter talking to a woman and her ten-year-old son. They had come in for *The Yearling* (imagine that) and we were sold out. The mother had told me that she desperately needed the book today so that her son could start reading. He had dyslexia, or some such thing, and she wanted him to have a head start on tackling the book. I told her that she could certainly spend the day on the subway looking around from bookstore to bookstore and she would probably find a copy. Or, I added with a hint of drama, she could have the book right now. I cringe when I think back to those days right before the end. Some of the things I said to customers . . . ugh. Hard sales have always made me feel shitty. But this was the changing culture at Miles of Books, and, like it or not, there were a few points I was obligated to make in a situation such as this.

Everything I said was true, really. It's not like we were running some racket. If she was in a bind and didn't mind investing a hundred bucks or so, she could have the book right now. And any other book, for that matter. With the touch of a button. I was showing them the ins and outs of the device when Jake walked in.

—Hey, Jake.

I hadn't talked with him since our run-in at Piper's a few days earlier.

—I was just showing this nice lady and her son the SwiftFoot.

Jake liked to butt in on SwiftFoot sales. He loved to talk about digital books. He just couldn't contain himself. But he brushed past the counter and didn't even look up. I turned back to the customers, a little chagrinned, and smiled.

—Must not have heard me.

I continued my presentation and they eventually passed. Too much to spend today, the mother said. But she was going to think about it. I walked back to the customer service counter to answer the phone. I placed an order for the customer on the phone and then went back to my morning shelving. I pondered Jake's cold shoulder. He might have been worried about the way he talked to me at Piper's the other night. He had been pretty drunk. No one likes to see people at work after something like that. That must be it. I would have to make a joke the next time I talked to him, I decided, to put him at ease.

I punched out at eleven o'clock, the shelving finished, one SwiftFoot problem solved, and two membership cards sold. Good day. Karen was working in the afternoon, but we had dinner plans at her apartment in Queens and then were going to the Mets game against the Pirates. I walked back to the breakroom looking for Jake. I wanted to say goodbye to him and clear the air before I left. I know from experience if someone thought they made a fool of themselves, they tended to stew if left to their own devices. I needed to let him know that I didn't think less of him because he'd gotten drunk. Hell, I'd gotten drunk that night, too, he just didn't see it. Jake was looking at the schedule posted on the back wall when I entered the breakroom. Someone was cooking a microwaveable lunch, filling the air with the scent of Salisbury steak. I walked to the refrigerator to retrieve my own lunch and sniffed audibly.

—Smells good.

Jake's back was toward me as he studied the schedule. He didn't say anything to me.

—Is the stuff in the microwave yours?

He turned around as if he hadn't heard me come in. He was pale but his cheeks were spotted a deep red, almost purple. His lips looked purple, too. I wondered if he was sick.

—No. I think Michael P is cooking it.

He turned back toward the schedule, running his finger along one of the lines to check a shift.

—Oh. Well, it smells great.

But Jake just kept staring at the schedule. I was trying to engage, let the water flow under the bridge, but he wasn't having it. One more try. I smirked.

—Hey. Your shifts don't get any shorter by staring at your schedule.

A terrible joke, really. I think I had heard someone else make that joke before. I didn't like it then, and I don't like it now. But, whatever. I needed to break the ice. I watched Jake for a moment, gauging his reaction. He didn't have one. Shrugging my shoulders, I opened the fridge and took out my lunch. I set it on the breakroom table, moving aside my cottage cheese container to find the can opener for my tuna. I realized that Jake was staring at me.

—What?

—Did you already punch out?

—Yes. It's past eleven. Do you need me to stay longer? Did someone call off?

—I need to talk to you. Why don't you go punch back in.

My face pruned.

—I don't need to punch back in. We can talk. What do you want to talk about?

—Please go punch back in. I'll meet you in the office.

He gestured toward the Michaels' old office. They had moved into Don's office, now, leaving the other as a file room. I glanced into Don's old office. Michael M was reading a memo, legs neatly folded one atop the other. Michael P had been staring at me but quickly looked away. His Salisbury steak had finished cooking in the microwave. I didn't tell him. I hadn't unpacked anything from my lunch bag yet, so I picked it up and put it back into the refrigerator. I turned toward Jake one more time, a question on my lips. He wouldn't look at me. He retreated to the empty office. I went back to the customer service desk and searched for Phil. His shift often started when mine ended. I wanted to ask him if he knew of something odd happening in the store. I punched back in at the computer terminal, but I didn't see Phil. Instead, Chelsea was there with her nametag around her neck, a scanner in her hand. I frowned at her.

—What are you doing here?

—They called me in early.

—Where's Phil?

—I don't know.

Then Chelsea darted away from me as if she just remembered a project she had left unfinished. I trudged back to the breakroom and into the Michaels' old office. Jake sat in a swivel chair. The office still bore the markings of Michael M's fastidiousness, with general tidiness and a smell of lemon cleaner. There were folders for everything, clearly labeled with their significances, and the appliances—the computer, the printer, the copier—were pristine, dust-free. They looked like sales floor models. Don's office had once been the opposite. An unending state of erosion and clutter. But under Michael M's watch, it too was lemon-scented perfection.

I hunkered down in a folding chair opposite Jake. As I sat down, he stood up and shut the door. He swayed a bit on his way back to the seat. There was a feverish look in his eyes. I kept waiting for the mood to break. I expected Jake to say something silly or confess another problem with Chelsea. But I knew, really, that something graver was afoot. When he spoke, his voice was fragile and practiced.

—I just want you to know that six people will be let go altogether. We already talked to four of them between last night and this morning.

—Let go . . .

—These aren't considered firings, they're layoffs. So, we're encouraging everybody to apply for unemployment.

—Wow. Geez, that's too bad. Who was it?

I didn't get that it was me. Even Jake's tight, austere sentences didn't clue me in. Fool that I am, I thought he was letting me know that some business was going down in the store. A courtesy, an inside tip from my buddy. How humiliating.

Jake cleared his throat. He looked down, and I realized he was holding my file. He paged through, studying the old reviews and little slips of paper detailing customer complaints and compliments that had accumulated over seventeen years.

—Did Terry Fernando get fired?

—No.

—Huh. How about Amber? Was she fired?

—Laid off, yeah.

—I figured she'd be one of them. Her membership sales …

—It's not just membership sales. We had to consider every person in the store—every single employee—and decide who we were going forward with. So, it's not really about who is a bad employee and who is a good employee—it's more about the ones we didn't decide to move forward with.

—Oh. I see.

I didn't. I didn't see one bit. Jake kept talking, his voice gravelly. His cheeks were deep purple now. His eyes wet.

—The book industry is changing, and Miles of Books needs to change to keep up with it. As a company, we're going to be running with fewer people, and in the near future, smaller stores.

He hardly finished this sentence before he broke into a violent coughing fit. It was really wracking him. I thought he might gag and throw up. I leaned forward.

—You ok?

The coughing abated and he leaned back. He looked angry at me now. His eyes were bright red. I don't know why everything clicked for me then, but it did. A great weight settled on my chest.

—Oh. It's me. I'm one of them. You're firing me.

The words didn't sound real when they came out of my mouth. They sounded like a bad imitation of me. Jake shook his head. His voice was stronger now, pushed into another gear by the anger he was able to summon.

—No. You're not listening to me. You're laid off. It's downsizing, so you can get unemployment.

—But you're saying I can't work here anymore.

Jake swayed in his chair, pained, and for the first time looked at my face.

—Yes.

The long-term effect of this development wasn't real to me. I couldn't imagine not working at the bookstore. It wasn't in my scope of reality. The only thing I could focus on was how stupid I had been over the last several minutes, not understanding that Jake was firing me. I felt so foolish.

—I just didn't expect . . . why did they have *you* do this? Why isn't Michael M in here?

I looked around as I said this as if Michael M might be lingering in a corner of the office. I tried to keep my voice steady and mostly succeeded. Of all the things I could be upset about, I don't know why that occurred to me first. It just seemed so poisoned, so backward and cruel to put Jake and me in this room together.

He looked back down at my file.

—This is part of my training as a manger. I have to do it.

We sat in silence. I watched Jake squirm in his chair, keeping his eyes anywhere but on me. I could hear my heartbeat in my temple. He wanted me to leave now, I think. My legs were numb. I'm not sure I could have stood at that moment.

—Did Phil get fired?

—Yes. Laid off. He was one of the six.

—And did you have to do that too?

—Yes.

The clock ticked loudly on the wall. Almost ten minutes had passed since I had sat down in this room. The time seemed to have gone by very quickly. On the overhead, someone paged for help at the cash area. Jake started talking again.

—Phil passed his certification, but then told Michael M he wouldn't sell the SwiftFoot. He said he would fix them, but he wouldn't sell them. They tried to get him off the sales floor—they offered him the receiving manager position—but he wouldn't have it.

So, I had to ask.

—And what about me? Why am I fired?

Jake snapped. He spoke roughly to me, with tears brimming his eyes.

—You didn't pass the certification, Charlie. It's like you didn't even *try* to pass the certification.

—I tried. I did.

—You missed twenty-three out of thirty questions on the written test. How is that trying?

He was disgusted with me—disgusted that I had put him in this position where he had to terminate me. The idea that I was facing an injustice began to fade. The cool, heavy pressure of regret settled on me. He was right. I could have tried harder on that test. I began to apologize and stopped. I couldn't talk. Or, at least, I couldn't say what I wanted to say. My lip curled. Even with Jake speaking to me like this, I couldn't muster any anger toward him. He was twenty-four years old. Twenty-four, and sitting here telling a man fifty years his senior that he was no longer qualified to continue his career. I was sorry for him instead of sorry for myself. Sometimes I just don't feel the way I'm supposed to feel. I don't know why.

I stood up.

—I won't bother you anymore.

I opened the door and walked through it. I heard Jake sob once behind me, like a caged dog whimpering, but I didn't look back. I crossed the breakroom to the Michaels' office and stood in the doorway. Michael M was typing on his computer, writing an email of some sort, and didn't look up. But Michael P saw me. He balanced a plastic plate of cut-up steak and gravy-washed mashed potatoes on his knees. He tapped Michael M on the shoulder. Michael M rotated in his swivel chair; his eyes narrowed at the sight of me. He folded his hands curtly into his lap.

—Charlie . . .

I wasn't about to let him condescend to me. The anger that I hadn't felt toward Jake erupted from me now. Words I never processed in my mind spewed from my mouth.

—You coward. Both of you. Having a kid do your dirty work. You're heartless and cruel. And you're that way for no good reason. This stupid, fucking job . . .

I grabbed my bag and stomped out of the breakroom. As soon as the door closed behind me, I realized that I had forgotten my lunch. I wasn't hungry anymore, but there was a can opener in that bag that I would lose if I didn't get it right now. I paused for a moment, but then decided to leave it.

I walked through the sales floor for the last time but I didn't even look around. I kept my head down, ashamed because I thought the staff knew of my firing. I thought about Don leaving the store and about Becky leaving the store. I didn't want anyone to be uncomfortable on my behalf. I needn't have worried. They avoided me like I was a raving homeless person staggering about the stacks. All save one person, standing by the customer service desk, hands neatly folded behind his back: Bernie, our deceptively insane regular. I could *not* deal with Bernie right now. I sped up.

—Hey, Charlie . . .

His voice sounded different. Slower. I paused by the desk and mumbled back to him.

—Hey, Bernie. Sorry, I have to go . . . catch a train.

—You too, huh? You're out.

—Yeah. I'm out.

—Hey, they're making a mistake. You're a good worker. A good guy. Good man.

—Thanks, Bernie. I gotta go.

—Good man . . .

And that was it. It was over for me, a bookseller no more, out of print like a ragged Western. It was sunny outside, with a cool summer breeze, and that felt good. My mind was stretched thin, nerves dead in my body. I decided to do some shopping.

29.
Strawberry Fields Forever

MOHAMMAD'S gruff voice from just beside the shoe tree.

—He is back there and around the corner. I asked him if he feels all right, and he won't answer me. I try to lift him from the ground, and he don't move.

Two pairs of feet walked swiftly across the creaky wooden floorboards of Second Lives. I sat cross-legged in front of a white bookshelf, my hands in my lap, my jaw slack.

—He said your name.

They stood over me now, looking down at a problem to be solved.

—He said *Karen, Karen, where is Karen?* So, I take the cell phone from his bag, and *Karen* is the only one in it. He don't know no one else?

—He never inputs numbers. I put my name in myself.

—He needs a new cell phone. This one—it is terrible. I have many phones when he decides to move on from this junk.

—All right. Thank you.

—I'd like to find the person who sold him this phone and hit him in the head.

—Ok. Thank you. Could I have a moment with Charlie?

—Yes, yes, of course. Let me know if you need me to call an ambulance. You all right, there, Shakespeare? New phones are in the front by the music.

I didn't look up, but I could smell Karen's perfume. My head was level with her knees. She wore khaki pants and small yellow shoes. I was overtaken for a moment with the remembrance of childhood. In fact, I felt like I was a child in that moment, heartbroken over some mishap, my mother standing over me, waiting for the tantrum to pass. Karen finally took a knee and then crouched down next to me, settling into a similar position. She wore makeup on her eyes and lips, her nametag from Miles of Books still hung around her neck.

—Mohammad said you've been here for hours. He says you haven't moved. He's worried about you.

I heard what Karen said but I didn't react. I was very slow at that moment, my face numb, my thoughts thick. I could have answered, I guess, but it would have been with an incredible effort. I didn't want to try. She kept talking.

—I know what happened.

She laughed after saying this, and that laugh seemed out of place.

—I'm fired too.

This woke me up.

—What? How could you be fired?

—I sorta lost my cool when I found out about you.

She clearly thought this was funny.

—I told Michael P that they had just fired the best bookseller they had and that he didn't know his ass from a hole in the ground.

I sat up straighter.

—Really?

She nodded.

—And I said something to Michael M about being a prick, but I can't remember exactly how I put it. I guess I pretty much shouted down any manager in range. They asked me to leave. I think Michael M called the police.

I looked around the floor of Second Lives, dazed. The incident with Jake seemed like a long time ago and not exactly real. My flesh felt gummy, made of rubber, hanging from my bones. When Karen spoke about my firing, it jarred me, reminded me that it wasn't just a bad dream. But this awakening was for the best. I couldn't sit on this dirty floor forever.

—Thank you.

The blood was flowing to my brain again as I pictured Karen walking around Miles of Books giving everyone the business. What a lady.

—So, what's up, Charlie? What are you doing here?

I grew forlorn once again.

—I don't know. I came here to relax. I sat down to look at the books on the bottom shelf, and I just didn't have the strength to get back up. I got—I don't know—dizzy or something. I feel ok now. I don't need a doctor or anything. Did you talk to Jake? Did you yell at him too?

—He wasn't there. He left sick.

I thought about Jake for a few moments while Karen watched me. In that moment, the world seemed like an impossible place.

—You don't need that job anymore, Charlie.

She wrapped her arm around my shoulder and hugged me into her side.

—You have a family now. You have me and Kate and my grandchildren. They can be your grandchildren, if you want.

—I can't contribute any money . . .

—Oh, come on. Get over that. No one cares.

—But what will I do . . .

—You'll find something. People find ways to take up their time.

To a certain degree, she was right. I don't know that I felt much better right away, but I did fill up my days. Karen didn't have a job anymore either, so we spent all our time together.

We went to a lot of baseball games over the next two weeks. The Mets were out of town, so we went and saw the Yankees in a series against the Blue Jays and then another against the A's. And let me just say, I don't know what people see in Jeter. I mean, he's fine, I guess, but enough already. I read more than usual. Too much reading, I suspect, for Karen's taste. One day while I was rereading *The Two Towers* she slapped the back of the cover like a middle school bully.

—Let's go!

I didn't take my eyes off Tolkien's words. I had read *The Lord of the Rings* trilogy before, of course. It was one of the few books I reread. I was at a part I liked and I didn't want to stop reading, so I answered without looking up.

—Where are we going?

—To the park. Today is the day they're having a Beatles cover band play songs at Strawberry Fields.

—There is *always* a cover band playing Beatles songs at Strawberry Fields.

I turned back to read about plucky hobbits fighting a giant spider. We were in Karen's apartment on the Upper East Side, so Central Park was only a few blocks away. I was comfortable, though, and trying to get lost in this book.

—We're going, Charlie. I told Kate we'd meet her. Bill is coming, too, and I want you there. You love the Beatles.

—I'm a Stones man.

This was a bald-faced lie and Karen knew it. I stared at my book. I was no longer reading, just holding it in front of my face, like a shield protecting me from the day. An idea lurked in the back of my mind that Karen was getting sick of my behavior. I was a treasure she found at a thrift store that turned out to be too broken to use once she got it home. I didn't want her to regret being with me. I didn't want to be a burden. But I also didn't want to get up. I was tired. My face felt numb. A flutter of fear ticked through my body with the steadiness of a clock hand. I had felt like this for weeks. I wanted to stay here, on this couch, with this book, and simply be left alone. Karen stood over me with her hands at her hips. She wasn't going anywhere. I wedged a slip of paper into *The Two Towers* and slid my legs off the couch.

—They're not only playing McCartney songs, are they? These bands are always heavy on the McCartney.

Central Park was beyond glorious that day, I guess. We passed some statues, a merry-go-round, a pond reminiscent of Impressionism and many other beautiful things. It was a nice day, a perfect day, really. It was probably seventy-five degrees with a steady wind. My face felt wooden, like a marionette. I had to laboriously pull the strings to keep a dead expression from my lips.

Kate, speaking in her mom voice.

—Bill wants to ask you a question, don't you Bill?

Bill was a quiet boy, tall for his age and good-looking. He leaned into his mother after she spoke and turned his head away from me.

—What do you want to know, Bill?

I wasn't annoyed by the child's shyness, not at all. But I had no energy. My voice felt flat, my inflection cross. I don't think it could have been helped.

—Go ahead. Ask him, Billy.

Strawberry Fields was just over the next hill. I could hear the band stomping through the chorus of "Ob-La-Di Ob-La-Da." Inspired by this, Bill turned his head back toward me.

—Did you really see a Beatles concert?

I had almost forgotten.

—Yes, I did. They were great.

Actually, the sound quality was nothing short of terrible.

—They played "Paperback Writer" toward the end.

Billy's eyes grew wide as I told him these tidbits. I could tell he wanted more, but I couldn't think of anything else to say.

—You were in that small room? With all those screaming girls? And the man that talks all funny, with the suit?

I didn't know what the hell the kid was talking about. Karen smirked. I figured it out.

—Oh. You're thinking of the Ed Sullivan Show. No, I wasn't there.

The boy was crestfallen and confused.

—I watched that one on television, just like everyone else. No, I saw the Beatles at Shea Stadium. 1966.

Bill nodded. He reestablished his grip on his mother's hand, his face pensive. It was funny that the kid liked the Beatles so much. I was a relic to him, from another age when giants walked the earth. So be it.

We broke the crest of the hill and started down a new path toward Strawberry Fields. We could see the band now, set up right behind the Imagine emblem. They weren't dressed like the Beatles or anything, just playing their songs. Billy let go of his mother's hand and started to walk faster. Kate and Karen matched his pace and I lagged. I felt hopeless. I knew this wasn't the right way to feel and that knowledge made me feel even more hopeless. It was a beautiful day and I was with a woman I loved. There was a child with us who enthusiastically loved the Beatles. What more could you ask for? I just couldn't shake the blues. My body was an organic machine capable only of producing anxiety and fear.

I cut across a grassy section in order to catch up with the Schneider family. Billy had run all the way to the front of the small crowd, standing on the squiggly engravings of the Imagine emblem, shifting from one foot to the other while the band leaned away from their microphones, talking about which song to play next. There was a vendor in a silver cart to the left of the stage. Kate and Karen had meandered over there to stand under the yellow sign and buy lemonades. I stood in the shade of a dogwood, its pink buds all fallen, littering the ground, rotting; I felt like hot garbage. Unwarranted turmoil wracked my body. I took a deep breath while the band started to play "All You Need Is Love." I stared vacantly at my shoes while they bounced along the sing-songy verses about how nothing is really achievable. I looked up at the band for the chorus.

All you need is love

All you need is love

All you need is love, love

Love is all you need.

I exhaled largely. *If only*, I thought. *If only that were true.* Karen surprised me by bumping into me from behind and I jumped. She smiled, her eyes expressive, and pushed a cool lemonade into my hand. I wrapped my lips around the straw and sipped. It tasted fantastic. I sighed.

30.

Down in a Hole

SUMMER turned to fall and fall turned to winter. I missed a season of promotions, a season of books. My spirits dropped down, down, down as the temperature began to lift us up out of March. Karen and Kate were forever trying to get me out of the apartment, and I constantly had to think up new reasons for my inactivity. When Kate told me about the cottage they kept in Upstate New York I said, *Shit! How many houses do you people have?* It was the first time I had used my sarcastic voice in a long while. Karen and Kate shared a look about me. But they were wrong to think this was a good sign. I was high on coffee, that's all.

I let them talk me into visiting the cottage. I didn't want to go, of course. I wanted to stay in Karen's apartment and read, read, read. I had gotten heavily invested in fantasy novels and was sprinting through Robert Jordan's *The Wheel of Time* series. I wanted to disappear, and this line of books was made for people who want to disappear. They're massive, if you haven't seen them. I appreciated their length more than anything. When unoccupied, I felt nauseated, like carsickness, like I was in the backseat being tossed around without control over my destination. Reading about magic and knights and the creation of a world steadied me. I didn't want to step back into the reality of Earth. Back on Earth, I was nothing but a too-quickly beating heart.

But people don't let you do what you want to do, that's a fact. Everyone tries to change your course, to dampen your resolve, throw in to doubt all your decisions. That's what Kate and Karen did to me with this cottage business. I didn't want to go, but I didn't have the strength to fight them. I was a real mess on the car ride. It was a long one. Five, six hours, up around the Finger Lakes. It wasn't good for me. My mind got weird with all that time in the car. We were in Kate's big van—Billy rode in the passenger's seat, Karen and I in the first row, Emma and little Drew strapped tightly into car seats behind us.

Karen and her daughter, they talk. They talk a lot. And when I'm not in the mood for talking, all that noise gets to me. I lose possession of my thoughts. They tend to bond against me, my thoughts do, when they sense weakness. They take over and live the hurtful lives of which they've always dreamed. I became suspicious of things. Something clouded my mind, and a sense of unreality took hold. The world morphed into a landscape of traps set to offend and annoy me. If that sounds scary, well, it is. I'm probably not safe to be around when my mind is dark like that. This had happened before, maybe a half-dozen times over the decades, when I was particularly down about something. But I had always been alone during those times, in my apartment, peaking out the windows in the middle of the day. There was a bad spell after Kurt's passing, of course. But I was practically alone then, too. Teresa wasn't much of a talker.

Now, I was in a car with women and children. There was no reason for me to be here. Who *were* these people? Why had they invited me into their lives? And was it even an invitation? Wasn't it more like they dragged me here? I started reconstructing the past year rapidly in my head. Somehow, in this reconstruction, it was Karen's fault that I had been fired from work. She had taken my even-keeled life away from me. She erased my 7:00 a.m. shifts, my cans of tuna, my mustache—all the constants I had diligently built over the years. She had deleted it all with the push of a button and left me this apologetic creature that could barely support itself. I was quiet for those five hours and surly when called upon to speak.

It was dark when we arrived at the cottage. Emma and Drew were asleep in their car seats. After opening the doors and turning on lights inside, Karen and Kate took the two sleeping children directly into a bedroom. Billy wanted to hold my hand when we got out of the car and I obliged. Karen had told me that Bill was afraid of the cottage, afraid of the dark, afraid of all this fresh air and green leaves. Pretty standard for a city boy. I was still turned-around and mean. I knew something was wrong in my head, so I kept quiet—mostly one-word answers. I lounged in the TV room staring at a wall while the ladies did the quiet night-time bustle. But there was a problem putting Drew down. He had woken up and now needed to be fed. It was a whole thing. They asked me to help Bill, read him a story, and sit with him in the dark until he was comfortable.

There was nowhere to run, so I did it. I read him two chapters out of *The Lightning Thief*, and he let me shut off the lamp after that. I got up to leave. I was almost out of the room when I heard him turn over. I stood against the door jamb, cutting a bent silhouette. He whispered.

—Charlie . . .

—Yeah?

—Could you sit with me?

—Yeah.

I walked back over and sat on the side of the bed.

—Do you want another chapter?

—No. Just stay here, please.

I sat there in the darkness until his breathing slowed. I sat there for a good while after that, too.

The land surrounding their cottage was a near paradise. A long, green lawn spread out from the back porch, twisting with sugar maple trees that spiraled to a cloudless sky. Fifty yards from the cottage, the grass turned to gray-black rock and the path of rock bent around a still, mossy pond. A wooden dock stretched a few yards into the water and a canoe, white but weathered yellow, clanked by its side, tethered to the dock and forever bumped into it under the tipsy sway of the pond. We rose early in the morning, just after the sun came up. Kate and Bill made breakfast—scrambled eggs, bacon, toast with puddles of butter in the center. We sat at a large oak table drinking coffee. The children talked loudly, often breaking into song. Karen and Kate told stories about when Kate was a little girl at the cottage—catching toads and fishing with her brothers. I ate half my breakfast and paged through book four of *The Wheel of Time*.

We strolled onto the lawn after breakfast. It was April, but unseasonably warm for this early in spring. Bill had laid fishing rods on the dock in preparation for a morning activity. They walked me through a wooded trail, lined with purple flowers, the leaves rustling in our wake as squirrels jumped about. A baby pool was set up and filled in the back yard so that Drew had a place to wade while his older siblings were in the pond. Karen rumbled through the musty, spider-webbed garage to find a set of iron horseshoes, dropping them by a sandy pit next to the house. Everything was all set. Time to have fun.

—Charlie, come to town with me. We need some things.

—Like what?

—Worms, for one. Can't fish without worms. And we need to stock up some groceries.

—I woke up too early. I think I'll stay here. Lie down.

I'm sure she was frustrated with me. But I didn't watch her face to see the reaction. Karen had been giving me a long leash as far as my mood went and maybe I was taking advantage of it. Maybe. Anyhow, I felt better this morning—not as out of sorts as I was on the car ride—and I thought a little time alone might get me right again. I settled down on the bed where Karen and I had slept the night before. The window next to the bed was open, the breeze from the lake blowing the white curtains like ticklish ghosts. It smelled really good in there, fresh. I turned to page 407 and set my bookmark on my stomach.

—What are you doing, Charlie?

Kate stood in the doorway, hands on hips. She wore a black one-piece bathing suit and a red bandana on her head, like Rosie the Riveter. She looked skinny and too frail to have such an aggressive stance.

—Just lying down for a bit. Do you need help with something?

—Get up.

—What? No, I'm tired.

She spoke with a growl in her throat.

—You just woke up two hours ago. Get up and play horseshoes with Bill.

I looked back at my book.

—Oh, he won't be strong enough to throw those things.

She stomped toward me and I flinched, thinking I was about to get smacked. Instead, she grabbed my copy of *The Shadow Rising* and attempted to rip it in half. She wasn't successful, mind you. Her attempt was pitiful. It's much more difficult to rip a book in half than you would think—even a cheap mass market like the one I had. She did manage to rip out a good chunk of the pages and crinkle the cover. She threw the damaged book to the floor. Then she yelled at me.

—Enough of this! Enough with being depressed! Get up!

I shifted up on the bed, planting my back against the headboard.

—I'm not depressed. I just don't feel good.
—Bullshit, you don't feel good.

She lowered her voice to a venomous whisper. She pointed her bony finger in my face.

—Right outside this window are three kids who would love to have you in their lives. There's a woman who would love to have you in her life. Everything you lost you could have again. But you're sitting in here wallowing, reading about elves.
—There are no elves in *The Wheel of Time* series.
—Shut up! Get out of the fucking bed!

Kate was crying now, staring at me in a rage. She huffed loudly and then stomped out of the room, slamming the bedroom door. I was truly alone for a few moments there. It was the worst I had felt in a long, long time.

Then I got up.

I walked over to the window and looked out. Emma held an emerald, snake-like hose over the baby pool. There was a mischievous grin on her face that burst into laughter as she shook the stream of water onto Bill. Drew sat in the grass nearby chewing on his fingers. Kate walked out of the backdoor, adjusting her bandana. She picked up Drew and set him on her hip, her arm cradling his underside. Behind them was the lake, crisp and windblown. Just like when I was in Central Park, I was reminded of impressionist paintings. Something about ponds and lakes did this to me. I guess ponds and lakes do that to everyone, right? I wished I had known Kate before the cancer. I wondered if she got into other people's business this much before the illness. I didn't think she had the right to criticize me. Yes, she was sick, but personal pain did not give her the right to pull rank. We are all equals in that war against ourselves. I shook my head.

Instead of thinking about her, I thought about Dennis, my friend from Geraldine's. Like I said, he had been dead for many years now and we had drifted apart well before his passing. Dennis was much more artsy than me—meaning he could spend hours in a museum and never get bored. I like art just fine—paintings and sculptures. But I only have so much patience for them. Let's be honest: paintings and sculptures and songs are all well and good, but they don't highlight the human experience like books do. Not as thoroughly. Dennis did not agree with this sentiment, not one bit. I remember him growing particularly angry when I told him that I did not like the paintings of Claude Monet. No lily pads for me, thank you. The paintings are too messy, I said, too chaotic. It hardly looks like lily pads at all. Maybe add a frog, I remember suggesting. He didn't speak to me for a week. Years later, on an afternoon when he convinced me to visit the Met with him, he became angry again.

Dennis, gesticulating like a passionate professor in the echoing white room.

—That's why!

—What?

I adjusted my glasses and peered closer at the four by eight mural.

—You're standing too close to the fucking paint!

A security guard bustled to life next to us.

—Hey! Watch your language, bud.

Across the room, alone in the corner, it all fit together. I just needed some distance to see it. Cyan leaves and deep purple petals. Yellow pistils, the red reflection, sun against water. I felt foolish at the sudden rush of emotion. I dabbed my eyes with a museum map.

Dennis exhaled and threw up his arms.

—We'll have to look at everything all over again!

Looking out the window at the pond, the children playing in front of it with their sick mother, I breathed out, deflated until I felt like I was hardly there. Yesterday, last year, the last decade, all the hours and days that had ticked away since that morning that I found Kurt in his crib—just a combination of minutes wandering like security guards down white hallways. Stopping to look: the green-blue of my embarrassment and anxiety-filled silence. Red of Kate's cancer. Yellow of her children's confusion. Deep purple of my estrangement from Teresa. Kurt's death. All these things slopped together like an accident. Maybe someday when this is all over, I'll see it from the right distance and dab the tears from my eyes.

I made a decision in that moment to see a therapist. Dennis had suggested this to me many times. He had seen one himself for years. If he was right about the paintings, maybe he was right about this too. And do you know, I felt better as soon as I decided on this path of action. As soon as it set in my brain in a way that I knew was real and that I would really do it, a veil of darkness lifted. It wasn't as powerful as the transformation that would follow, but it was something. It was noticeable.

I sat down on the bed, reaching over to the suitcase that I had yet to unpack. Fished out some white socks and pulled them over my feet. Strapped on my tennis shoes and doubled knotted. Enough already. I went outside to play.

31.
The End of Illness

KATE fell ill in the beginning of May and had to be hospitalized again. It was bad this time. Karen practically moved in at the hospital to be with Kate, transforming me into a stand-in father to Bill, Emma, and Drew. Their actual father was a busy man. He could only take them on weekends. During the week, they were with Charlie. Well, me and the nanny, Sissy, who now worked around the clock.

I had never spent much time with children. I was sure, in fact, that I had never been charged with a child for an entire day. I didn't know anything. Karen wrote volumes of notes for me and Sissy about what they ate, how they played, bedtimes, mealtimes, time-outs; you name it. Sissy found the notes patronizing. I studied them like the Torah, pouring over the words whenever the smallest problem arose. Kate, when she was feeling well enough, phoned relentlessly from her sickbed.

On Tuesdays, after Bill caught the bus and I dropped Emma off at the elementary school, Sissy stayed at home by herself with Drew while I went to see Dr. Mallory. During our first visit, I wasn't sure if Mallory was her first name or her last name. Calling someone by their first name after a Misses or Mister or Doctor is something that children do, and I was a bit put out until she gave me her card and I saw that her full name was Dr. Tamara Mallory.

I didn't tell Karen that I was seeing a therapist. Only Sissy knew, and that was purely out of necessity, since I couldn't think of a lie I'd be able to keep up as to why I needed to be somewhere every Tuesday at ten o'clock. I'm not someone who has a lot of appointments.

I didn't want Karen to know. I can't say why, exactly. I suppose I was embarrassed. Of what? Beats me. It's not like Karen didn't know I was a headcase. In fact, looking back, she probably would have been proud of me for taking the initiative to better myself. But I hid these sessions away like Poe's tell-tale heart beneath the floorboards.

There was considerable paperwork to fill out during the first session, and that was fine with me. Take it slow. I didn't want to plop down on the couch and start spilling my guts right away. Turning page after page in the waiting room, I answered all the questions while an episode of *The Price Is Right* played on a small television mounted in the corner. There was a student from Vermont with a bizarre laugh on the show who I had just begun rooting for when I was called in.

Dr. Tamara Mallory was a tall woman, black hair, dark complexion, Middle Eastern or Indian, I suppose. Her office smelled nice, not flowery and perfumy but fresh, like a stick of expensive men's deodorant. There were two paintings on the wall, from the same artist, if I had to guess. Solid swaths of pale pink on a white background flanked by hard baby blue bars. She shook my hand and asked me to sit. There was no couch, just a soft leather chair that I sank into. She sat down on its twin a few feet away. She leaned forward with her elbows on her knees. She kept this posture for much of our conversation, unless she was taking notes about something I said.

Dr. Mallory wanted to know about my medical history and was pleased to hear I wasn't on any regular medication. Most people my age are on all types of pills. And maybe I would be, too, if I went to a doctor regularly. She wanted to know why I had come here, what were my symptoms. Though I had written this down on the forms in the waiting room, I explained again. I was experiencing high anxiety, I said, I had trouble sleeping, I felt tired all the time, I get annoyed easily and can be unreasonable when I feel pressure.

—I suppose I just don't feel right. And I know I'm becoming a burden to those around me.

—You think of yourself as a burden to others? Why?

—Not always.

—But when you do feel that way, why do you feel it? What proof do you have that you're a burden?

—Proof? I guess I don't have any proof. But it's not a courtroom, is it? I know if I had to deal with someone like me, I'd be annoyed.

Dr. Mallory sat back, jotted something down in her notebook and then leaned forward again, her elbows on the tops of her thighs, her hands balled together.

—During these times, do you have thoughts of suicide?

—Oh no. Not that.

She looked at me for a moment, her large, brown eyes unblinking. She was quiet. I don't know if she believed me.

—Ok.

It was true. I didn't ever have thoughts of doing myself harm or killing myself. But, to be completely honest, in the middle of those nights, the really bad ones, if I could snap my fingers and not exist anymore, I would snap. Just blink out into blackness and have sudden relief from all this. But that's different. That's not what she asked, and I wasn't going to tell her that. This was the first appointment, after all. This was a softball conversation.

Next, she wanted to know about my general history—what was my relationship like with my parents, what was my career, was I married, did I have a lot of family around, friends. I told her about being fired from Miles of Books and about Karen and Kate and the kids. She took some notes. I told her about my father's problems with alcohol and my mother's strange distance. She took some more notes. I told her about my first marriage; I described Teresa.

I paused. Dr. Mallory looked up from her note-taking. She leaned forward. I grinned in a weird way and tilted my head.

—Can we stop there?

—We still have some time.

—I know. But it's the first session. I just . . .

Then I didn't say anything else.

—Sure, Charlie. We can do whatever you're comfortable with.

Don't worry, I eventually spilled the beans. We had a second session where I feel like we didn't accomplish much of anything, and a third where we talked mainly about how I was handling not having a job for the first time in my adult life. Then, during the fourth or maybe fifth session, I told her about Kurt. She got the whole show from me, waterworks and everything.

Dr. Mallory diagnosed me with Major Depressive Disorder. No surprise there, I guess. She wanted me to try Prozac and I agreed. So much for my medicationless streak.

It was a Tuesday in early June. I had been taking a little green pill every morning for four days and felt absolutely no change in my mental state. The only difference I felt was an increase in how much I was sweating. I've always been a sweaty person, I'm ashamed to say. If it's above eighty degrees on a summer day, I need a handkerchief to wipe my forehead when I venture outside. But a few days into these pills and my armpits had turned into faucets. I was changing my shirt three times a day.

Kate had been in the hospital for five weeks, lying in bed while the last days of school fluttered away like art class paintings dropped in the street. I stood in a clean, linoleum hallway with Drew at my side, a pacifier wedged in his mouth, waiting at a blond, wooden door for Emma to be let out of kindergarten. I heard the teacher speaking to the children, slowly and clearly. She said goodbye to them, and then an instant chatter arose. The door opened. I scanned the little heads bobbing past. I picked out Emma as she waddled with the pack.

—Hey, sweetie. How was school?

—Good.

She took my free hand in hers. Kate's children were so quiet. They were so well-behaved. I worried about them. Bill waited outside the school, leaning against the concrete steps descending from the front door. He had grown into a miniature man during the last few months, changing so quickly that sometimes I saw him without recognition. He was good-looking, with dusty brown hair and large eyes. I was told he looked like his father. I nodded to him.

—Good afternoon, sir.

—Good afternoon.

Bill took Emma's hand and we began to walk toward the subway.

—Are we going today?

—Yes. She's awake.

I didn't take the children to see their mother every single day. Days when Kate was particularly ill or sleeping, we skipped. The stress was apparent on the children when they had to go to the hospital, worry and confusion etched their faces like laundry in need of an iron. It was hardest on Bill because he understood, to some degree, what was happening.

—I need new shoes.

Bill's serious tone implied that he had been thinking about this proposition for some time.

—Really? The shoes you're wearing look to be in good shape.

—Everyone else has the shoes with air pockets in the soles. I need shoes like that.

—Do you think they'll make you jump higher?

—No.

—Well, why don't you think about it for a couple more days? I want you to be completely sure that you want to buy new shoes and aren't just following a whim. Understand?

—I *have* thought about it. I want them.

—It's not always good for a child to get what he wants when he wants it.

—Why not?

—It could make you a bad person.

—No, it couldn't.

My cell phone vibrated in my pocket just outside the subway terminal. I saw Karen's number on the screen, pressed talk.

—Charlie . . .

I could tell by her voice that the time had come.

—Do you have the kids with you?

—Yes. We were about to board the subway.

—Get here as quickly as you can.

I hung up the phone and placed it in my pocket. Drew, latched to my side, was singing "The Itsy-Bitsy Spider," doing the movements with his free hand. Bill and Emma stood at the top of the subway entrance, staring at me. Bill read my expression well.

—Is something wrong?

—Maybe. I don't know. We're going to take a cab.

—We need a car seat for Drew . . .

—He'll sit on my lap.

Karen waited for us in the lobby of the hospital. I carried Drew and held Emma's hand through the oversized rotating doors of the main entrance, Bill trailing behind us. We all stopped in our tracks when we saw Karen. She frowned heavily, her eyebrows knit and pleading. Her hands were at her waist nervously clutching each other.

—She's gone.

Emma broke my grip and walked over to hug her grandmother's leg. Bill didn't say anything, just dragged over to a sofa chair in the lobby, crashed into it, the back of his head to us. I stood there dumbly, holding Drew. Eventually I walked over to Karen and leaned my head into her shoulder.

Bill sat in that chair for a long time. I had thought he knew that his mother wasn't going to make it this time, but he didn't. How could he? She had always gotten better in the past. We adults have seen enough cancer to know that it never really goes away. We've lost enough of our friends that, unless it's someone particularly close, we get to a place of quiet acceptance in a blink. Not Bill. He didn't have that sour knowledge yet. Karen curled her arms around his shoulders over the back of the chair and talked in his ear for a while. I wonder what she said. I wonder what I would have said in her situation, if I could have thought of anything to say at all. But whatever it was, it worked. Bill pulled himself up, now nothing more than a bundle of arms and legs with his grandmother. We trundled in a daze to the elevator and were lifted to the now-familiar room on the fifth floor.

There were people in the hallways going about their everyday lives. They watched television on the mounted screens. There was a lively ping pong game in progress. They laughed, some of them. They didn't know where we were going. We had been just like them a few weeks ago. Now we were slow-walking, morose soldiers, going to aid a lost cause.

A nurse was in Kate's room and scurried away when she saw us coming. We walked in, Drew and I first and then Emma, Bill, and Karen behind us. Kate was there, her eyes closed, a red bandana on her head, her hands folded on her stomach in a way that I had never seen her relax. Sometimes people look at the dead and say things like, *It looked as if she could just wake up.* Kate did not look like that. Sunken cheeks, blotched skin, pricked up arms. She was gone.

Bill ran to the bed and grabbed his mother's hand, buried his face in her chest, shouted nonsense that deranged into strangled sobs. Emma stretched out her arms, indicating to Karen that she wanted to be picked up. Karen lifted her and they walked to the bed. Karen stood over her daughter. She was still for a moment, Emma in her arms. Then she shook once, almost like a hiccup. She shook again, crashed into a chair behind her, still with Emma in her lap, convulsing as the tears ran down. Drew was in the crook of my arm. He didn't know what was happening, I don't think. He began to cry but he didn't understand what for.

I had emotionally prepared myself for Kate's death. Talked to Dr. Mallory about it and everything. We knew within a week of this last hospital admittance that it would probably be the end. I was ready, steeled against her peaceful body lying in a white bed, thin and impossibly frail. I had not, however, properly prepared myself for Karen. For whatever reason, it is more difficult to see a strong person cry than a weak person. That's just the way it is, I guess. And it was especially difficult to see the strongest woman I knew broken down completely into emotional chaos, hysterical worrying, and now that the time had finally come, a deep, hopeless sadness. She calmed down after a while, stopped shuddering and stared coldly out the window. Karen looked like a wax figure of herself. The children, like me, were more affected by their grandmother than by Kate. They eventually gathered around Karen, dripping with tears, their faces blotchy and red.

I don't know how long we stayed in that room. It was an echo chamber of sorrow. Measurable pillars like time, hunger, exhaustion, ceased to exist. I guess someone, an unfortunate nurse or doctor, came in and gently told us it was time to leave. I don't remember it happening, but there must have been a chauffeur out of that room, or we might never have left.

Karen once said that a child should never die before their parents, and she was right. But it's tough the other way around too. Days later, Kate's three children stood in the graveyard like China dolls propped up in the grass. Karen leaned against my side and shuddered once more.

I stood in the middle of this mire and kept my shoulders straight. I had avoided scenes like this for years, decades, even. I thought that seeing Kurt's little wooden box sink into the ground was enough tragedy for a lifetime—I was a veteran of sorrow, and it was my right to withdraw from this type of emotion, let others take the brunt. But standing here, while the bullets of grief flew over my head, a spark of bravery caught in my chest. I could do this. As strange or even profane as it might seem, Kate's final illness and death left a hollow opening that I could climb into like a cocoon to emerge a better man. I could do it. I *would* do it, I promised myself.

32.
Life After Kate

THE cheaper storage units were across the Hudson in New Jersey. We went there to rent one for my books. I had access to Karen's money now, but I didn't like to spend it. Old habits. Now that I was moving in with Karen the danger of looking like a cheapskate lurked around every corner. I would certainly be using all of Karen's nice things because, besides the books, I didn't have much. What I did have I sold. Karen had a better television, a better bed, and no need of an extra chair.

I didn't even ask if I could bring all my books; I knew I couldn't. Normal people don't want to live in a library. I planned to take nearly five hundred to my new home, a reasonable amount by my tabulations. I fretted for nearly two weeks over which ones would make the move with me. On the way to Jersey, I still wasn't sure the selections were entirely fair. I tried to make a deal with a wholesaler to take the rest before the move, but Karen stopped me. She convinced me to keep the books in the unit and go retrieve a new batch whenever I needed them. I don't think Karen understood the point of the books. Many of them I didn't even *want* to read. I just wanted them around. If I couldn't have that, I may as well get rid of them. I don't know why, but that type of need is hard to express to a woman.

I never liked New Jersey much—no one who lives in the city likes New Jersey much—but I did appreciate its overlooks. Particularly in the North Bergen area where the land juts up over the river, the sights are something to behold. These sights were behind Karen and me as we surveyed the storage unit that we had spent the morning filling. Karen whistled low.

—That is a lot of books, Charlie.

Drew sat in the corner of the storage unit scribbling on a piece of paper with a purple crayon. It was a Wednesday, so we still had a couple hours before we had to pick the other children up from school. Spring was well under way, and I think all of us, Karen as well as Emma and Bill, looked forward to the free summer months ahead.

The first anniversary of Kate's death lurched nearer and the scars that had so recently healed were feeling tender all over again. But the hurt was certainly lessened. The memories were sweeter than they had been during previous months. The grief used to be a broken bone, but now it was more like painful stretching. There was something good about it almost, something healthy. Dr. Mallory thought I was doing especially well, and she said so. She asked often about how Karen was holding up. I'd tell her a bit, but then redirect the conversation back to myself. The little green pills were amazing once they started working. The energy I had after a cup of coffee in the morning—it was like I was ten years younger.

Karen and I saw Kate's jackass of an ex-husband at her funeral. Bill did indeed inherit his father's face. The bastard dragged his feet during the following months when asked to take the kids permanently. He had an excuse for everything. He had remarried some time ago and now had two new children. He claimed he didn't have enough room in his house for Kate's kids, but if Karen would just hold on to them a little longer, he had designs on moving into a larger house. I wasn't so sure about him. It seemed to me he wanted to put his old life behind and didn't care, or didn't have the emotional capacity to understand, what he was doing to Drew, Emma, and Bill. Anyway, the kids stayed with Karen as the months ticked away.

Breathing in deeply, I tried to take stock of all the books in the unit at once. I tried to understand the amount of time I had spent searching them out in thrift stores, time spent reading them, thinking about them, running my fingers down their spines like a studious chiropractor. I would miss these books. When my life had nothing real in it, these books had been my reality. It would be difficult thinking about them in this dark storage unit, shut away from curious eyes. It was like I was burying some old version of Charlie, shutting him in a tomb, rolling the stone to block him in. I had an urge to climb in there with the books, have Karen shut the door behind me. I shook my head.

—I don't know why we're doing this. We should just sell these things. Or give them to Mohammad, even.

—No. Let's hold on to them for just a little while longer.

The books stayed in storage all summer and, I admit, I thought about them sometimes. At night, after the children had gone to sleep and I had had a beer or two. I walked around the three paltry bookcases Karen and I kept in the apartment. Sometimes, I closed my eyes and visualized row after row of black shelves going on for infinity, lined with faded covers of varying thickness, the musty smell of my old apartment.

When August rolled around, Karen still had the children and I had not once been to New Jersey to retrieve a book. I again told Karen that I thought we should get rid of the lot. I hated to think of them locked up. But, no, she said to me again, let's just hold on to them a little longer.

Emma and Bill went back to school in September. It was awkward, because Bill had told his friends he would be in a new school this year, living with his father in another district. He had to explain the unexplainable to a pack of fifth grade wolves. I know it was hard on him. Drew attended a half day of preschool four days a week. People say it all the time, but it really is shocking how fast time goes when children are involved. On a Monday in early September, Karen and I were alone together for the first time in two and a half months. We had plans to check out a new restaurant in the city for lunch, so we were at the Upper East Side apartment. The weather was warm for September, sticky still, like July usually is, and Karen looked quite stunning in a blue dress and white top. She was extravagantly dressed, I thought, for just going to lunch on a Monday. And she was acting strange as well. I arched my eyebrows.

—Are we ready to go?

She had both hands behind her back, standing in the kitchen. She was definitely up to something. I let her play her game.

—We're not going to lunch, Charlie.
—But I'm hungry.

She produced a slip of paper from behind her back and showed it to me. I was almost a lawyer some years ago, so I recognize a deed of ownership when I see one. I read through it quickly and then tried to picture on my mental map of New York City where, exactly, the property was located. It was right across the street.

—Your old bookstore. The one that closed across the street from here.

A nervous smile swayed on her face, like a shy toddler meeting a relative for the first time.

—I bought it, Charlie.

I looked up from the deed, bewildered.

—You bought it?

—I thought we could open it back up.

I looked down at the deed again and then back at Karen. I rushed to the window and looked down, down the many concrete feet to the street level, to the closed store.

—Can you afford this? How much was it? You bought it?

—I can afford it. We can afford it.

—But it's old.

—We'll fix it up.

—No. No, you need things to run a store that we don't have. Cash registers …

—People just use an iPad now, Charlie. We can do this.

—But it's empty. We don't have any books to sell!

She shook her head, laughing.

—We don't? What do we have in Jersey, then?

I couldn't speak. It began to fit together. This was why she didn't want to get rid of my books. They were our first shipment, our first stock. I felt dizzy for a moment and had to steady myself with a hand against the window, staring down at the store. At our store.

She sidled up next to me.

—We can do this, Charlie. We can.

She was convincing me. Every time she said it, I started to accept that maybe, possibly, we could do this. And either way, I was getting my books back. I was getting a job, a store. I was a bookseller again. I teared up.

She had been scheming and plotting for months to pull this off, just like when she set up Jake and Chelsea at the ball game. In that moment, in that rush of emotions, I thought that maybe another plan was evident, too. I thought the purchase of this bookstore was the tying of some cosmic knot, evidence of the Master's Hand at work, the picture in its entirety, finally seen from the right distance. This was it. This was why I was fired from Miles of Books. It was all so clear. In that moment, I was overcome with a peace I had never known. Looking back on it, I sometimes wonder if all the frustration and heartache of a life is the equal of one of those moments. If years of unbalanced scales can be righted by a short period of serenity. Maybe.

Karen and I kissed. We hugged. She spoke into my clavicle.

—What do you think?

—I think that this will work out just fine.

It didn't.

The distance between fantasy and reality is about a hundred miles of shit. It took us a full year to get the place in shape. And an ugly year it was. There was some demolition that needed to be performed. Karen and I decided that a wall had to come down to open space for more bookcases. After smashing into the wall, it turned out there were water pipes embedded. We weren't sure how our contractor missed that. Turns out the man wasn't licensed. Live and learn! The pipes had to be rerouted and the water damage from the accident taken care of. With this work going on, we received a notice from the city that there were noise complaints against us from our neighbors. We were not allowed to start construction until after nine o'clock in the morning. All right. Then the unisex bathroom smelled like a sewer even though no one had ever used it. That was an issue. There was the light switch problem, when all the panels behind the switches became burning hot to the touch. I psychosomatically smelled smoke until that hazard was fixed. When winter set in some months into construction, the place wouldn't get warm. We had the furnace turned up to seventy-eight degrees and we were shivering. After an extensive and pricey investigation, we found that the thermostat wasn't reading correctly. Ok. Then, we had a large swath of wall painted green—a green that Karen and I had picked together after much deliberation. The painters finished. She looked at it. She didn't like it. It got painted again.

This was all very frustrating for me. I wasn't used to days filled with problems. I wasn't used to ordering groups of rough-looking men around. I wasn't used to making decisions that cost thousands and thousands of dollars. I didn't like it. Dr. Mallory heard a lot about it. Karen, though she was more comfortable with the situation than I was, didn't like it either. We came back to the apartment in Queens at six or seven o'clock at night and tried to spend time with the kids, but we were beat.

And the kids. That was another issue. Things had gone downhill with the kids. My impression that they were a well-behaved lot had changed, though the unsaid pressures put upon the youngsters shouldn't be discounted in my judgements. Kate's pile-of-rat-shit ex-husband was hardly returning Karen's phone calls at this point. He hadn't moved yet, was still in a small house in Staten Island that he claimed couldn't house the three rapidly growing kids. This stressed Karen out more than the store, honestly. At the beginning, right after Kate's passing, she kept these struggles close to the chest so that the children didn't know there was a problem. In her weariness, this calm front was lost.

She received a phone call about two months before the store opened from one of Kate's girlfriends. Bill was in the dining room doing his homework, Emma sat curled at my feet using a plastic loom to make bracelets, and Drew lurched in the corner of the kitchen, smashing a toy truck into a wall repeatedly. Pretty normal Thursday night. I had *Ghostwritten* by David Mitchell open in my lap.

—Hello, Caroline! It's so nice to hear from you . . .

Her tone changed almost immediately. Instead of catching up, there were several *Oks* and *Ummms* and *I sees* right in a row. My book sat unread in my lap as I tried to listen over Drew's rough play.

—Right. No, I'm not surprised. I mean, it makes me furious, but it doesn't surprise me.

I strained to listen closer. Karen was saying things that I was missing. Drew smashed the truck again and again.

—I know. No, I won't tell him that you and I spoke. He doesn't need to know how I know.

Drew's crashing stopped abruptly. I breathed a sigh of relief and leaned in to properly eavesdrop. Then the crying started. Drew was sort of a whiny child, if I'm being honest. Cried ten times a day. Karen cupped the phone and spoke to him.

—No, Drew. Nan's on the phone. Go show Charlie, please.

He ran into the living room red-faced, eyes in a cartoony bulge, brandishing his broken truck like it was proof of an absent God. There was some wailing and gnashing of teeth.

Karen, shouting into the phone now.

—I'm sorry Caroline, I have to go. No, no, of course I'm happy you called. No, really. Thank you. I needed to know.

Before his grandmother hung up the phone, Bill popped out of his seat at the dining room table, letting his chair crash to the ground.

Drew sucked in his breath as I held him and looked to his older brother. Bill had my attention now, too. Emma, never one to lose focus, kept up her Silas Marner impression on the loom. She didn't even look up when Bill shouted.

—How am I supposed to do my homework with all this noise?

He threw his pencil against the table, and it bounced across the room.

—This isn't fair! Other kids have their own rooms and their own desks. I have to sit here where babies are shouting and you're yelling on the phone.

Drew started crying again, this time a quiet blubber. He didn't like to be called a baby. He leaned against my forearm, wracked with misery. Outbursts like this could be expected from Bill on a weekly basis. Karen and I didn't really know what to do about it.

—I just won't do it! I won't do my homework. I'll go watch a *fucking* movie!

Swearing. That was new. Something should certainly be done about that. And it seemed Karen knew just what to do. She threw her cell phone against the living room wall, shattering it. Ok. Drew stopped crying again, looking at the shards of electronics sprinkled across the ground. The blood drained from Bill's face. Now it looked like *he* might cry. Emma was at a particularly tricky part with her knot-tying. Karen reared up in front of Bill.

—Don't you use that language with your grandmother! What's wrong with you?

Bill heard the words but took a moment to compute. He sifted through the two sentences and found the accusation. His scowl returned and he fired back.

—Nothing's wrong with me! Nothing! It's all of you!

—Emma is sitting in the next room quietly playing. She's not going to bed for another hour. Go up to the room and do your homework there, if you're so concerned about silence.

—But this isn't fair!

—What's not fair? I don't even know what the hell you're referring to.

—Now *you're* swearing!

—Go up to your room! Now!

He snatched up his notebook and loose sheets of paper with the math problems printed across them and stomped out of the dining room and through the living room. Drew clutched my elbow as if he thought his brother might strike him. Bill stomped up the stairs and screamed in anguish as he slammed the door to his and Emma's room. Emma searched her stock of threads for an elusive hue.

Karen shot into the living room after him, tears in her eyes, looking up the stairs. She was steaming, ready to chase after him and fight some more. Maybe about the door-slamming, maybe about interrupting her on the phone, maybe rehashing the swear word. If none of these worked, something new would spring up. It was their routine of anger and it dominated our nights, I'm sorry to say.

—Karen, sit down.

She had a wild look in her eyes. She turned toward me, searching her mind for something cruel to say. Drew softly cried in my lap. I patted the couch cushion next to us. Her face melted, just a little bit, and she sat.

—What was the phone call? That was Caroline?

—Yes.

Her voice was still hard. Her body was rigid on the couch, weaponized, ready to blow. She took a breath and closed her eyes. She struggled to calm down.

—He went on vacation.

—He did?

—They went to the Caribbean. He took his new kids and everything. Caroline saw their pictures on Facebook.

—He's not paying for his own children and he puts pictures of a tropical vacation on Facebook?

—He's an idiot, Charlie.

—Yes.

Drew was sitting atop the David Mitchell book, so I slid it out from under him. I put it on the side table next to my tea. Drew leaned into me, his wet face dampening my collar. He was quiet now, vacant. It was almost his bedtime. Karen stewed next to me, simmering in the injustice.

—I'm going to sue him, then.

I didn't say anything to this. She had wondered aloud to me in the past whether she should take legal action to force the children on him. But in those conversations, we had wondered if the point would not be lost. Our feeling was that the children should be raised by their father. But if their father were being ordered by a court to take them in, wouldn't the relationship be ruined? Wouldn't they be better off staying with Karen, if that was the case? There was enough money. And she loved them.

—He needs to take them. I don't think I can do all this. I already did this once. It's not fair. It's not fair to me.

I didn't know if she was going to follow through on this threat or not. Karen had made plans in the past that dissipated once she calmed. This proposed lawsuit could die before it got off its feet.

But still . . . she seemed different these last couple of weeks. What with the hassles of the store and the attitude of Bill, the slipperiness of Kate's ex-husband and the lingering specter of Kate herself—maybe Karen had finally had enough. Maybe it was time. Karen and little Bill did agree about one thing: something about this life they were sharing seemed unfair.

33.
The Grand Opening

YOU have to have a grand opening, apparently. And when we were ready, that's just what we did. Karen hired a party planner and everything. The celebration was ready to go before the construction was finished. The interior of the building was set the way we wanted it by the end of January. I was depressed that we had missed the Christmas season because those six weeks between Thanksgiving and Christmas would have been just the thing to start off the store with a bang. But what are you going to do? We were knocking down walls at the time.

In early February, we brought in my books from storage and quickly realized that they weren't nearly enough to fill the space. Halfway through organizing the sections the way I wanted things, it became clear that we were going to have long rows of brand-new shelving with nothing on them. I panicked. Karen hopped on her tablet and found a place on the internet that sold pallets full of used books. Ok. We bought two. These pallets were good for filling the shelves, but they presented a rather serious problem. We had named the bookstore Romance & Literature, because that was basically what we wanted to sell. My lot was the literature (for the most part) and Karen had purchased the beginnings of a reputable romance section from a wholesaler. We knew the random pallets we had purchased wouldn't follow our guidelines exactly, but they were further off than we anticipated.

They came through the back door on a snowy Wednesday, covered in plastic, resting on two splintery wooden pallets. I had been looking forward to the perusal process and cut them open immediately. The books were in good condition, I'll give them that. But the selection was terrible. There was a healthy percentage of cookbooks, which we really didn't want. The history was old, old stuff from the seventies. There were out-of-date travel books, which were basically worthless. And the fiction was obscure and in inappropriate quantities—six copies of *Fluke* by Christopher Moore. Five copies of the second Steve Martin novel. Three copies of the book adaptation of *Batman Returns*. Come on! I set them up. There was really nothing I could do about it. These were the books we purchased; these were our stock. I felt confident enough in my fifteen hundred that I knew we had some good stuff mixed in with the slush.

The grand opening was something else. The party planner did her job well. We had a violin player. There was a crowd. Karen's husband's old business associates were still some powerful people, and they came out in droves. I got the feeling that Karen's husband's friends liked Karen a lot more than they had liked her husband.

—So, this is the new guy?

Red-faced, checkered suit jacket, silver hair, pouring whiskey into his big, round gut.

—You snatched up quite a prize, didn't you . . . uh . . . what's the name?

—Charlie.

—Charlie. Right. Everyone was after *Ms.* Karen the second Jerry croaked. Let me tell you that. But she wouldn't give it up.

Wife next to him, slim, brunette, elegant, embarrassed.

—Larry, please …

—We're *talking* here, Mar. Charlie, I mean it. Karen was hot property. You know how she is—all forward and flirty. She was like that when she was married too. We all thought she had things on the side, the way she talked to people. But she didn't. Everyone wished she did. She didn't.

Embarrassed wife, trying to elegantly take the drink out of Larry's hand.

—That'll be enough, Larry. Charlie's very busy tonight.

—I mean, I don't know a cock and balls in the Upper East Side that wouldn't walk out on his lady for a shot at Karen.

—Larry! Enough!

—I mean, I don't need Jerry's money, but I sure wouldn't mind—

Desperately apologetic wife, dragging him to the door.

—He's on these new pills for his back pain. I'm so sorry.

Awkward, sure. But they bought a set of Shelby Foote's *Civil War* on the way out the door, so it was worth it. A lot of the people from Karen's past were like Larry and Mar. People with money who weren't aging gracefully. I didn't get it. I mean, wasn't this their life goal? To have money when it was time to retire? But they weren't doing it right. I don't know. It's possible that I just don't understand success.

—Charlie, grab the register, please. My friend Sherry wants to check out.

Karen's friend Sherry was very nice. Bought three books from the *Outlander* series. People were eating the hors d'oeuvres Karen had ordered—mini crab cakes and some type of hot dog on a skewer. They drank the yellow champagne. They laughed heartily and tipped the violin player. They bought books and made pledges to shop only at Romance & Literature. But Karen seemed down. I thought at first that she didn't like being reminded of all these people and her old life. And then I thought, maybe she missed the life she used to have. This gave me the chills. I wasn't part of that life.

She stood next to me after Sherry checked out. Her customer service smile masked her face, but her eyes were wet. Something was churning in that brain.

—What's going on?

—It's a great opening, Charlie. I used to go to things like this all the time. It's a good turnout. Did you see Rosa and Ludmilla?

—I did.

A woman approached the cash register wielding a blocky copy of the medical classic *Gray's Anatomy*. A gift from our two pallets of used books. I had been introduced to this lady earlier—Jeanie or Janie. Couldn't remember. Dolled up old gal. Old New York, pearls and the whole deal. Smiled like Times Square. Set the tome on the counter.

—I just love your store.

—Thank you.

—You two are so cute.

—Thank you.

—I hope this book is like the TV show.

—Oh. Well . . .

—I know that sometimes the shows stray from the book's plot. But I'll work through it. Sometimes I like to see the original material, you know?

Karen, cracking wise.

—You'll love it, Jeanie.

Karen and I looked at each other as she exited. Finally, Karen smirked. I shook my head.

—Not a good way to create repeat customers.
—She'll never open it, Charlie.
—Glad to see you smiling again.
—Yeah.

She leaned against the counter, observing the dwindling crowd.

—You feel ok?
—I feel . . . hollow, Charlie.
—. . . and not just tonight?
—No. Not just tonight.

She looked out over the people who used to populate her life. She took her glasses off and rubbed her eyes. She wore those glasses a lot more nowadays.

—I mean, it's worse tonight. All these people, their kids grew up with Kate. Kate is still a little girl to them. Not a dead person, a little girl. I . . . shit.
—Right. It'll get better.
—No, it won't. We have a problem, Charlie. I can't raise those kids.
—You can if you have to, though.

—I don't think so. I'm too tired. When Kate was alive, I kept going and going and going. No problem. But now that she's gone, I'm just . . .

She wiped tears from the corner of her eyes with her thumbs.

—I'm angry all the time.

—Don't be like that.

—I am.

—What are you angry about?

—Different things every day.

—Do I make you mad?

—Yeah.

—How? I'll stop.

—It's different things all the time. It's not your fault.

—I could help out more.

—You could.

I didn't like that answer. I did quite a lot, actually. But now wasn't the time to defend myself. Karen needed encouragement. I was about to suggest she get more exercise, eat better, take more breaks from the kids if she needed to. This would have been the perfect moment to tell her about Dr. Mallory. I could have suggested Karen go and see her. Or see somebody. It was just what she needed. But instead of telling her, I hesitated. Looked at the counter and shrugged my shoulders. Maybe I would have worked up the courage if given enough time. But then we had an unexpected visitor.

His hair curled down behind his ears, almost to his shoulders. His black eyebrows were graying and bushy, his small brown eyes studying us like we were an Escher painting. His white dress shirt was thin and flimsy and through it I could see the outline of Marvin the Martian printed on an undershirt beneath.

—Phil!

—It *is* you two. I heard about this place, but I didn't believe it.

I shook his hand.

—How have you been?

I really missed the guy. I worked with Phil for nearly ten years and—poof!—he was gone from my life on that awful last day at Miles of Books. We chatted for a while and his mannerisms were like passages from a favorite book. It warmed my heart, seeing Phil. It was nice to see we had both landed on our feet. At least, I hoped he had landed on his feet. After a little small talk (Phil wasn't big on small talk) Karen asked the tough question.

—So, are you working somewhere Phil?

—Oh . . . yeah.

He sounded despondent.

—Yeah. I tried to find another bookstore, but there aren't many of those around anymore.

—So where are you at? Is it still retail?

I had an awful image of Phil in a referee's outfit working at Footlocker.

—No, I'm at the school.

—School?

—NYU. New York University.

—Oh, very good.

God, this was like pulling teeth. I hadn't seen Phil in over a year and he was quickly reminding me how annoying he could be. What, was he a janitor at NYU? A groundskeeper? Just say it already! But Karen summoned her patience and continued the questioning.

—What are you doing there, Phil?

—Um, I guess it's a little hard to describe.

—Give it a shot.

—All right. Have you ever heard of the Navier-Stokes equations?

Holy shit. We had to shut him down before he got started. There were still nearly thirty people at the opening to which Karen and I had to attend. We couldn't sit here and listen to a Phil dissertation. I was about to tell him to forget it, he worked at the school, very good, let's end it there. But I think Karen was enjoying herself with Phil's social peccadilloes.

—Have I heard of *what*?

—The Navier-Stokes equations? They predict blood flow in the human cardiovascular system?

Phil made a scoffing sound in the back of his throat.

—Well, they *try* to predict it.

—Phil, what the hell are you talking about?

—I made up a new equation to model blood flow in the human body and most of the bioengineers at NYU think it could replace the standard, which is the Navier-Stokes. So, I have to go in every day to test my theories. It sucks.

Karen looked at me, her eyes slits, and then back at Phil.

—Are you telling us you're a . . . bioengineer or something?

—Sort of. I mean, my doctorate is in Bio*fluid* Mechanics.

—Doctorate?

—Yeah. Doctorate. So, this store is really cool, you guys. Where did you get all the books?

The crowd hung around for a few more hours, drinking, talking, buying books. Phil was the last one to leave. He asked Karen and me if he could work part-time at the store. When we told him that we weren't sure if we could afford an employee, he said he would do it for free. We agreed. I think Phil drank nine or ten glasses of champagne in the short time he was at the opening. So.

So, the evening was a success. It was nice. I had a nice time. I don't know that Karen did, though. Our conversation about her hollowness haunted me. It haunted me that night and it still haunts me today. I knew what she meant; I had been hollowed out several times myself. It's a hard thing to shake. Still, I wonder if there was something at that early stage that I could have done to turn the ship around. That conversation wasn't the first indicator and it certainly wasn't the last, but, in retrospect, it seems like it was an important one.

34.

A Little Reunion

OPENING your own business is much like being a man of great faith. Now and then something good happens—something magical even, like a customer buying an expensive book. At those moments, you must say to yourself, *Look! There's proof! I'm doing the right thing, here.* But there are also times when you sit in overwhelming silence wondering if you've wasted your life.

That was how I spent my days, for the most part. Sitting at the desk in Romance & Literature, walking the stacks at Romance & Literature, reorganizing the Romance section by series instead of by author and then, two days later, switching it back. You would think that I read a lot during this time, but you'd be wrong. I did the sitting and the pacing and the reorganizing. And I guess I looked out the window a lot.

We opened at eleven o'clock every morning and closed at seven every evening. Karen worked with me if there was something to do, but mostly she showed up twice a day to give me breaks. Everything smelled piney and fresh when I came back from the breaks.

The weekends were better. There was a pretty good flow of people on Saturday and especially on Sunday afternoon. Honestly, if Phil wasn't there to help out, I might have been overwhelmed a few times. We didn't see much of Karen's friends, but that was ok. There were other people in the area and a church just down the street that brought patrons by.

There were so many customers who asked if I sold coffee that I decided I should start selling coffee. Give the people what they want, right? I bought an industrial coffee maker and a retail subscription to the *New York Times*. I put a sign in the window indicating that the coffee was free, and I started opening at eight in the morning instead of eleven. This was a good idea. I didn't make any money, mind you. I gave the coffee away and selling newspapers bears nearly no profit. But people stopped in on their way to work and they saw the store. I had some regulars and those regulars came back in the evening to shop. The business grew. If we were a run-of-the-mill small business functioning primarily on loans, we probably wouldn't have made it six months. But with Karen's cash flow, things kept going until they got better. By November of the following year, we were almost turning a profit and gearing up for what we thought might be a successful holiday season. We had started paying Phil for his time and were even thinking about bringing on another employee for the weekends in December.

I stopped seeing Dr. Mallory. It happened gradually. I missed an appointment here and there when I was busy. But when we moved to an eight o'clock opening at the store, I stopped seeing her altogether. I certainly could have continued with the therapy. Karen had plenty of time to cover me on Tuesday mornings, but I never told her that I was going. She didn't even know I was on the antidepressants. When we talked, I spent a lot of energy trying to get her to see the changes in me. She never acknowledged that she noticed.

Dr. Mallory's office called a couple times and I didn't reply. I knew I'd have to go back when my prescription ran out and that knowledge became a source of dread. I had many sources of dread. There was a sense that my life was a piece of fruit, decaying from the inside. The skin still looked good, but sooner or later the brown spots would rot to the surface.

I was finishing up with a customer on a Wednesday night, just around six o'clock, when the bell over the entrance jingled. I said hello without looking up. Carefully counted out my customer's change, told them to have a pleasant night, to enjoy the book, to please come again. When I finally turned to the new customers, my heart skipped a beat. It was Jake and Chelsea. And Chelsea was holding a baby. Why was Chelsea holding a baby?

Jake with a bashful smile.

—Hey, Charlie.

I stood with my mouth open. I didn't move. They must have thought I had a stroke. Let me tell you, it had been a long day. I had discovered a leak on the ceiling of the store. A small waterfall erupted in the sci-fi section during a storm that afternoon. Some books got wet. I don't need to get into it, but just know that I was tired and had a great many things to do the next day. So, my overloaded mind didn't deal very well with the shock of seeing Jake and Chelsea.

—You have a baby?

They laughed. Chelsea hugged the little bundle to her chest. She nodded.

—Yeah. This is Clarabelle Fletcher.

I teared up. I had missed her mush mouth.

—That's a . . . that's a beautiful name.

Jake took a few steps down the science fiction aisle, looking around in wonder.

—Charlie, this is a great store.
—Thank you.
—It reminds me of your apartment.

I could tell already that we weren't going to talk about the incident at Miles of Books. I could just tell. And that was good. I really didn't feel like talking about it. Not just because I was frazzled over the thing with the ceiling, but because I had gotten past the incident, buried it, moved on. Talking about it would just be a waste of time.

I closed the store up a half hour early so that we could talk privately and fetched a few beers from the back room. I kept a mini-fridge and a television back there. Sometimes in the summer, if Karen was feeling especially blue, I would stay at the store after close and watch the Mets game. She didn't want to see me when she was having a bad night. She never told me that, but it was clear. She stayed in the bedroom if I was in the TV room and moved to the kitchen if I was in the bedroom. I didn't like the dance. When I saw one of those nights coming, I stayed at the store.

The Fletcher family and I moved over to the lounge area in the back. Chelsea sat in a wing-backed recliner and Jake and I shared a bench. Clarabelle cooed and stretched out one of her pink hands, reaching. I hadn't talked about Miles of Books for a long time—hadn't even thought about it, really. I was excited to hear some news.

—So, how are things? How's the store?

Chelsea and Jake looked at each other. Did I say something awkward? Was I not supposed to talk about the store? If that was out of bounds, what the hell *were* we going to talk about? Chelsea filled me in.

—We don't work there anymore, Charlie.

—Yeah, we moved to Cincinnati about a year ago. We're just in town for a wedding.

—A year?

—Yeah.

Chelsea blushed and Jake raised his eyebrows and looked at something in the corner of the store.

Oh. I got it. A baby surprise.

—Well, it must be nice to be so close to your parents.

Chelsea smiled.

—It sure is.

They asked about Karen. I didn't burden them with too much. They already knew of Kate's passing, but I put a rosy spin on the situation with the children, Karen's state of mind, our splintering relationship. No need to get into all of that. We talked about Romance & Literature, about Phil, who they were thrilled to hear was working for us, and, of course, about books. Jake was reading *Moneyball* and Chelsea an Umberto Eco collection of essays. I had read *Moneyball*, but not the Eco. It wasn't a bad night. We even drank another round of beers.

It was nearly nine o'clock when they began putting on their coats to leave. Clarabelle wasn't asleep yet and they wanted to get her back to the hotel and into her crib. I stood with my hands folded behind my back as they bustled about with their blankets and bottles and pacifiers. Chelsea stood up straight, realizing something, looking at me.

—You haven't held her yet, Charlie. Here.

She offered the fragile package and I took her carefully in my arms. Clarabelle was warm and soft and very, very light. I was shocked at how little she weighed. I searched her tiny red face for signs of Jake or Chelsea, but I couldn't see any. Babies all look alike to me when they are less than six months old. It could have been anybody's baby. It could have been Kurt. Her eyes were large and black. Brown, if you kept looking at them. I kept looking.

35.

Deep Purple Paint

It happened that night. I got home around nine forty-five. Emma and Drew were asleep and Bill was in his room, reading. Karen sat at the dining room table with a glass of wine. That's how I knew; before she said anything, I knew the time had come because of that glass of wine. Despite the sadness and tumultuous times, Karen never started drinking or anything silly like that. She faced the problems head first and soberly. But not this one. This one required a drink or two.

—Charlie, we need to talk.

—I know.

I could have fought it. I certainly could have complained. I had done so much for her and her family, I didn't deserve this treatment. I could have said that I never wanted this relationship, that she dragged me out of my comfortable life and into hers for the past few years. It's not fair for her to tell me to go away now. Maybe I don't know the way back. And I definitely could have brought up that night, that first night that we were intimate together, when she told me that this was forever. She said it. She did. She said that this would stay as it is until the end.

But these points would just serve to hurt her, and I didn't want to hurt her. It would be like hurting myself.

Karen was infatuated with me at one point, I'm sure of it. Did she love me? I don't know. Kate thought that I could be her mother's companion after she died, that I could take care of her mother. I suspect Karen thought the opposite. I think Karen was looking to the future as well, to a time when Kate and her weaknesses weren't around, and she needed a replacement. Karen thought I could be someone to look after. Someone that needed her help. I guess, eventually, I wasn't either of those things. Maybe I grew up a bit after Kate died. Yeah, growing up in the seventh decade—it happens. Maybe I'll grow up even more now that I've lost Karen. Sometimes I wonder why the milestones in my life have to be made of pain.

So, being separated from her—is it a good thing in the long run? No. No, I wanted to stay with Karen. I wanted things to get better between us, like they were when we first started seeing each other. I guess I was a lot like Bill in that regard, visiting his mother in the cancer ward, fully expecting her to walk out of there any day. The relationship between Karen and me was not going to work out. That was a fact. So, time to change. What would Dr. Mallory say? Time to reassess. No one was going to pick me up like Karen did after my firing, and I couldn't spend years lost in grief like I did when Kurt died. No time for that garbage. I focused on the good things that came out of being with Karen. One great thing about Karen was that she didn't seem to know she was old. She took in new experiences like a young person. I picked up some of that from her—I learned how to learn again. I learned how to make friends. I realized that I didn't have to fall out of sync with the world like so many people do in old age. And the kids—they were certainly a net positive from this whole mess. I learned the drudgery and ecstasy of raising children, if only for a short while. They were more important to me than all the time I spent with

Karen. Or maybe that's an exaggeration. Maybe it's all one big thing, inseparable. I'll tell you this: I can think about Kurt now because of Drew and Emma and Bill. It still hurts, yes, but it doesn't poison me anymore.

To think about Karen sets my heart swooning and the memories of those last few months are riddled with regrets. When Dr. Mallory asked me about Karen, I should have really dug deep and given thoughtful answers. I shouldn't have let Karen sit in the bedroom alone all those nights. I should have pushed her like she pushed me. I still think I could have saved us. If I had admitted to myself that we were headed down the path to ruin early enough, I could have done something—I don't know what, but something.

And really, I could have avoided all of this, the whole damn thing. In my mind, I often go back to that moment when she touched my lips with her finger outside Miles of Books. Right then, I could have averted my eyes as she walked away. I could have decided right then not to think about her in that way. I could have shut the door on all the heartache that was to come. But I'll keep it. Sure, I will. I wouldn't erase that time with Karen. I'll keep every second of it. Tennyson had something to say about love and loss and now I know he was on to something. If you don't know the quote, you can look it up on your phone.

Shit.

At the end of March, I was invited to see Bill perform in his seventh-grade orchestral concert. He'd learned to play the oboe. I'd sat through some torturous nights in the apartment listening to him squeak out scales while his private tutor corrected him, so I figured I should see the results of that cacophony. They played theme songs from movies but the only one I recognized was *Star Wars*. It was all right, I guess. Bill seemed to know what he was doing.

Afterward, I was invited for drinks at the Queens apartment with the rest of the friends and family who had gone to the concert. I reluctantly attended. I hadn't been around the Schneiders for a while and this socializing put my anxiety on high alert.

Karen wanted me to keep working at Romance & Literature after we separated. This might seem like an odd request, but if you've ever split with someone you lived with, you know the breakup isn't clean and quick. I was deeply rooted in Karen's life and she in mine. There were plenty of details that needed attending, and it was some work to weed each other out. I didn't leave Karen's apartment and move into my own place for nearly two months. I worked at our store during that time. It wasn't as awkward as you might think, but enough that I knew I didn't want to be attached to Karen in that way if we weren't together. It hurt; I'll say that.

Even though Romance & Literature was built entirely on Karen's dime, she insisted that we owned it together. That we had built it as a team and were entitled equally to the meager profits it was now turning. When I made it clear that I no longer wished to be involved with the store, she offered to buy me out. I refused, of course, and she insisted. I wasn't really in the position, financially speaking, to decline with any kind of gusto. And there were some valid reasons why I was owed some money. I mean, I had purchased more than half the stock. I had worked for basically no pay for over a year. But it was a tidy sum she gave me, and I am fully aware that it was charity. Just thinking about that money makes me feel heavy and embarrassed. But what was I supposed to do? I'd still be living in Karen's guest bedroom without that money.

Karen hired Phil as a full-time manager. It turned out that there were some crucial flaws in Phil's blood flow equation. He wasn't going to change the course of history with his work, unfortunately. He was invited to stay on at NYU but he didn't want to. He hated it. He hated the people he worked with and he hated laboratories.

While part-time at Romance & Literature, he had begged Karen for more hours so that he could quit. When she offered the manager position, he began immediately. Didn't even tell his lab partners, just stopped showing up. It was wild. I figured he lost about sixty thousand dollars a year on the job swap. He didn't seem to care.

With the cash from the buyout, my social security checks, and my military money I probably could have sailed off into the sunset. But the thing about the sunset is, it's boring. I was so bored.

I was bookless in my new apartment because my entire collection was now being slowly sold at Romance & Literature, so I set about re-buying them. It gave me a fairly inexpensive hobby, wandering around the city's thrift stores paying spare change for literature to replace the ones I'd given away. But it wasn't enough to fill up a life. I started spending entire afternoons at Second Lives. Mohammad seemed happy to have me at first. We talked quite a bit during those months, and I now count him as one of my good friends. But after I asked him if I could work there—even for free, I said, volunteer—things became awkward. A distance grew between us. We were still friendly, but there was now a distance.

When Karen called and invited me to Bill's orchestral show, I marked it down as the lone activity on my calendar, a few squiggly pen lines on a white-washed chess board. I didn't perform too poorly at the Queens gathering. Bill's father was there and his new stepmother. Bill Sr. had finally taken the kids, just after the new year. When he caught wind that Karen was going to begin legal action, he suddenly found room in his house for them. He didn't seem as bad as I was led to believe.

Bill Sr., a faded, tired version of his son, silver-lined temples. He shook my hand.

—Charlie, I know what a help you were to Kate and Karen with these kids. I've been meaning to properly say thank you.

—Oh, no need for thanks. I didn't do anything special.

The new stepmother stood next to him and I shook her hand, too. Beth. She had short hair, almost buzzed in the back, and large, watery eyes. Emma hovered around her at knee-level, occasionally hugging one leg.

Beth looking down at her barnacle.

—Hey, bub. Why don't you hit Charlie with your Lincoln line?

Emma turned red and buried her face behind Beth's thigh. I tried to encourage her with a question.

—Lincoln line? What's that, Emma?

—Emma's class recited the entire Gettysburg address. It was a showcase at her elementary school last week. Each grade had a little performance. C'mon, bub! Hit Charlie with the Lincoln line!

Muffled in the corduroy of Beth's leg.

—Now we are engaged in a great Civil War, testing whether that nation, so . . .

—. . . conceived . . .

—So conceived, and so dedicated, can long endure.

I reached over and patted her on the head.

—That's very good, sweetheart.

So, Beth—she's a good woman. She cares about the kids as if they were her own, and that's all you can ask. It's not the greatest situation in the world, sure, but that's what happens when a parent dies young, I suppose.

Later, Bill approached me in the living room and extended his hand. Since he was the man of the hour, I hadn't had the chance to talk with him yet. God, he was tall.

—Hello, sir. Excellent performance.

—Thank you.

—You've come a long way with that oboe.

We didn't talk about anything special, but it was good to see him. Good to hear his voice. Karen sidled up next to him, Drew holding Karen's hand. Drew had had some problems with school. I wasn't completely up-to-speed. I knew there were some behavioral issues, and he was assigned an adult helper to sit with him during class. But he was the most affectionate of the three kids, he came over and hugged me. I kissed Karen on the cheek after.

—Thanks for coming, Charlie. The kids were excited to see you.

—Thanks for having me.

There was a beat or two of strained silence.

—I understand Emma had an event the other night? The Gettysburg Address?

—Oh, yeah. It was cute. They're always doing something. I don't want to flood you with invitations to all these things.

—I would have come.

—Oh, all right. I'll invite you next time.

—I want to come to all of them, if that's ok. All the events.

Karen, smiling and crushing Drew into her side with a one-armed hug.

—Ok, Charlie.

Phil was there, believe it or not. He had become a fixture at Schnieder family events. Hanging around with his open dress shirts, his Marvin the Martian tee, stinking like cigarettes. I was having a beer in the kitchen and he beelined for me.

—Stop down at the store so that I can give you money for the game.

No *hello*, no *how have you been*. We hadn't communicated in months, and this is the first thing he says.

—What? Game?

—Mets. We're going to the second game, right?

And so we did. Just Phil and me on a cloudy Wednesday in April. The Mets lost to the Nationals, 1-5. They had four fielding errors. Four. But it was a good time, a pleasant afternoon, and I was happy that Phil had suggested we go. I think I talked his ear off a little bit. I told him about what I was reading, but also about my empty days, my loneliness, and my yearning to be with Karen again. Phil was an odd sounding board for these types of laments, and I was unaccustomed to lamenting. But it happened. He processed the conversation better than you might think.

—There.

Phil pointed at an old gent, dressed in a blue and orange jacket, working as an usher at the end of our row.

—Right there.

—What are you talking about?

—You should do what that guy does.

—The usher?

—Yeah. You need a job, Charlie.

—You think? I mean, my money situation is fine.

For some reason, this sent Phil into hysterics. He laughed—like, really laughed hard as if I had just told him some great joke. Good God.

—What's so funny?

—Working isn't about *money*, Charlie.

We stood up to leave. I tucked the game brochure into my jacket. Phil dusted peanut shells off his pants, spilling the rest of the bag across the seats and floor around us.

—You just spilled your peanut shells everywhere.

—Usher will get it. That's what they pay him for.

We stopped at the customer service desk on the way out of the stadium. I asked about getting an application and the nice woman behind the glass told me that I had to apply online. Phil let me use his computer a few days later—that was a whole thing, let me tell you—and after a couple interviews, I was hired. My customer service experience definitely paved the way.

And do you know what? It's not a bad job. I get to see all the home games and talk about baseball the whole time I'm at work. There's a lot of standing, but I'm used to that. Sometimes you have drunk people, which I wasn't used to, but if it's bad I just notify security. The ushers tend to stick together and I get along with most of them pretty well.

By the time I had really settled in, the summer was over. It was the last game of the season. The Mets hadn't done much, they were above five hundred but weren't going to the playoffs. There were a few weeks more that I could work—cleaning up the stadium, winterizing, and things of that nature. But then I was off for the winter with the promise of rehire next spring. It was good. Perfect? No. But good.

At the ballpark, ten minutes before the first pitch. I folded my hands behind my back and flexed my shoulders. It felt like a fall night even though it was still officially summer. Brisk. I looked out onto the field as they threw the first pitch.

Acknowledgments

Thanks to my editor, Chastity West, for your keen eye and thoughtful suggestions. Thanks to Allison Randal and Onyx Neon.

Thank you to the many people who read early drafts: Tim Pitoniak, Laura Miller, Billy Mott, Siobhan Mackey, Tom Sweterlitsch, and Arden Nicoletta. Thank you to my family.

Thank you to Jenny and Afton for the time and the encouragement. I love you both.

www.ingramcontent.com/pod-product-compliance
Lightning Source LLC
Chambersburg PA
CBHW010836250626
47157CB00011B/3291